WATCH YOUR BACK, KATE

"Saw Mr. Garney Wilcox the other day, but before I could speak to him and ax about his mama he
hopped into a big fancy car and was gone."

"You saw him here?" Kate asked, puzzled.

"Shore did," said the old woman. "Don't know
what he was up to. Might 'uv been peddling butter
and eggs, but shore wasn't passing the time of day
with old neighbors."

She started to laugh at her own joke, but suddenly her rheumy old eyes fixed on something behind Kate and went dark with fear.

Kate turned. A scrawny little man with a knife
in his hand was bearing down on them.

AH, SWEET MYSTERY

CELESTINE SIBLEY

HarperPaperbacks
A Division of HarperCollinsPublishers

This is a work of fiction. The characters, incidents, and dialogues are products of the author's imagination and are not to be construed as real. Any resemblance to actual events or persons, living or dead, is entirely coincidental.

HarperPaperbacks *A Division of* HarperCollins*Publishers*
10 East 53rd Street, New York, N.Y. 10022

A hardcover edition of this book was published in 1991 by HarperCollins*Publishers*.

Cover illustration by Merritt Dekle

First HarperPaperbacks printing: December 1992

Printed in the United States of America

HarperPaperbacks and colophon are trademarks of HarperCollins*Publishers*

10 9 8 7 6 5 4 3 2 1

For Lawrence P. Ashmead
and Walter Mathews, grazie.

CHAPTER 1

Kate Mulcay knelt in the rough grass in her front yard digging holes for daffodils. The sun was warm on her back and the winelike fragrance of ripening muscadines drifted down from the poplar tree where the wild grape vine hung in swags, its leaves already freckled with autumnal gold.

Her dog Pepper, with his Dalmatian spots and his hound build, and her cat Sugar, so-called because she was as white as, dozed in the filtered light, which lay like a benison on the tangled fencerow. For once there were no cars or trucks on the old dirt road, and power saws and bulldozers committed to building subdivisions in the woods toward the river were blessedly quiet. Three speckled guineas, as neat as Quaker ladies going to meeting, clucked contentedly over seed that had fallen from the bird feeders. They had strayed into her yard a year or so ago and stayed, and this time,

Kate thought placidly, she would have to find time to search for the nest, where there was probably a clutch of eggs. She wanted to be there when the baby guineas hatched because they were such fragile little creatures, so vulnerable to dogs and foxes and snakes that she had never been able to raise one.

She did right, Kate thought, pushing her hair off her forehead with a gloved hand and sitting back on her heels, to stay here after Benjy died. She had dreaded loneliness, the special recurring ache of remembering and missing. She hated the wrench of having woods and fields turned into expensive subdivisions with landscaped mansions full of strangers surrounding her plain little log cabin. It seemed pointless to drive thirty miles to and from her job at the *Atlanta Searchlight* in bumper-to-bumper traffic that was beginning to spill over onto the old country road.

But on this autumn day, with the smells and sounds of fall around her and the feel of the damp earth and the silken husks of the daffodil bulbs in her hands, she felt tranquil. Benjy wouldn't have shored up and made habitable that funny century-old lopsided cabin behind her if he hadn't been convinced that she loved it enough to stay and to enjoy it even without him. He knew he had cancer, even if she hadn't believed it.

Kate counted the daffodils. Eight more to go. She would get them in the ground and have time to pull the honeysuckle vines out of her prize white althaea before sundown.

Suddenly the peace of the autumn afternoon was shattered.

The Gandy sisters from down the road jumped over the fence she and Benjy had carefully erected around the cabin, old chestnut rails laid in the time-honored zigzag pattern of the mountains. They of course knocked down the top rail.

"Miss Kate! Miss Kate!" cried Sheena, the one named for the jungle queen. "Somebody's kilt Mr. Garney Wilcox!"

"Murdered him cold!" put in Kim Sue, the one with the overbite.

Distracted and not thinking, Kate murmured, "Good riddance. He needed killing."

The Gandys, nine and ten years old, were shiny-eyed with satisfaction.

"Yes'm," said Sheena, "right in his own mommer's house."

"What did you say?" Kate asked, her trowel poised in midair.

"Right in Miss Willie's root cellar," said Kim Sue.

"'Twas not her root cellar!" contradicted Sheena. "'Twas on the stair steps."

"Aw, shit," conceded Kim Sue. "Them steps go down to the root cellar, don't they?"

"You don't know!" shouted Sheena. "You didn't go over there with papa and the law. You didn't see the dead body!"

"You didn't neither!" retaliated Kim Sue. "He was all covered up when they put him in the dead wagon!"

"All right, girls," said Kate, putting her trowel in the basket she carried over the yard for hand tools.

"Come on in the kitchen and have a Coke. I'd better call somebody."

It wasn't grief or even shock over the death of Garney Wilcox that ruined Kate's Saturday afternoon stint of gardening, perhaps the only one she would have in a week. She herself often thought she'd kill Garney Wilcox if she had a chance—a mean avaricious jerk who was ruining the countryside with his real estate "developments"—what a misleading word!—and breaking his mother's heart.

But his mother, Miss Willie, Kate's old friend and neighbor since she and Benjy moved to the woods of north Fulton County twenty years before, was something different. Kate loved Miss Willie, a valiant, wise country woman who had been the strength and comfort of the whole area in years past. Miss Willie had walked down the old wagon road the day Kate and Benjy brought the first shabby load of their belongings to the little three-room cabin, which had stood vacant except for mice and birds and even snakes for thirty years.

"Willie Wilcox," the old woman had introduced herself with a touch of formality. "I'm so proud to have you'uns for neighbors. Hit's gon' be mighty heartening to see lights in the old schoolhouse agin. When you'uns putting the electric in?"

Wires were due to be run in that day, Benjy told her, if the electrician they had hired could find the house. Meanwhile, Kate offered Miss Willie a packing case to sit on and they had the first of many happy

4

laughter-laced visits while Benjy brought in and set up bedstead and stove.

Miss Willie had come to what they called "the Cove" as a bride forty-five years earlier when the area was still country with mule-plowed fields and creek-side moonshine stills the only sources of livelihood. She had grown up in the adjoining mountain county, which she referred to as "up in Churkee" (for Cherokee), and even in her seventieth year she retained the flavor of the mountains in her speech, the love of mountain beauties in her heart. All wild things were her friends. She alone among the gardeners Kate knew could transplant lady slippers and trillium, dogtooth violets and sweet shrub from the woods to her dooryard without shock or damage.

She knew all the practical things essential to rural living—when to plant delicate early peas and new potatoes, the exact night in May, rain or shine, when watermelon seeds should go in the ground. She followed the signs in the almanac, which she could have written. She was weather wise, the settlement's oracle on hog-killing time, and she often was called upon to calm and separate feuding colonies of bees. Her clothesline had the whitest sheets blowing in the breeze, even after most of her neighbors had acquired washing machines and dryers. To Miss Willie nothing was more efficacious than boiling clothes in her old black three-legged iron pot with homemade lye soap.

The only thing in her life which Miss Willie couldn't handle with confidence and abounding love was her stepson, Garney. She often told Kate that she married Cy Wilcox because of his motherless son. She loved the little boy on sight and gladly left her home in "Churkee" to settle down in the Cove to "wife" Cy and "mother" little Garney, who was still in diapers when his own mother died. Cy died before she had completed the job of raising Garney, but she managed.

The way Miss Willie managed often seemed to Kate to be little short of miraculous. Her herbs and quilts were advertised in the state's *Farmer's Bulletin*, bringing a growing trickle of mail orders and even customers to the old farmhouse. Butter from the rich, creamy milk her cows gave was greatly in demand in the little town of Roswell six miles away. Once a week Miss Willie packed it in towels wrung out in icy water from her well and drove the old Ford truck Cy had left her into town to peddle.

She loved supplying the small-town housewives with the bounty from her kitchen and cow pen and even branched out to offer them her butter-and-egg-rich pound cakes and vegetables from her garden. She took so much pleasure in talking to people that she hated to take their money. But Garney didn't.

Even as a little boy the money was the only thing Garney could stand about those peddling expeditions. He was embarrassed and shamed to be knocking on doors and, cap in hand, as Miss Willie insisted, offering farm produce for sale. When he got old enough to ride the school bus to high school in the little town, he flatly refused to be a part of her selling.

For a time Miss Willie compromised by letting him drive the truck and wait in it while she knocked on doors. But when some woman customer, accompanying Miss Willie to the curb, saw him and chided him for not helping, he quit altogether.

Miss Willie didn't fault him for it. He was, she told Kate, a "minded" person, which obviously meant that he had a mentality far above the mundane chores of cleaning out stalls and plowing. His real mother had been an educated woman, good at reading and writing, Miss Willie said, and she expected that Garney had inherited this splendid intellect.

"I wish I could of give him something like that," Miss Willie had once told Kate wistfully. "But twarn't no schools close when I was a-growing up."

"Bullshit," Kate had said, to Miss Willie's horror. Granted that you had to shovel the stuff—and lucky to get it for the garden—and almost daily step in it, but there was no call, Miss Willie had said, to use the word.

Kate had meekly cleaned up her vocabulary and listened while Miss Willie told of her plan to send Garney to Peach State Tech, a small vocational junior college not far away. It would cost "cash money," she admitted, but she had a plan for that.

"You know old house plunder is now called 'antiques,' " she had told Kate. "There's a woman that opened up a store over on yon highway not selling nothing but them old things. She's a-coming to my house and see if she wants to buy any of my stuff."

"Oh, Miss Willie!" Kate had wailed. "All your nice old things! She'll talk you out of your grandma's clock and your rope bed and all your platters and churns. And she won't pay you half what they're worth! Those things are irreplaceable!"

7

But Miss Willie had been stubborn. Garney needed money, and she didn't need a thing for herself but a bed and a stove.

Kate had made up her mind to be there with her friend Nan, a fair-minded antiques expert, when the new entrepreneur invaded Miss Willie's old house. But a murder trial Kate had been covering for her newspaper was cranking up again in south Georgia. It had resulted in a mistrial the first time around, and they were going to try it again. She had to be there. In the excitement of the trial she forgot Miss Willie's antique sale, and when she visited that evening she was dismayed to find the old house practically empty.

The old woman had sold nearly everything she owned except her bed and her stove and one thing more. She had sent her old parlor organ to Kate's house, where it sat in the middle of her "big" room— which passed for living room, dining room, and study. Its mellow golden wood glowed softly in the cabin darkness, its voice deep and sweet when Kate touched a key.

When Kate had confronted Miss Willie, the old lady's wrinkled face was luminous with pride and triumph.

"Always wanted something to give you, and when that woman's cold eye fell on mama's organ I figgered money couldn't buy it. I want you to have it. It's got a hundred years of love and good tunes in it and I ain't a-pricing that."

Kate had accepted it, choking up with affection for the donor and resolving to keep it not for herself but in case Miss Willie needed it or wanted it in the future.

Now, as she served the Gandy children Cokes and, on impulse, threw in a plate of fresh baked cheese straws, her eyes rested on the parlor organ and she knew she had to hurry. Whatever things happened to Garney, however much he deserved it, she had better get to Miss Willie in that hideous nursing home down the road.

Garney had put her there months earlier when one of the new subdivision neighbors had found her wading in the creek and reported to him that she was demented. It wasn't the first time city people had been dismayed to find Miss Willie abroad in the woods and fields on a moonlit night or in predawn hours. Their dogs barked at her and some of their children ran from her, and they themselves found her earth-and-smoke-smelling old clothes and her way of speaking incomprehensible.

"Crazy," said the people in the pink stucco house.

"Probably got Alzheimer's," said the people in the French provincial.

It was a word Garney latched onto in triumph. That was exactly what his mother had, he decided, and the only thing to do was to pop her in a nursing home where she would be well taken care of.

Again Kate had been out of town and unable to go to the rescue, even assuming she would know what course to take. Obviously Garney and his pudgy, painted-faced little wife, Voncile, were in charge, and even Miss Willie, when Kate finally got to her, seemed resigned.

She was tired and listless and the old face, which had mirrored the beauty of the sky and the woods around her as surely as a body of water, was now empty and arid as a drained pond.

"I'm eighty-five years old," she had told Kate. "Ain't much sense in keeping on. Garney and Voncile say my mind is gone and I'm just to stay here and be took care of."

Kate had failed utterly in her effort to incite her old friend to rebellion. She had jeered at the notion that Miss Willie needed to be taken care of. She had urged her to come and spend a spell in her old school-house to recover from the shock of being wrested from her home and institutionalized. And, failing all else, she had wept, telling Miss Willie that she was lonesome. It had been to no avail.

Now Miss Willie's beloved son Garney was dead. Kate had to find out how and why and get to Miss Willie.

She reached for the telephone with one hand and shooed the Gandys out the back door with the other. As a longtime newspaper reporter who sometimes solved crimes, she knew the county police at the Morgan Falls Courthouse annex would tell her what had happened.

She unzipped and let fall her muddy denim skirt and stepped out of her sneakers as Pete Blount, a local boy who worked for the county, answered the phone.

"Yep," he said. "Pretty dead. In fact, thoroughly dead."

"What do you mean?" Kate said. "Dead's dead."

"Well, old Garney got it several ways. Blow on the

head. A raw electric wire scorching him to a crackling. And I don't know what else. He vomited a lot, so the medical fellow is looking for poison."

"Oh," said Kate weakly. As she was hanging up the phone, she managed, "I'll get back to you."

She had to call the paper. She had to get into some clean clothes. She was headed for her loft bedroom when the Gandys set up a cry from the grape arbor, where they had been surreptitiously prospecting for Kate's prize scuppernongs, the tawny amber grapes she reserved for wine. Her thoughts were interrupted by Sheena's voice.

"Miss Kate! Miss Kate!" keened Sheena. "Mommer said tell you to come and take a ride in our new car. We got us a BMW."

"A BM—" Kate gasped, pausing by the upstairs window on the way to the bathroom.

"Yes'm," said Kim Sue. "Daddy sold Grandpa's old cornfield and we got us a new car."

"Crazy," Kate muttered, "everybody's crazy." She stepped into the shower. The Gandys didn't even have a bathroom in their house, but when the developers shelled out for the old cornfield, they bought not just a make-do car, the kind Kate always had, but a luxury car. *Maybe they can live in it when builders send bulldozers to push their house down,* she decided wryly.

The night police reporter was already at work on the story of the little rural homicide when Kate called. With the way crime had burgeoned in Atlanta recently one more murder, especially one that was apparently unrelated to sex or drugs or his favorite, the Mafia, didn't interest Carl Yancy much. He took some notes from Kate and whistled lightly at the angle of multiple methods of murder.

"How redundant," he murmured, thanking Kate and hanging up.

She rushed out to her car and headed south for the nursing home. There were newer ones and nicer ones, Kate knew, but Garney and Voncile had not troubled to find one of those. The old gray two-story residence, which had once served as a boardinghouse and been converted to take the elderly and the ill, looked bleak in the gathering dusk. The big trees in the yard—like the old folks in the house behind them— had given up early, and dropped shriveled and brown leaves on the walk and across the porch. They rustled drearily as Kate climbed the steps and rang the bell.

Lulu Pitman, plump and officious in her stained blue nylon uniform, let Kate in but without the customary cordiality arising from her lifelong acquaintance with the old log schoolhouse. Her parents and grandparents had gone to school there, she always reminded Kate, with as much pride as if they had gone to Harvard or Yale. Now she said briefly, "It's after hours, Kate. No visiting."

"Lulu, I've got to see Miss Willie. Does she know about Garney?"

"What about Garney?" asked Lulu, suddenly curious.

"He's dead."

"Lord God," said Lulu. "That'll finish the old lady. No, we hadn't heard. What happened? Was he sick?"

12

Kate didn't want to feed what she knew would be Lulu's rich appetite for details and didn't want to take the time. She said briefly that he had been found dead and the police were investigating.

Lulu stood back and admitted Kate into the dimly lit, urine-smelling corridor leading to Miss Willie's room. In compliance with some fire code or other the offices and personnel quarters had been moved to the second floor and the downstairs rooms, once spacious, were divided into first-floor cubicles for the patients on the theory that it would be easier for them to escape in case the splintery old house caught fire. The place had been painted inside and the carpet, Kate suspected, was new, but it smelled the way it always had —of urine and decay, of grease and overcooked rutabagas. There were voices in the enclosed back porch, which served as a dining room, but only the sibilant whisper of leaky plumbing broke the silence in the hall.

Kate found the door to Miss Willie's room open and the old lady sat in a stiff little straight chair by the window with only the light from the hall to see by.

"Miss Willie," Kate said softly, putting an arm around the thin shoulders in the faded old outing gown.

The old lady looked up, her dark eyes brimming with tears.

Kate leaned over, kissed her on the forehead, and smoothed the thin gray hair.

"Miss Willie," she tried again. "Garney . . ."

Miss Willie nodded. "Dead," she whispered.

Kate paused. Lulu hadn't been told. Apparently Miss Willie had.

"You knew?" she said.

"I done it," said Miss Willie.

"Aw, no," Kate said soothingly. "Don't say that."

The old woman stared at Kate a moment and then looked back out the window, where the night sky was rosy from the reflected lights of the town of Roswell. The bare trees in the side yard made a black tracery against the luminous air.

Miss Willie jerked around in her chair.

"Go," she said. "Git!"

Surprised, Kate straightened up and reached for the old lady's hand. "I'm sorry, Miss Willie," she said.

Suddenly the old woman pulled her hand loose and cackled.

"Like a fish on a crow!" she snorted.

Kate sat down at the foot of the bed and tried again. When did Miss Willie hear? Did she know what happened? Wouldn't she feel better to lie down for a while? Had she had any supper?

Miss Willie glared at her. "Git!" she cried, and turned her back.

Kate left, worried and sad. *Like a fish on a crow,* she mused as she walked to the front door. The old country saying for the improbable, if not the impossible. Miss Willie knew Kate wasn't grieving for Garney, in spite of her "I'm sorry." Perhaps Miss Willie was angry that this should be so. That the idea that anybody would grieve for him was as likely as a fish riding on the wings of a crow.

Lulu came out of a room across the hall to let her out. Kate paused.

"Lulu, has anybody been to see Miss Willie today?"

"Naw," said Lulu. "Nobody hardly ever comes to see her except you and that little Carson girl. You know, the one that's friends with Garney and Voncile's young'un Cheri? She comes a lot. Near 'bout everybody else that ever knew Miss Willie has sold out and moved away."

She smirked knowingly and poked Kate in the ribs. "Garney and Voncile comes when they got papers for her to sign."

A light rain, more mist than water, had begun to fall, and the leaves on the walk to the gravel parking lot were slick beneath her loafers. Kate walked carefully, thoughtfully. She needed to call somebody, Carl Yancy at the downtown police pressroom or maybe Pete Blount before he went off duty. She'd stop at a pay phone at the filling station. Carl had gone to supper. Pete answered at the Morgan Falls office.

"No, I don't think anybody's told Miss Willie yet," he said. "First, they couldn't find her. You know Garney always told everybody she was in one of them modern places in Roswell or Marietta. They didn't check out. Voncile was out shopping and they couldn't find her for the longest. When they got to me I knew the place, but I told them Miss Willie's been off her rocker so long she wouldn't know what they was talking about, so there's no rush."

Little you know, Kate thought, but she hung up without saying it. If Miss Willie was going to maintain that she killed Garney, there was no use letting the police think she was in her right mind.

Kate fed Pepper and Sugar and found a piece of bread and cheese and a can of beer for herself. It was too early for her to go to bed and too dark for her to go over to Miss Willie's house, even assuming the police hadn't made it inaccessible.

She stood in the front yard and looked toward the grove where the old Wilcox house had stood for a hundred and forty years. A thin stand of trees partially obscured the backs of half a dozen half-million- to one-million-dollar houses, each set in a de rigueur three acres, which now stood between her and her old neighbor. Streets and sidewalks and curbs replaced the road they had used. Now lights glowed back of French doors and stained-glass windows and the reproduction bubbly glass of twelve-over-twelve panes of saltboxes and southern colonials. One incongruously vibrant blue swimming pool had been lit up, although it was too chilly for use. But beyond them all the dark hulk of Cy Wilcox's hill rose, unpaved, unlandscaped, unlighted, and unoccupied.

Cy's pa had bought a thousand acres along a little creek back when land in north Fulton County could be had for fifty cents an acre. It was said that he made the best moonshine in the area, and once when Kate and Miss Willie walked along the creek, which ran through the dooryard, following through deep woods toward the river, they found a stack of rocks where a still fire had been, and some rusty cans that had been left behind when the revenuers raided the still the last time.

"Pore thing," Miss Willie had said. "All he

knowed to do for cash money—and they put him in the pen.''

He had learned to read and write in the Atlanta Penitentiary and they said he never complained about serving time. He liked the electric lights and the steam heat and was not reconciled to the discomforts of the country after that.

His son, Cy, had not cared. He planted cotton and corn and was satisfied with a farmer's living. *And no wonder,* thought Kate. *He had Miss Willie with her good cooking and her pretty quilts and her fine vegetable and flower garden. He had been a comfortable man.*

Looking out across the subdivision to the dark rise of hill, she wondered if there was any comfort left. Garney and Voncile had bought in town, leaving the house vacant after Miss Willie left. Some of the new people in the subdivision had bought their land from Garney's share of the acreage, which Miss Willie deeded to him when he grew up, and they promised to keep an eye on the old house. They were pleasant neighbors, seemingly country lovers, so Kate assumed they had protected it from vandals. She would see tomorrow.

She turned toward her own cabin, and as usual her affection for it brought a lump to her throat. She and Benjy used to like to look for country lands before they were married. They would slip off from town, her job at the newspaper, his with the city police department, when news and crime were slow, and go prospecting. There was an old country store up on the Canton highway where they could buy sardines and crackers and Vienna sausage and cold drinks for impromptu picnics, and from it they wandered down the old wagon road which led to the cabin. Benjy had in mind acreage with maybe a lake site. Kate saw the cabin and lost her heart to it. Its scant one-acre site didn't trouble her. She wanted to live in a log house. It answered some childhood need going back to James Fenimore Cooper. Benjy looked at its raddled roof, its vacant lopsided window openings, from which the old shutters had long since rotted and fallen off, and he said she was out of her mind.

But they went back and took better picnics and Benjy saw the chimney with its pattern of dry-laid rocks climbing to the shake roof, and he said, "Maybe." The log corncrib would make a good workshop, he said, and back of it the land looked rich enough for a small garden.

They pooled their savings and bought it, and by the time the local carpenters had helped them to shore it up, clear out the well, and install electricity, they were ready to get married and move in.

Kate stood now in the darkness, looking in through the lighted door. She could see bright braided rugs and books and lamplight. Benjy had loved it as much as she did, and they had been happy there, although both were city-reared. It was small but big enough for two people. Now at night sometimes she opened the door to let in the dog Pepper and the cat Sugar and she knew it was because the three rooms suddenly seemed too big for one person. It was company having a deep-voiced watchdog on the rug by her bed, and she willingly pulled up her feet to accommodate the big white cat for the warmth she brought to her bed.

Sometime in the middle of the night Kate awakened to find Pepper's cold muzzle in her face. He whimpered, the signal to go out.

"You don't need to go out," she argued crossly as she fumbled for her slippers. And then she saw that the mist had vanished and an almost full moon flooded the yard with silver. Pepper couldn't stay indoors on a bright moonlit night. Something through the woods and over the creek or at least down the road called to him, and he begged to go.

Kate let him out the kitchen door and stood a moment watching him lope, tail high, through the yard. She found herself remembering how Miss Willie loved to roam on moonlit nights.

When the moon was full, Miss Willie often said, she was bound to get outdoors in that magic light. "A born lunatic," she told Kate with satisfaction. "Always have been crazy on a full moon."

She's not crazy, Kate told herself as she shut the door and headed back to bed. For all the tears and the newly caustic manner, Miss Willie's face held its usual intelligence. But why did she say she killed Garney? Miss Willie wasn't given to figures of ephemeral speech. If she meant she had done something to kill his spirit, she would have said so. But it was death, plain and final.

"I done it," she had said.

The whole idea was patently silly, Kate decided, reaching for one of the gardening books she kept by her bedside for middle-of-the-night wakefulness. Miss

Willie was old and frail and confined to that nursing home.

Kill a big grown man? Like a fish on a crow!

Kate opened Ron Freethy's book *From Agar to Zendry* at the chapter headed "Green Cunning," read a few paragraphs, and then put a finger between the pages to hold her place and think about it. The author's eighty-nine-year-old great-grandmother was called "the little witch" because of her skill with plants. She had that age-old "green cunning." Miss Willie certainly had it, Kate mused, thinking about Miss Willie's frost-touched and fading flower beds by the front door of the now empty house.

Kate loved all English books about cottage gardens and proposed to have one in the log cabin's small yard. Miss Willie had never heard of cottage gardens, but she had an instinct for spreading a bright, fragrant patchwork of all the old-fashioned flowers and herbs across the earth. Kate could see her coming through the woods with a basket on her arm. It would brim with poppies and larkspur, lamb's ears and cornflowers, all just dug from Miss Willie's own beds and kept fresh with damp moss. Miss Willie would top the load with her own trowel because she always helped to plant anything that she brought. Plants uprooted pined for the earth, she said, and she made Kate hurry to restore them to it. If she saw a bare spot in the jumbled symmetry of Kate's patch she might put a cabbage there, and once she brought a bee skep she had woven herself from wheat straw and broomsedge.

Kate resolved to go and get Miss Willie and keep her in the log cabin until the grisly details of Garney's death had been settled and the funeral held. She would call Voncile in the morning and get permission. It didn't seem likely that Garney's dumb, greedy little wife would care. Her only interest in his mother had been the five hundred acres remaining to her after she had halved the land with Garney. It was prime residential land, selling for thirty-five thousand dollars or more an acre, and Voncile probably had it already, or would get it. What did she care about Miss Willie?

The next morning Kate had to have two cups of coffee before she could brace herself to call Garney's widow to ask permission to take Miss Willie out of the nursing home. The only thing worse than talking to Voncile on the telephone would be having to see her in person in her pretentious, expensive, overdecorated Buckhead condominium. Voncile was an idiot, but now that Garney was dead she was presumably in charge of his mother.

The widow answered the phone herself in a suitably subdued, black crape voice. For a moment Kate actually felt the sympathy she felt compelled to express.

Recognizing her, Voncile's voice abruptly changed.

"You're not fooling me with your 'sorries,'" she said shrilly. "I know how you felt about Garney! You're in cahoots with his murderer!"

"Now, Voncile," Kate began placatingly. "I'm a friend and a neighbor, and I know Miss Willie is grief-stricken. I just thought—"

"You thought—you thought!" screeched Voncile. "You and that old murderer are in cahoots. No, you can't have her come and 'stay with you,' " she went on, mimicking Kate's voice. "I won't give leave, and the police sure as hell aren't gon' give her a chance to run off."

"Miss Willie's not going to run off," Kate said, laughing a little. "She'd be right here in my cabin, close to her old home, and it might make her feel a little better."

"Who cares how she feels?" cried Voncile. "I'm surprised at you. Your father and your husband cops, and you want to harbor the killer of my darling, my dearest love! No! She'll hang for this."

She banged down the receiver and Kate, slowly returning hers to the cradle, caught herself editing Voncile. Electrocuted, not hanged . . . and then she pulled herself up sharply. Neither applied here. She had been thrown off, she thought ruefully, by Voncile's way of talking in country song titles. Her "dearest love," indeed. More like her co-conspirator to rob Miss Willie of everything she loved and imprison her in a nursing home. The only comforting thing about it was that their intimacy might be what Ambrose Bierce, defining the word, said was a relationship into which fools are drawn for their mutual destruction.

CHAPTER 2

Shining Waters Subdivision began just beyond a thin stand of pines and scraggly shrubs separating the backyards of the big new houses from the gravel road and mercifully screening from their view Kate's shabby old cabin. Kate often thought they would have her zoned out of the neighborhood someday when the area went completely elegant, living up to its glittering name. She and Miss Willie had laughed when the developers hit upon that name. The little stream that wended its way through the woods, across Miss Willie's yard and toward the river had always been called 'Shine Creek by the locals. The name probably appeared on no map and was known to few people beyond the handful of natives who had made whiskey on its banks and the revenuers who had cut up their stills and sometimes caught the operators and hauled them off to do a year and a day in jail.

But the developers had a talent for ferreting out old country names and turning them to their own uses. It was possible, Kate thought, scrambling up a clay bank, that Garney himself had told them that the lively little stream, dancing over rocks and falling in crystal cascades where the land turned steep, was called 'Shine. On their own initiative they had robbed it of its history and corrupted it into prettiness.

Kate had often walked with Miss Willie along the creek, gathering foamflowers and bluets in the spring and beech leaves to be soaked in glycerine to make glistening deep green winter bouquets. They had paused and inspected old still sites where rocks still marked the furnace base and the square tin cans still called "jars" lay rusting in the sun.

Once under a sweet shrub Kate had fished out a tall round metal can, as big as a five-gallon gas can. When she brushed the dead leaves off it she caught the green of tarnished copper.

"Look, Miss Willie!" she said. "It's copper!"

"Shore," said Miss Willie. "Hit's what they call the money piece. Wonder how them revenuers come to leave it behind without cutting it up."

Together they rubbed the metal and poked sticks into two short pipes which projected from its sides, digging out dirt and leaves.

"What's a money piece?" Kate had asked.

"Condenser," said Miss Willie. "Hit's where the vapors turn to liquid and git drinkable instid of smellable. After it comes through there you jar it and sell it."

She looked dreamy.

"If the price is up you can buy you a Jersey cow."

"Ha!" Kate laughed. "I know who made 'shine here! Can I have this money piece?"

Miss Willie chuckled. "Child, what would you do with it? You ain't planning on making white whiskey, air you? Take it, if it suits you."

Kate had set the tall metal pot on her hearth to hold fire tools, and from time to time Miss Willie would bring her another artifact from the old days when the manufacture of white lightning along 'Shine Creek was the only local industry. Kate had a T-shaped length of pipe hanging on her kitchen wall and an oft-polished little copper funnel on her windowsill. She suspected some of the tall blue half-gallon mason jars that held dried beans and rice for her use had once held untax-paid whiskey for the Wilcox family. And one day she had boldly asked her old neighbor if she had indeed made moonshine herself.

"I've made a lots of things," Miss Willie had said with dignity, dismissing the subject.

Now in the early Sunday morning sunshine Kate followed the remnants of the old path that led to Miss Willie's house, obliterated here and there by Shining Waters's curbs and paved streets, disappearing under well-tended lawns and emerging again in the woods beyond. There had once been a wagon road to the river, but grading machines had taken care of that. The results, Kate had to admit, were more attractive than the little patchy and scattered dumps old settlers had created there, but she had loved picking through the castoffs of long-ago householders.

"It's such neat garbage," she had once exulted to

Benjy. "No nasty old bottles and cans. Just nice holey blue granite pots and pans, and look at this—a home-made meal bin! A good old primitive with only a few mouse gnawings around the bottom."

"Too poor for bottles and cans," he had said. "They didn't eat out of the store."

Kate had hauled the meal bin home, scrubbed it with lye water, and put it in the kitchen to hold potted geraniums, which didn't hide the mouse gnawings but made a pleasant distraction.

Now there was no sign of the engaging little dumps. Stone lions guarded one driveway, which Kate carefully skirted. Several yards were sequestered behind handsome iron fences and brick walls, beyond which oak-leaf hydrangeas, dogwood, and crape myrtles turned scarlet and gold against impeccable stucco and stone house walls.

Pepper, galloping ahead of her, suddenly stopped and started barking. A couple in matching blue running outfits came walking slowly up the hill.

The man waved and spoke soothingly to Pepper.

They were the Gardiners, Ron and Valerie, closest of the new neighbors, and very pleasant when she saw them, which was not often. They lived in a fortresslike gray granite turreted castle. She thought they were childless and she wondered why a couple needed so much room. But it was possible that they entertained a lot. She saw cars coming and going when she happened to look that way at night.

Now the man, a short, plump, freckle-faced fellow of thirty-odd years, beamed on her cordially.

"You're out early," he said. "Walking, or running for your health?"

Kate shook her head, sharing her smile with the slim, dark-haired girl who stood beside him. "I'm not," she said, "but I admire to see such energy in the neighbors. Did you run, or are you about to?"

"Valerie here did the running," he said. "I puffed along behind her. She's a regular whippet."

It was a good metaphor, Kate decided. Valerie, probably still in her twenties, didn't have an ounce of spare flesh on her lithe, long-legged young body. Her dark hair, falling in a shining tide below her shoulders, was probably the heaviest thing about her. Her smooth face, with its creamy skin and long, dark eyes, was unsmiling, expressionless.

"Ah, you're going over to the murder scene," said Ron, screwing up his pudgy red face in distress. "I hear they think the old lady did it. I don't see how, but they said she confessed."

"Poison," said Valerie in her velvety contralto, speaking for the first time.

"Aw, no," said Kate. "That's ridiculous. But, yes, I thought I would look in over there. I don't know why. It's probably sealed."

"She gave us poison mushrooms," said Valerie petulantly.

"Aw, hon, I don't think she meant to," protested Ron. "She's an old lady and didn't know any better."

Kate looked at them aghast. Of course Miss Willie would know better. But why would she give the Gardiners poison mushrooms?

"Are you sure?" she asked. "I can't believe it."

Valerie regarded her wordlessly and moved ahead. "I'm going in," she said to her husband.

Ron, looking more like a sweating fifth grader on the school playground than a husband, winked at Kate and followed.

"See you," he said.

"Oh, Lordy, Lordy!" Kate prayed quietly. "Miss Willie, don't be in this mess!"

Pepper had busied himself spraying a signature on several of the Gardiners' sidewalk plantings but, perceiving that Kate was ready to go, he went unerringly to the thicket where the path disappeared in the underbrush and with a triumphant yip and wave of the tail commanded her to follow him.

Kate stopped at the edge of the clearing and looked at the ancient farmstead. Gray and lonely, paintless for a hundred and forty years, its clapboard walls sagging and splintery, it had a certain grace she had always loved. Now behind the police department's crime scene yellow tape it looked like an aged beldam decked out for Mardi Gras. The tape necklaced the hard-swept yard, running from the fenceposts in the front yard to the scarlet and gold sassafras trees in the backyard and around the side to the smokehouse and the well house. There was a bench under the biggest sassafras tree, where Miss Willie had liked to sit on a hot day to shell peas or cut her corn off the cob. It was outside the crime scene ribbons and Kate dropped down on it, grateful for the fragrance of the tree's mitten-shaped leaves. Miss Willie didn't know a lot of history and geography, but she had it on the authority of family—and possibly Indian—lore that it was the sassafras tree which drew the first explorers to America. Its roots, unequaled for making spring tonics or easing childbirth, had been the first thing they sent back home over the sea. She didn't understand why people wasted their time digging ginseng, called "sang," to ship to China when they could have had the sweet fragrant sassafras roots.

Respectful of the police's fragile barriers, although there was nobody there to enforce them, Kate sat on, missing the smoke that once rose from the kitchen chimney, missing the cackle of hens and the sight of sheets like snowy sails and bright-colored quilts sunning on the clothesline which ran from the well house to the corner of the back porch. The porch, divested of old kitchen pots overflowing with geraniums and begonias, blazing Christmas cacti and the delicate vermilion skeleton of devil's backbone, seemed bare and unfriended. The water shelf, which once held a bucket and washpan with a sturdy flour-sack towel hanging from a nail beside it, was shorn of all but the police department's bright yellow ribbons.

The barn off to the side with a buggy shed next to it was off-limits, but Kate didn't think it held anything of interest since the departure of Miss Willie's old mule and milk cow. The old truck was kept in the buggy shed, but she could not be sure it was still there without crossing the police line.

The early morning sun lay a golden light on the cracked and weathered boards of the porch floor, and because the air was clear and rain-washed, Miss Willie's favorite view, the mountains of her childhood home fifty miles away to the north, was visible in amethyst peaks and valleys beyond the river and the woods. Remembering last night's rain, Kate wondered if it had obliterated any footprints leading to the house or if the crime scene boys had found and measured and photographed them. Miss Willie had kept the yard swept clean, using, to Kate's horror, dogwood branches for a broom. Dogwood, to Kate's generation, was sacrosanct, a tree of inviolable beauty. Miss Willie's hard-pressed mountain-bred kin valued the little tree for its use as well as its beauty. Its granitelike wood had been sold for years to English textile mills for spindles. The stubby branches that were left did make good yard brooms, and it wasn't likely that the packed earth they had swept clear of twigs and leaves and chicken droppings for half a century would retain a clear footprint.

But the flower beds on either side of the path and spaced about the yard in circles and triangles and diamond shapes were soft and receptive to prints. Kate studied them from a distance. All were empty of flowers and weed-grown now, but one closest to the back door still held tansy and wormwood and catnip and sage. An old rambler rose which sprang up in the herb bed clambered over the kitchen wall and held aloft half a dozen late blooms. Maybe, Kate thought wistfully, she could still bring Miss Willie home and let her rejoice in the unexpected autumn bloom.

Pepper, sniffing in the weeds at the edge of the yard, had scared up a rabbit and given chase. Kate sat on, remembering the place as it was before Garney, the real estate entrepreneur, had seen its money-making potential and taken it away from Miss Willie.

A deep sadness descended on her. She was sad for her old friend and days that were, but she knew that she was most of all sad for herself. Day in and day out she went on with her work at the newspaper, glad to be wanted, grateful that the approach of retirement age would not send her home and into senior-citizenhood. She wrote a column a few days a week, covered an occasional story, assisted with book reviews, and was available as a kind of office memory for youngsters who knew nothing about Atlanta's or the newspaper's past. Her contacts with readers were good and durable and held to be of value by her employers.

But murder . . . how it had once been the assignment to fill her with fire and fervor as a reporter! She had loved playing amateur detective by the side of the best of the pros, Benjamin Franklin Mulcay. Their fathers had served together on the Atlanta police force until Kate's father was felled by a holdup man's bullet and went home to spend the rest of his days in a wheelchair. Benjy's father, a captain, had retired and moved to the mountains, subsequently dying of a heart attack on a deer hunt.

Kate and Benjy had known and hated each other in earliest childhood when their families gathered for police outings and picnics at Grant Park. But there came a time when murder struck close to Kate, taking two of her co-workers at the *Atlanta Searchlight* and threatening her. Benjamin, just home from the Marines, was assigned to the case. When it was solved but seconds before Kate was to have become the third victim, he knelt beside her and took her in his arms.

They were married six months later. Thereafter

Kate's exuberant interest in murder was tempered and kept in line by the steady knowledge and expertise of lieutenant, then captain, and finally Major Mulcay of homicide. Her excitement, her intuitions, sometimes amused and exasperated him, though as the years passed he increasingly realized they were trustworthy.

Now Benjy was dead and she was old, wrinkled, bereft.

She knew that Miss Willie could not have killed her stepson, but her ardor for proof seemed to have vanished into that hole in the red clay earth where Benjy was buried. Experience said that the best way to clear Miss Willie, if her infirmities didn't save her, was to find the real murderer.

But how? Where? Kate didn't know.

Pepper came back empty-jawed from his rabbit hunt and collapsed with a sigh at Kate's feet.

She leaned down and cuffed him gently on the muzzle.

"Let's go," she said. "Church time."

Kate's colleagues at the newspaper and Benjy's fellow policemen sometimes expressed surprise that they were regular churchgoers. This stereotyping amused the Mulcays. The picture of newspaper reporters as hard-bitten and profane, of cops as tough and unfeeling, wasn't altogether false, but neither was it infallible. Both of them knew that many newspapermen and -women wrote well because they were nurtured in their youth on the cadences and rhythms of the Old Testament. In many poor homes in the South the Bible was the only book. It led the young people to become acquainted with the literature and the music of the church, if nothing else.

Benjy's first chief, an elegant white-haired man who had been on the force with Benjy's and Kate's fathers, spent every vacation of his life attending camp meeting at old Shiloh Campground south of Atlanta. He followed in the footsteps of ancestors who had gone every summer for a hundred years to the cluster of little shacks, called "tents," which encircled an open-air arbor. Families came, often with the milk cow hitched to the back of their wagons, at lay-by time on the farm for a season of feasting, worship, and spiritual refreshment.

Kate and Benjy went to church, sometimes they thought acceptingly, because they were reared to, rather than as an act of piety or fresh-springing faith. There was a rightness about being in the little white clapboard Presbyterian church on Sunday morning, and they hoped humbly that they would, as Kate put it, "be better and do better." They knew they fell short, that doubts often assailed them, that the pursuit of criminals wasn't conducive to a life of Christian charity.

Still they had gone, and Kate, showered and dressed in her best brown linen suit with the soft white shirt, felt lonely now but not alone as she took her place on the Spartan white-painted bench as the small congregation lurched tentatively into an old hymn.

Benjy, she thought, missing his enthusiastic baritone rising from a place beside her, *I don't know what to do. Show me. Miss Willie is having one of her "darksome" times. And me, too.*

The young minister, not long out of the seminary, spoke eloquently of the needs of people in the community. The choir countered with "Behold a Stranger at Thy Door." The psalter seemed peculiarly appropriate with Psalm 37: "Fret not thyself because of evil doers, neither be thou envious against the workers of iniquity. For they shall soon be cut down like the grass and wither as the green herb. . . . The steps of a good man are ordered by the Lord and he delighted in his way. Though he fall he shall not be utterly cast down. For the Lord upholdeth him in his hand."

Substitute "good woman"—Miss Willie—for "good man," Kate said silently to the thin page and read on responsively, her mood subtly improved by the service, as always.

After church a small group gathered around the minister to compliment him on his sermon, shaking his hand and moving a little way to pause under the old oak trees and chat with one another. Kate spotted the Pritchetts, who ran the nursing home, and hurried to speak to them.

"Tell me about Mrs. Wilcox," she begged. "How is she doing?"

"Independent as a hog on ice," said Lon Pritchett, a newcomer from the Midwest who delighted in the local idiom, usually using it wrong.

Kate was puzzled. "Her son—"

"That's right, Lon," said Esther Pritchett, pulling at his sleeve. "Mrs. Wilcox seemed very sad and depressed to me when I went over for the coffee and songfest this morning. She would not even come out of her room and let her friends console her."

"We-ell . . ." said Lon Pritchett uncertainly. He had run afoul of his own cliché. He didn't really know how Miss Willie was. He considered all his charges to be as independent as hogs on ice or as happy as dead pigs in the sunshine.

Kate turned her attention to his wife.

"Does she eat and sleep well and get some exercise?"

"I don't think she eats or sleeps at all," Mrs. Pritchett said worriedly. "But she walks. Our other guests say she paces the hall, and before lockup time at night she walks back and forth in the yard and on the sidewalk. Once—" she looked at her husband, who was safely chatting with somebody else—"once she was found walking downtown. That really upset Lon. She had been missing for hours."

"I'm coming back to see her," Kate said decisively, not asking permission. "We're old neighbors."

"Wait," said Mrs. Pritchett hesitantly. "Let's ask Lon. There's a policeman . . ."

Lon was emphatic in his refusal.

"Sorry, kid," he said. "I got my orders from her daughter-in-law *and* the police. Strictly incommunicado, you know, until this murder bit is solved."

The phone was ringing when Kate walked into her kitchen.

"Katy, chile," said Shell Shelnutt, the city editor. "You got anything you can't turn loose of tonight?"

"Why?" asked Kate cautiously.

"Because the home team needs you. I'm short-handed as hell and those pretty Red Dogs are making a strike in the housing projects. I know you know those heroes and they wouldn't object if you struck with them. We can find out what kind of roundup they make of dealers and drugs, but we really need you to go along and see how the folks in the projects react. It ought to be dramatic."

"Okay," said Kate. "What time?"

"First dark," said Shell, a country boy, liking the term and easy about being imprecise because he knew Kate, the old pro, would find out for herself when the Red Dogs planned their outing.

Kate went to take off her church dress and make herself a sandwich, smiling a little at the way the elite Red Dogs drew sarcasm from old hands on the paper and even on the police force. For her money they *were* pretty and they were heroes, geared to risk life and limb in the performance of the most dangerous duty around. She loved their slim black uniforms, their bullet-proof vests, their boots, even the ugly semiautomatic pistols the city had just seen fit to equip them with. There was a macho elegance about the understated absence of brass buttons and the usual police insignia. They were athletes, few as old as thirty years, picked from a surfeit of volunteers from the fifteen-hundred-man force because they were also seasoned in police work with impressive track records and had been found to be cool under fire.

There were twenty-five of them, as vigorously trained as Green Berets for battle, and Kate, who had watched some of them grow up in policing, loved their impudence, their insouciance. If the drug traffic could be stopped, they could do it.

"Ah," said an old department friend of hers and Benjy's once, "the drug dealers are not afraid of us. They're afraid of each other. Red Dogs are just an inconvenience to them."

He had grinned, knowing full well that the jails were filling up fast with dealers brought in off the streets and they would soon go out on bond. But at least there was a lull in their reign of terror, and Kate's heart went out to the people living in the public housing projects—old people too terrified to venture out of their little apartments, children not allowed to play in the yards. Drug dealers were indiscriminate about their killings. They shot out streetlights, fired their pistols into the air to announce their presence, and drove by in fast cars, spraying with bullets the houses where the innocent lived, on the off chance they would hit a rival dealer or somebody who had squealed on them. Often as not they hit a child or an old grandmother.

She would be glad to go with the Red Dogs.

On her way to the Red Dogs' kennel, which they shared with a variety of other city offices, a new, plain, unembellished building on the south side of town, Kate decided to stop at the medical examiner's office to learn which of the various attacks on Garney had hit the mark. His body would have been taken to Grady, the city-county hospital, for a doctor to "pronounce him," as the police said. When his obvious and irreversible death had been made official by some weary, overworked young intern or resident, they would move his body half a block away to the medical examiner's building on a short street, the name of which always delighted Kate's sense of the ludicrous— Coca-Cola Place, one of the first on-purpose homes of the world-famous fortune-making elixir. Chief among Atlanta's claims to fame, the drink had been brewed there early before it went on to help finance the building of hospitals and clinics, parks and some of the handsomest northside mansions on a street wags called Rococola Row. Now the street called Coca-Cola Place was the next-to-last resting place for the mysteriously dead. The beaten and the burned, the starved and the shot and the poisoned were brought here to be cut open and probed and divested of the last vestige of privacy. The triangular-shaped building which became the headquarters for Coca-Cola in 1898 was no more, although at the time Asa Candler had said it was "sufficient for all our needs for all time to come." Plain, utilitarian, furnished with slabs and coolers for the dead, the city-county morgue dominated Coca-Cola Place.

Kate turned off the Ella Fitzgerald tape she had been listening to. On some days Ella's "Gooodmorning, Heartache" seemed to be sung for her, but she felt no pport with "Clap Hands, Here Comes Charlie." Sd a parking space in the lot adjoining the mu-t behind the medical examiner's build-epared to unbuckle her seat belt and Lincoln Continental drew up by building and Voncile, supported by her daughter and another young girl, lumbered toward the door, weeping noisily.

Official ID, Kate realized, and she didn't want to be there.

She slouched down in the car so Voncile, even if she came that way, wouldn't see her, and fixed her attention on the lavender Lincoln.

Was that Voncile's personal car, or was it shared by Garney? If so, did he drive it to Shining Waters Subdivision? Or had he another car which the police had impounded?

She rebuckled her seat belt, started the engine, and headed for a telephone.

Corky Martin, an old baseball player turned cop and a friend of her father's, answered at Fulton County Police headquarters. After an exchange of pleasantries, Kate got to the question. What kind of car was Garney driving?

"Beats me, Kate," said Corky. "We didn't find one anywhere near the scene. There were tire prints in the driveway but lousy ones. You know how that hardpan is after a rain."

"Well, how do you think he got there?"

"The perp brought him and left him, I reckon," said Corky.

Kate let out a long sigh of relief.

"That sure lets Miss Willie out, doesn't it?"

"Huh?" said Corky, who had known Miss Willie for years. "I never would try to pin anything on that old girl. Although . . ." he paused, "she has confessed."

"Oh, I know," said Kate lightly. "Bless her '~

Her mind isn't as clear as it used to be, and the shock of her dear boy's death probably didn't help it any. We can forget Miss Willie."

Corky agreed and they hung up, but Kate couldn't exactly forget Miss Willie. Something about the old lady's words, "I done it," troubled her. There had been grief there but anger as well. Who was Miss Willie angry with? Not Garney, surely, as much as she loved him and as willing as she had been for him to put her in the nursing home and take everything she owned. She hadn't balked at that, had in fact accepted his and Voncile's decision docilely.

Kate backed out of the municipal market lot, flattening with her right front wheel a bunch of collards, which had fallen out of a market garbage can. She wrinkled her nose at the imagined smell of decaying cabbage in the hot autumn sun and headed down Edgewood Avenue to Five Points, historically the center of Atlanta, where banks and office buildings overlooked another evidence of Coca-Cola's role in the city —Woodruff Memorial Park, named for Robert W. Woodruff, the capitalist-philanthropist who headed the company for many years and bought up and donated a chunk of expensive center-of-town real estate and turned it into a dreaming acre of trees and grass and flowers. With a burgeoning population and the in___table exodus to the suburbs, Five Points was no ___ ___ ___e heart of the city's financial and business ___ ___ banks and office buildings still towered ___ ___park, but the real activity seemed to ___ ___lower beds and benches. A jazz ___ ___ A black preacher thumped his Bible and exhorted a small group to repentance at the other. Families picnicked, young lovers lolled on blankets in the grass, and a male dancer in pink tights whirled and pirouetted along the center walkway.

Kate liked the in-town pastoral scene and would have lingered if she hadn't had a previous engagement with the Red Dogs. Instead she turned left on Pryor Street, passing the courthouse and then a block away the city hall and the gold-domed capitol. Past these and a few more governmental buildings the old section of town began, once the stylish thoroughfare of ornate Victorian mansions, which the city's founding families built when they came back to find themselves homeless after the Yankee General Sherman had set a torch to the town. Now it was virtually a slum except for the football-baseball stadium and a small, beautiful cancer hospital run by the Dominican nuns in the center of a walled garden. Kate knew from previous visits there that in the midst of downtown squalor the nuns nurtured the state's biggest oak tree by the hospital's back door.

A block away she parked the car on the street and climbed the stairs to the plain, unglamorous three or four rooms of Precinct One, the Red Dogs' base. A dimpled young fellow she had not met before greeted her.

"I'm Sergeant McElroy," he said, smiling. "You're Miss Kincaid? Come on in. Glad to have you aboard."

Kate lifted her eyes to his baseball cap with the words RED DOG embroidered over the bill. "My goodness, are you old enough to be a Red Dog?" she asked, dropping her bag and suit jacket on a folding chair.

41

He grinned. "The good never grow old, ma'am," he said. "But I'm twenty-eight. You'll be traveling with Sergeant Alvarez," he went on. "I'll take you to meet her. She supervises this operation."

Kate carefully did not say, *A woman?* She remembered when the Atlanta Police Force had but two women, both plainclothes detectives, both assigned mostly to cases of domestic violence, varied from time to time by trapping mashers in movie theaters. To have a female supervising a Red Dog unit surprised her and made her glad. Her father had felt that women had a place in policing, and Benjy had even given her credit for what he called "copship."

She was interested in meeting Sergeant Alvarez.

"First," said Sergeant McElroy, "will you please sign this and we'll get you a vest?"

Kate dutifully took his pen and a seat by a folding table.

"Are criminal charges pending against you?" asked the sheet headed WAIVER FOR CIVILIAN OBSERVER. "Do you have any medical problems?" *Well, a toe ache,* thought Kate, newly conscious of a freakish hurting in her little toe. It happened only in moments of tension, and she always ignored it. And a touch of poison ivy on her arm, where gardening gloves ended. Maybe the police needed to know. As she considered the question a giant black man in a gleaming leather jacket and wide-brimmed hat came up.

"Ah, Whit!" she said with pleasure. He was an old acquaintance going back to the days of the heartbreaking missing and murdered black children case which had saddened and baffled Atlanta for months. He had been recruited from a Detroit police department in the massive search for thirty-one poor youngsters. He had stayed. Kate had met him in court and been impressed by his cool professionalism. He had not been totally convinced of the guilt of Wayne Williams, the young black man who was tried and subsequently convicted of the death of two of the children and sentenced to two life terms.

But Whit had been tireless in his effort to assemble the rug fibers which connected Williams with the case. When Williams went to trial it was out of Whit's hands, but Kate knew that for years he had worried that the stoic, occasionally obnoxiously cocky young fellow who was serving time for the crimes might not be guilty. He had a recurring suspicion of circumstantial evidence. So did Kate.

Whit walked away. She went on to the questions: "Have you been convicted of a crime?" Then the waiver promising not to sue if she was hurt while riding as a passenger in a city of Atlanta bureau vehicle. And finally, "Name and address of person to be notified in emergency." *Ah*, thought Kate, *that is a puzzler. Who would be willing to get involved?* With Benjy gone, she had no family except some nieces and nephews of his and the people at the newspaper, whom she considered family. But that would do. She wrote down the name and number of Shell Shelnutt, the city editor. It would serve him right.

Whit stood by holding a bulletproof—or nearly so—vest.

"Put it on, Mrs. Mulcay," he said, the light making his flawlessly white teeth dazzling against his blue-black face and glittering on his gold-rimmed shades. "We don't want to lose you."

"Pooh, who would shoot at me?" said Kate, standing and holding out her arms for the vest.

"Probably nobody, if they recognized you," Whit said, smiling at her affectionately. "People in this town seem to like you. But you'll be in bad company with these Dogs. You know that, don't you?"

Kate looked around the room at two or three young men who had wandered in and were studying a map spread out on a table.

They were young, but they looked enormous and invincible to her.

"I just don't want to get in their way," she said.

"You'll be lucky if you can keep up with them," Whit said. "They run like greyhounds. Most likely they'll leave you behind and pick you up on the way back."

"You're not going with us?" Kate asked, noting the leather jacket and the broad-brimmed hat.

"Plainclothes tonight," he said, grinning, knowing full well that there was nothing really plain about the silver-studded black jacket.

Sergeant McElroy waited for her by the door and courteously took her arm as they descended to the driveway. *Sop to an older woman*, Kate thought, smiling. His mama raised him nice, but it was no way to treat a fellow Red Dog, and that's what she would be for the next hour or two.

He opened the door of a maroon van with smoke-colored windows blotting out the view of the interior, and helped her in, going around to the driver's side.

"Some snazzy police car," murmured Kate, smoothing the maroon velour upholstery with her hand.

The young sergeant nodded. "About what the dope dealers use when they're not taking their stretch limos. We aim to look like we're them—until we grab one or two of them. But you're going with Sergeant Alvarez. She's less showy."

Sergeant McElroy took to the South Expressway with verve, rushing into a line of traffic with such authority that Kate reached automatically to check the buckle of her seat belt.

The south end of town seemed as peaceful as any little country hamlet from the eminence of the expressway. Streetlights, spaced in orderly rows against the darkness like yellow zircons, diminished the glow of lighted windows in the scrubby little houses and crumbling apartment buildings. Kate's eyes rested on them with affection born of nostalgia. To the west against a still rosy sky lay the campus of the Atlanta University complex, five impressive black colleges which got their start with two New England schoolteachers and a boxcar shortly after the Civil War. Kate had visited them often to interview distinguished visitors, to cover the speeches of Martin Luther King, Jr., and to listen to the memorable mixture of carols and spirituals to be heard there at Christmastime.

The university campus had gathered to itself the homes of professors, the city's black leaders, affluent doctors and lawyers, and in an earlier time the black aristocracy of the day, Pullman porters and mailmen. The view from Diamond Hill, Kate remembered from sitting in a little walled garden back of a legislator's home, was the best view of downtown Atlanta to be seen anywhere. But the progression of streets and homes down the hill was dingy and dilapidated, growing more so as they drew nearer to the expressway. Kate remembered when it was a respectable neighborhood, once grand, even, but gone now to seed.

The one murder she had covered there early in her reportorial days was rare to the point of unprecedented at that time. An old woman had bashed a young girl in the head with a sash weight and stuffed her body in a trunk in her basement, and the hardworking, churchgoing citizens of the fiercely slicked-up bungalows up and down her street were shocked and unbelieving. Now murder was almost as daily as sunrise and sunset, and if there were sorrowing people they were usually only the relatives of victims.

On the other side, the southeast section, lay the federal penitentiary and all around it poor, sad, neglected little houses with trash and garbage drifting over their yards. Once the Lakewood Fairgrounds nearby had been one of Atlanta's proud conceits, with agricultural shows, automobile races around its lake, and, to the delight of a child, the big carnivals with merry-go-rounds and Ferris wheels. Streetcars, the clang-clang-clang-goes-the-trolley kind, had run to the fairgrounds in those days, taking loads of excursion-happy families. Now the fairgrounds were no more. A new ampitheatre functioned occasionally, and once a month there were antiques shows.

Kate fought back a sense of melancholy for what she knew was there, or used to be, rather than what she saw. If she allowed herself she would remember people, and this was no time to be distracted with old stories from the past. The Atlanta-Fulton County Stadium, home of baseball's Braves and football's Falcons, lay on the immediate left, a gigantic, empty blue and white cup. Acres of parking lot around it were flat, unoccupied, except close to old Washington Street, where there was a cluster of parked cars, nosed into a wagon-trainlike circle, their parking lights on.

Sergeant McElroy wheeled his van smartly down the Georgia Avenue ramp, crossed Washington Street, and joined the circle. He jumped out, obviously intent on rushing to the right side and opening the door for Kate.

"Uh-uh," she said hastily, "I'll get it."

Within the circle of parked cars a dozen Red Dogs, shadowy figures in their black uniforms, stood together, talking. A slim young woman, wearing the Red Dog uniform but bare-headed, saw Kate and McElroy, separated herself from the group, and came to meet them.

"I'm Sergeant Alvarez," she said, holding out a slim brown hand. "You'll be riding with me. We're hitting the Rose of Sharon housing project first."

She turned back to the circle of young men.

"You got it, fellows. You team leaders know where we're going in, front, back, and sides."

The men nodded and separated. Sergeant Alvarez led Kate to a plain black sedan, walking rapidly despite the heavy load of metal which encompassed her slender body. Beneath the bullet-proof vest, the edge of which barely showed at the throat of her black tunic, was an automatic pistol, handcuffs, radio, and an ammunition packet.

Kate, unencumbered except for the metal-lined vest, which felt surprisingly light and pleasantly warm against the cool of the autumn evening, increased her stride, feeling apologetic that she carried no burden of law enforcement gear. Her leather bag, swinging by its shoulder strap, and a notebook and ballpoint pen in her jacket pocket were heavy enough.

"I know your stuff," Sergeant Alvarez said conversationally as she started the car and hit the accelerator a wallop which sent it shooting up the expressway ramp. "Don't check me, though. I don't read much. I have three television sets in my apartment."

She grinned, showing very white, slightly crooked teeth. Her face was lean and tea-colored, her eyes small, widely spaced, and dark, her black hair short and curly. Kate guessed her age at mid-thirties.

"You've been in Atlanta forever, haven't you?" Sergeant Alvarez asked.

"Forever," said Kate firmly. "How about you?"

"Feels like forever," snorted the sergeant. "I got out of the Marine Corps here five years ago and decided to stay awhile. I'm from New York and there's nothing to go back to there, no family, no home. I've seen everything the Big Apple's got to offer. Hate it."

"Ah, a shame," murmured Kate. "It's fascinating to me."

"Tourist," said the sergeant shortly. She pressed down on the accelerator and smoothly passed half a dozen civilian cars.

"You ever get arrested for speeding?" Kate asked lightly.

"You think I'm a wild driver, huh?" asked the sergeant good-humoredly. "I do speed, I guess. But I feel itchy tonight, like I better get there."

"When you're in a civilian car like this—" Kate began.

The sergeant flipped a knitted red stocking cap that rested on the dash, revealing beneath it a fat blue light, identical to those on top of police cars. She touched a button and a siren wailed shrilly, and was silent.

"Oh," said Kate, relieved. "The police won't get us, then."

"No, but I shouldn't break the speed limit unless it's an emergency," Sergeant Alvarez said. "I just keep feeling like this may be the night. . . ."

The blocks of the housing project where dope dealers were expected to be had already been designated on the map back at precinct headquarters, courtesy of plainclothes detectives in the area since early afternoon. Entrances to the project were well known to the squad, as well as all passable interstices and alleys between the buildings. The first team would go in the front way, followed simultaneously by the backyard team, hitting the garage and garbage can area, reenforced by six-man units spilling into the side yards. Kate was to stick with Sergeant Alvarez, and when they had arrested dope sellers and buyers, if any, Kate could safely enter the buildings and conduct her interviews.

The black sedan rolled into the parking area of an

ugly treeless assortment of old apartment buildings with sagging and torn window screens, scarred and muddy lawns, and garbage everywhere. *What a hideous, senseless mess*, Kate was thinking, and Sergeant Alvarez, unbuckling her seat belt, clearly knew the unspoken comment.

"Public housing," she said. "They don't care. I know. I grew up in housing in New York."

Ahead of them the motorcade of police cars, only one of which was marked, stopped suddenly. The doors opened silently and quickly, and the Red Dogs hit the ground running. Kate squinted to see where they went, and then she realized that Sergeant Alvarez was also on the ground running. She fumbled with the door latch and, thanking her stars for her early morning exercise walks, gave pursuit.

The scraggly grass under her feet was damp and slippery, and she had trouble staying upright on a steep bank. If need be she would sit down and slide, she thought. Then she heard a gunshot. She froze, legs spread apart for balance.

Who was shooting whom?

She peered into the darkness beyond the floodlit project yard. Two Red Dogs were walking out, bringing between them a young fellow in a dark blue sweat suit and white Reeboks.

Kate went closer and Sergeant Alvarez materialized at her side.

"White kid buying," she said. "Those shoes got him. The pros wear boots like ours, except I got mine at the PX for twenty-five dollars and they pay ninety dollars a pair for theirs. Seller got away, I'm afraid."

"How about the gunshot?" asked Kate.

Sergeant Alvarez laughed. "That was a dealer advertising his wares. Didn't know we were on the ground. They shoot guns into the air to terrorize the residents into silence and to notify the customers they're ready for business. Two of our boys were close enough to nab him, but I'm afraid he got away."

"Ninety-dollar boots did it," said Kate.

Alvarez turned suddenly to look behind her and saw other Red Dogs coming through an alley between buildings, pushing ahead of them a black man in handcuffs. "Oh-ho, they got him!" she said happily, and went to meet them.

Kate hovered curiously on the edge of the little gathering, listening as the Red Dogs fired questions at the prisoner. Where was the dope? Did he have heroin or crack? Where did he throw it?

The prisoner grinned tauntingly and said nothing.

"Get the dog," Sergeant Alvarez directed. A policeman with a Doberman on a leash was beside her at once.

Meanwhile, doorways and windows were filled with people, waiting, watching curiously. Little children came out and sat on steps. One little boy trundled his tricycle up and down the sidewalk between soggy paper bags, beer cans, and paper cups and plates from a fast food emporium.

It's past his bedtime, Kate thought pityingly. *Why isn't he safe inside?*

She walked over to where a plump black woman stood with a toddler clutching her skirt. "Some excitement, huh?" she said conversationally.

"Sho is," the woman said, smiling cordially. "We just moved here and we watch most every night. Better than television 'cept the chillun can't play outside. Always gun-shooting till the polices git here. We be glad to see them."

Kate reached for her notebook to get names. A slim black woman with a baby in her arms stepped out the door and stood beside them, her eyes on the handcuffed pair in the group of Red Dogs beside the police car.

"They get him?" she whispered anxiously.

"Yeah, honey," said the older woman. "You be all right now."

The young woman, light-skinned and rather pretty except for the pinch of fear around her mouth and the haunted look in her eyes, shook her head.

"He'll be out by tomorrow," she said despairingly.

"Maybe not," the older woman said. "If they find the stuff. You could hep."

"No! No!" the girl cried hopelessly, turning away.

Kate followed her into the dusty hall with the single unshaded light bulb and scabby walls. The girl walked slowly, listlessly toward a door at the end of the hall. Kate knew she was that stereotype—a single parent with maybe another child or two, intimidated by a dealer with threats to herself and the children into letting him set up headquarters in her apartment. It was an old story, well known to the police, but Kate had never interviewed anybody caught in that trap. They were terrified, as this girl most certainly was now, but it was worth a try.

"Wait!" Kate called to the girl, who glanced skittishly over her shoulder. "Can I talk to you a minute?"

The girl disappeared into the back apartment, slamming the door behind her.

Before Kate could get there and knock, a door midway down the hall opened and a very old black woman, with wrinkled skin the years had dusted with gray like the blow on a ripe plum, grabbed her sleeve.

"Ain't you Mrs. Mulcay from up Roswell way?" she inquired in a tone ludicrously social under the circumstances.

"Ah, Jenny!" cried Kate, recognizing a one-time neighbor and reaching for her hand. "I'm glad to see you. I didn't know what had happened to you."

"Thought I had passed," said the old woman, laughing. "Not me. Not yet. I keeps up. Saw Mr. Garney Wilcox the other day, but before I could speak to him and ax about his mama he hopped into a big fancy car and was gone."

"You saw him here?" Kate asked, puzzled.

"Sho did," said the old woman. "Don't know what he was up to. Might 'uv been peddling butter and eggs, but sho wasn't passing the time of day with old neighbors."

She started to laugh at her own joke, but suddenly her rheumy old eyes fixed on something behind Kate and went dark with fear.

Kate turned. A scrawny little man with a knife in his hand was bearing down on them.

"No!" whispered Jenny.

Paralyzed, Kate waited, her eyes on the long knife

blade, which was the brightest thing in the badly lit hall.

She threw her body against Jenny's, hurling them both through the half-open door, praying to get it closed in time. Suddenly she heard the knife clatter to the floor a foot or two behind her and a grunt, followed by the sound of a body falling.

She turned to see Sergeant Alvarez, handkerchief in hand, picking up the knife and turning the body of the man who had held it with the toe of her twenty-five-dollar boot.

"S'okay," she said to Kate. "We'll go now. The boys'll bring him."

Shivering, Kate followed her out of the building and toward the car.

"Look," she said. "I think you saved my life—or Jenny's. What did you do? How did you stop him?"

"Easy," said Alvarez, grinning. "I was in the Marine Corps."

"But you weren't there—and then you were," Kate mumbled. "I don't see—"

"Aw, don't give it a thought," the sergeant said, standing by the car and looking around her. "We got another passenger. Patrolman Ellis is going with us. They need the room in the car he came in."

A pudgy young fellow in a regulation police uniform arrived and smiled and nodded as Alvarez made the introductions and opened the door for Kate, who noticed that her hand shook as she reached for the door handle. She felt leaden, unable to move, and she kept looking over her shoulder to be sure the police had gotten the little man in the hall.

Sergeant Alvarez waited at the wheel with growing impatience and Kate forced herself to climb in beside her. She reached for the seat belt and was fumbling with the buckle when Sergeant Alvarez yelled.

"Everybody out!" she cried. "Get out! Get out! Somebody in here's got dog shit on their shoe!"

The two policemen were out of the car scraping their feet on the curb before Kate could move for laughing.

"Oh, gosh . . . gosh!" Kate kept saying. "You disarm a man with a knife and then—" She broke up laughing.

"S'okay," said Sergeant Alvarez. "You don't need to get out. It's me."

She swiped at her boot with a dirty paper cup from the sidewalk and, apparently satisfied that it was clean, climbed back in the car, smiling sheepishly at Kate.

Kate studied the thin dark face with new interest. Sergeant Alvarez wasn't a pretty woman, but there was a harmony in the bone structure, the high cheekbones, the almost aquiline nose, the deep eye sockets. And competence and courage shone there better than makeup would have.

"What's your first name?" Kate asked curiously.

Sergeant Alvarez took her eye from the street and gave Kate a sidelong glance. "I wish you hadn't asked that question," she said.

"Melanie," said the policeman in the backseat.

"Melanie Scarlett," said Sergeant Alvarez bitterly. "My mama saw the movie in Puerto Rico."

Kate was laughing again before she could stop

herself. "There are a lot of you Melanies and Scarletts around," she conceded after a moment.

They made one more stop on the way back to precinct headquarters. Dooley's Recreation Center in Zone Three, what they called the Combat Zone. It was a combination truck stop, convenience store, liquor store, and pool room, and the Red Dogs had interrupted more than one shoot-out between drug dealers there.

Tonight all seemed quiet, and Kate, limp from her experience at the housing project, elected to wait in the car. Sergeant Alvarez disappeared into the little convenience store while her team combed the alleys and backyard around the complex. Kate, watching, was startled to see Sergeant Alvarez coming with a Mickey Mouse-shaped ice cream on a stick.

"Want one?" she inquired between licks.

Kate put her head back on the headrest and gave way to the giggles.

"Felling knife-toters one minute and eating Mickey Mouse the next," she said weakly. "What kind of woman are you?"

"Dunno," said Sergeant Alvarez, licking Mickey's head and starting the car. "Flexible, I hope. But you know we ought to have better vests. That one you're wearing will slow down a bullet aimed at your heart, but it wouldn't stop a knife to the back."

Kate finished her story, typed "30" on the computer, and then "Print." When she had a copy of it in her hand, she spiked it and returned to the computer to hit the SEND key. After two or three experiences with copy lost forever in the bowels of the computer, she was careful, no matter how tired, to wait for the printed copy.

And tonight she was tired, so tired she would almost forgo having that piece of paper in her hand, her personal safeguard against the vagaries of electronic systems. She paused a moment by the city desk to let Shell know she was going and then limped wearily toward the elevator. Her trick toe, which had been quiescent during the Red Dogs' caper, shrieked with pain now, and on top of that the patch of poison ivy on her wrist itched fiercely. It would be good to get home to the little cabin and crawl beneath her grandmother's old double wedding ring quilt.

But when she got to the cabin and fed Pepper and Sugar and climbed the stairs to bed, she remembered that it was not her grandmother's quilt but one Miss Willie had given her that served as a spread on her bed now. She really did like the old log cabin coverlet, made in a pattern of dark grays and blacks, the colors that predominated in the wardrobes of settled women when Miss Willie was a girl. She had given the quilt to Kate, deprecating the quilting.

"Don't look at that," she had said. "I learnt on this quilt when I was seven or eight years old. It was my first quilt, and Ma joked that my stitches was so big they'd lasso my bridegroom when I growed up and married. But it didn't take that. He was caught before he had a chanct to sleep under my kivver."

Remembering, Kate sat on the side of the bed and thought about Miss Willie caught up in the idiotic suspicion that she had killed Garney. And what was Garney, of all people, doing at the Rose of Sharon Project clear on the other side of town, far removed from the expensive subdivision developments which obsessed him?

It was pointless to think that anybody there had brought him to the country to kill him. Sad people trapped in squalor didn't journey thirty miles north of town to Shining Waters Subdivision to kill strangers. And what about herself, Katherine Kincaid Mulcay? Was she the target for that glittering knife or was it old Jenny, who used to wash everybody's fine tablecloths in Roswell? People would not trust their best linens to anybody but Jenny. She had to be eighty years old. *Why would anybody want to hurt her? Or me?* Kate asked herself again.

The memory of the knife and the cold dark face behind it made her wonder if she should lock the cabin door before she went to bed. She looked around at her little house. She had never worried about burglars, having nothing to interest one. The old rope bed, the chestnut bureau, the little rocker . . . they pleased her, but they weren't valuable. She had no jewelry except the plain gold wedding band, which had been Benjy's mother's, and a string of cultured pearls he had given her. No money.

But fear is a spreading infection, and suddenly she was afraid. She turned out her bedside lamp, the better to see the yard, which had always been balm to her tired body and aching heart in time of trouble. The crooked apple tree had been there, pulled to earth by honeysuckle and poison ivy, when she and Benjy bought the place. They had loved liberating it, hacking away the grasping vines, pruning the lichened old branches, fertilizing and watering. Now in the half-light from the kitchen window it looked deformed and sinister, a hunchbacked shadow. The woods, which came to the edge of the scrappy little lawn, were a friendly shade, autumnal color, or black lace against the sunrise on a winter's morning, but now were suddenly concealment for watching strangers.

Kate padded barefoot down the stairs to the kitchen door and turned the key in its lock. Sugar perched on top of the primitive, buttermilk-and-bluing-stained hunt board, opened a sleepy eye, and looked at her in boredom. Pepper, through with his supper, pawed at the screen door for admittance.

"Come on in," said Kate, unlocking the door and opening it wide enough for the big dog's body. "Come in and make like a watchdog."

With a heavy sigh, Pepper settled himself on the rag rug by the kitchen door.

That's it, Kate told herself, turning out the tin-shaded grocery store light over the kitchen table, leaving only a little nightlight burning by the back door. *The drawbridge to the castle is up. I'm going to bed.*

She would have liked a cup of tea, but she didn't want to turn on lights and make herself visible to any random passerby or—just a freakish possibility—anybody waiting in the yard. She needed a bath, but remembering Tony Perkins, playing the crazy young killer lurking in the shower in the old Hitchcock movie *Psycho*, she decided to go to bed unwashed. Nobody was more vulnerable than when naked and in the bathroom.

She felt uncommonly cold for the time of year and fished out her favorite wintertime plaid outing nightshirt and pulled it over her head.

Miss Willie's quilt, smelling of cedar and lavender sachet, felt good, and Kate closed her eyes for sleep. But sleep was slow to come. She kept seeing the venomous face back of the upraised knife. She saw Sergeant Alvarez as a length of electric wire, covered with brown insulation but pulsing with explosive energy beneath it. She saw the frightened girl with her baby and the sweet-faced mother watching mayhem from the front door as if she were at a church social.

The filthy buildings and the garbage-strewn yards distressed Kate. She remembered when Techwood Homes and University Homes, two of the first public housing projects in the nation, had been virtual showplaces. The shade trees, which still lined the streets, were young and verdant then, and the lawns were carefully kept. Many residents had planted zinnias and marigolds by the front steps and had small, tidy vegetable gardens in the back. White sheets blew on clotheslines in the fenced backyards, and Atlanta congratulated itself that what had been a slum area was beautiful, low-rent housing.

President Franklin D. Roosevelt and Mrs. Roosevelt, in town in the 1930s for a speech in Georgia Tech's stadium, had swung by Techwood to unveil a marker designating it as the first public housing project in the country, and had visited University Homes, the first project of its kind for blacks, to the thunderous applause of thousands of loyal supporters.

A lot of housing projects had been built since then, and as far as Kate had seen they were no sooner finished and occupied than they became eyesores and hotbeds of drug traffic.

There was a story, told to her by an old reporter, that when the housing projects were initiated, Secretary of the Interior Harold Ickes came to town and threw the switch which dynamited a brace of shanty dwellings, making way for the revolutionary public housing. *Somebody should come back and throw another switch*, Kate thought sleepily, dozing off to a vision of twenty-five strong young Red Dogs armed with brooms and mops and rakes doing a cleanup job.

CHAPTER 3

For a few seconds Kate didn't know what had awakened her. Then she realized Pepper must have barked but she hadn't heard him. It had to have been a brief and perfunctory bark, for now he was whimpering cordially, his greeting reserved for people he knew. Between his whimpering and tail-thumping she heard a hoarse whisper. "Hush, Pepper, hush!" And then, "Kate! Kate! Come to the door."

There was something so ghostly about it that Kate hesitated to answer or turn on a light. Her digital clock on the dresser showed ten after midnight. Nobody came to see her at that hour.

The voice spoke again.

"Kate! Kate! It's Willie. Let me in."

Pushing back the covers and without bothering for slippers or robe, Kate hit the floor and ran for the stairs. She turned on the back porch light and then turned it off quickly. Miss Willie stood there in her nightgown and robe and beside her there was a plump teenage girl in an aqua running suit. Judy Carson, Kate decided, Cheri Wilcox's friend.

"What in the world?" Kate cried, putting her arms around Miss Willie. "How on earth did you get here? Come on, come on in."

"Traveled in the truck like always," said Miss Willie sharply, and then, exhausted, she sank into the little cane-bottomed rocker by the kitchen stove.

"I need a stay-place," she said wearily. "You got room?"

"You know I have," Kate said. "You want to come up and get in bed now? You look worn out."

"Be good," said Miss Willie submissively. "Anything will do—pallet, pad on the floor."

"Ah, my bed's all warmed up for you," Kate said. "Come on and crawl in. I'll sleep down here on the daybed." She turned to the girl. "How about you, Judy, will the sofa do for you?"

"Yes'm, but I'm not staying," the girl answered. "I just brought Miss Willie. I gotta get home before they miss me."

"Well, wait a minute," said Kate. "Let me get Miss Willie settled. I want to talk to you. Be right back."

She put an arm around the old woman and slowly propelled her toward the stairs. Miss Willie took the shallow, wide steps with a firmer, stronger tread than her age and state of exhaustion would seem to allow. Kate helped her to sit on the side of the bed and remove her robe and slippers. She lifted the wrinkled, whey-colored old feet onto the bed and pulled up the covers.

"You all right?" she asked. "You want a glass of milk or some hot cocoa?"

"No, honey, just rest," said Miss Willie.

"Let me go see about Judy," Kate said. "I'll be right downstairs if you need me."

Miss Willie's hands were smoothing the old quilt over her chest. "Mama," she said softly, remembering, and closed her eyes.

"What happened, Judy?" Kate asked when she got back to the kitchen and found the girl slumped down in the rocker Miss Willie had vacated.

"She wanted to leave," Judy said. "I been keeping her truck hid out for her, and I knew if I didn't drive it she'd do it herself. And at night and all . . ."

"You were right," Kate said. "I'm glad you brought her. Let me make you some cocoa and some toast."

Judy shook her head. "I gotta go," she mumbled, without moving.

"Where have you been hiding the truck?" Kate asked. "I didn't know what happened to it. Thought she might have sold it."

Judy's plump pink face broke into a sly smile.

"That's what everybody thinks," she said. "Cheri's mama and daddy and them. I'm the only one that knows except Cheri and Miss Marlowa Walton."

"Miss Marlowa Walton!" Kate gasped. "What has she got to do with it?"

Miss Marlowa Walton was the fragile aristocratic last leaf on an old Roswell family tree, a hundred years old if a day, living alone with only a black woman to do for her in the finest white-columned, camellia-gardened, magnolia-shaded antebellum house in the state. How did Miss Willie and this child enlist her help in hiding a ramshackle old truck that was nearly as old as both women?

"Miss Willie just told her," Judy explained as if that were reason enough. "She said it was her last propitty and she didn't want nobody else to have it. Miss Marlowa knew Mr. Garney was a greedy son of a bitch, gon' sell Roswell and the rest of north Fulton County to them developers, and she give permission. We keep it under the scuppernong arbor. No scuppernongs much this year, and the vines make a long curtain, kind of. It's a good place."

"I'm sure it is," said Kate, thinking with wild amusement that no policeman in the county would dare to invade Miss Marlowa's elegant acres looking for a missing truck, even if they claimed it was stolen. Nor would Voncile.

"I better go," Judy said, standing and pulling down the aqua running suit over her plump young thighs and hips.

She stopped at the door and turned back.

"Tell Miss Willie I'll come see about her when it gits good and dark tomorrer. And . . ." she paused, searching Kate's face as if for evidence that she was trustworthy, "I forgot—will you tell her I forgot?—it's four months."

"Four months?" repeated Kate. "What does that mean?"

"She'll know," said Judy, lifting her white eyebrows in a mysterious smile. "Well, good night."

She was gone, and Kate heard the old truck start up back of the toolshed, where it would be screened from view of the road.

After she had tiptoed upstairs and found Miss Willie snoring, Kate picked up an afghan and settled on the little spool daybed in a corner of the living room. But she couldn't sleep. She had forgotten to ask Judy if Miss Willie had permission to leave the nursing home. If she had slipped away without asking, there was probably a full-scale search for her going on now. Should she call and tell them where Miss Willie was?

A mental picture of them coming with one of their ambulances and forcing the old lady out of bed and onto a stretcher stopped her. Miss Willie was no stretcher case. She was a strong willful old woman who had a right to decide where she wanted to be. Kate knew her own feeling about that would carry little weight with the authorities, and she turned restlessly, wondering what she would do if the nursing home people, pushed by Voncile and even the police, arrived. Too bad, she thought ruefully, she couldn't call on her new friend, Melanie Scarlett Alvarez, for backup muscle.

Then there was Judy's cryptic message. Four months. Four months till what? It sounded pregnant, but Judy didn't look pregnant. And why tell Miss Willie? Miss Willie's generation wasn't accepting about teenage, out-of-wedlock pregnancies. And besides, Miss Willie had enough to worry her. She hadn't mentioned Garney's death, but it must be weighing heavily to make her summon strength enough to flee the nursing home. She came, Kate decided, out of a hunger to be in her own house and to see for herself where Garney had died. Kate resolved to take her there in the morning.

Kate awakened to the smell of coffee percolating, and she stumbled to the kitchen to find Miss Willie, a dish towel tied around her waist for an apron, stirring a pot of grits.

"Oh, Miss Willie, I was going to bring you coffee to your bed!" she said apologetically.

"Hate my vittles in bed," said Miss Willie firmly. "Hit feels good to be afore a cookstove agin. Them home people do the best they can, but hit ain't my kind of cooking. You want eggs?"

Kate shook her head. She started to say, *Just coffee,* but she smelled biscuits. Miss Willie's tender flaky biscuits hadn't perfumed her kitchen in many a month. She opened the door to the old jam cupboard in the corner and brought out a small jar of blackberry preserves.

"Boy, we're feasting!" she said happily.

The sun slanted in over the kitchen table, striking fire to the old carnival glass sugar bowl and picking up the blues and reds of Kate's mismatched yard sale Fiesta plates. Miss Willie set the biscuit pan on a pot holder to protect the already scarred little pine table and sat down opposite Kate.

She buttered a biscuit complacently, sliced herself off a bite of ham, and stirred redeye gravy into her grits. Kate looked at her in awe. The frail, submissive old friend who had surrendered helplessly when Garney and Voncile took her house away from her and put her in a nursing home had vanished. The woman of strength and resolution, handling her own life and even making biscuits for her friends, had reappeared.

"Miss Willie, I'm so glad you're back!" Kate said.

Miss Willie nodded, chewing her ham. "That home . . ." she paused to make a face mocking the word, "ain't no place to be."

"Do they know where you are? Does Voncile know?"

"Not yet," admitted Miss Willie, unconcerned. "I aim to tell them today. But I got a heap to do first. You go on about your business. I'll clear away here and feed Pepper and Sugar and make my plans."

"Miss Willie, they'll come and get you," protested Kate.

The old woman stared out the window at a brown thrasher picking up seeds under the bird feeder.

"Them rascals rather eat off the ground, no matter how many seeds you put on the feeder for them," she said irrelevantly.

Kate grinned. Miss Willie was clearly competent to be left in charge. Kate might as well go on to work.

She was dressed and standing in the kitchen door wondering if it really was wise to leave Miss Willie alone when the old lady came out of the bathroom, smelling of soap and talcum powder but still in her night clothes.

"Me and Judy ain't got sense enough to bell a buzzard," Miss Willie remarked. "I had me a valise with my wearing clothes in it and we left it in the truck! Would you have time to bring it home when you come?"

"Oh, sure," said Kate. "I'll get it now and bring it back before I go to town, so you can get dressed. Miss Marlowa will let me get to the truck, won't she?"

"Just tell her Willie Wilcox sent you," the old woman said importantly. "Me and her has been friends since I used to sell her butter and eggs. Done her a favor onct and she's returning it now."

"What kind of favor?" Kate asked.

"Let not your right hand know what your left hand doeth," Miss Willie misquoted the Book of Matthew smugly. "And Kate," she added, "you just as well not to know where I'm at."

"Gotcha," said Kate, heading for her car.

Kate pulled in back of a camellia hedge which encircled the driveway to the Marlowa Walton mansion, hoping her little car would not be visible from the street. Black Ida answered the old-fashioned tinny sound of the doorbell, which quivered and reverberated in the dim recesses of the old house somewhere. Kate assumed that Ida knew everything Miss Marlowa knew and it would be all right to ask her permission to get Miss Willie's clothes, but she hesitated, not being sure. She asked for Miss Marlowa.

"Child, she be's sleeping," said Ida.

"No such thing!" called a voice from the stairs. "Ida, you tell tales. You know I never lie abed this late."

Kate glanced up to see a tiny old woman swathed

in a purple velvet robe standing midway the staircase, her short-cropped hair bristling, her mouth painted a deep fuchsia. "I never sleep, and Ida knows it!"

"Miss Marlowa, I'm Kate Kincaid—" Kate began.

"I know who you are," snapped the old woman. "I can see. If you'll wait a moment or two, I'll be down. My mother would be horrified if I were to receive a guest in my kimono. Ida, show her into the sitting room."

Kate and Ida exchanged smiles. "Her mama been dead for fifty years," murmured Ida, leading the way to a room at the end of the hall.

And I haven't heard of kimonos in at least twenty-five, Kate said to herself, entering the small, book-lined room with a thin wood fire burning in the shallow grate, which was framed by a marble mantelpiece. The day was already too hot for a fire, but Miss Marlowa, from the appearance of the velvet "kimono," was likely to be chilly, and Ida was looking after her.

Kate declined the rocking chair Ida trundled toward her and the coffee she offered, and went and stood by the tall uncurtained window looking out on the backyard. It wasn't a well-tended yard, but its bone structure, probably formed a hundred or more years ago, was still sound—a drive outlined by boxwood, gigantic oaks spaced to wall off the busy street to the south of the house and provide summer shade, a rose arbor with late-blooming Maréchal Niels crowning its weathered lattice, camellias everywhere.

A brick walk, thickly carpeted with thyme and edged by birdfoot ivy, curved toward a well house and a barn and beyond that the grape arbor. Judy had been right. Vines, unpruned for many a fall, hung to the ground, concealing anything that might be behind them, including an ancient pickup truck. Kate smiled at the competence of Miss Willie in picking such a hiding place.

She heard Miss Marlowa's footsteps in the uncarpeted hall and turned to see the old lady, in a fuchsia pants suit which matched both her lipstick and perilously high-heeled sandals, standing in the door.

"Ida, coffee!" she cried imperiously.

Even as she spoke Ida came through a swinging door from the kitchen bearing a little silver tray covered with a lacy white cloth on which there was a small silver pot and two thin cups, which Kate suspected were Haviland, from her acquaintance with a few she had inherited from her own grandmother.

"Sit ye down," directed Miss Marlowa gaily. "I haven't had a guest for morning coffee in a coon's age." And then suddenly, "Did Willie Wilcox make her getaway?"

Kate looked at her, startled.

"Oh, I know Willie's on the lam," said Miss Marlowa placidly. "Everybody in town knows she killed that scoundrel stepson of hers. She confessed right and left, and I congratulated her."

"Oh, no," whispered Kate. "She couldn't . . . she wouldn't."

"Would and could," said Miss Marlowa. "Willie's a strong woman, and if she thinks murder is necessary she can do it. If I ever saw a time when murder was indicated, it's now. Would you care for a piece of sweet potato pone with your coffee?"

The incongruity of heavy, homely sweet potato pone with this daintily served morning coffee made Kate laugh. "No . . . no, ma'am." She giggled. "I've got to take Miss Willie her clothes and get on to town. May I look in the truck?"

"Yes, certainly," said Miss Marlowa, putting down her cup. "While you're doing that, Ida can make some sandwiches for Willie to eat on the road, and I'm going to get her Mama's sable coat. Mama was a big woman like Willie, and wherever she goes sable will be a comfort to her. Id-ah!"

Kate passed Ida on the way out the back door and the black woman sniffed grumpily. "That sable coat's a dog bed. Ain't gon' be no comfort to nobody."

But she brought it, a plastic-covered bundle, and tucked it in the backseat of Kate's car, along with a brown paper bag which presumably held sandwiches "for the road."

The kitchen door was locked when Kate got back to her cabin, and while she tried to remember where she had stowed the extra key Miss Willie came down the steps from the bedroom and let her in. Her homely, weathered old face was wreathed in smiles.

"Voncile come a-looking for me," she said triumphantly. "I laid low and let Pepper handle her. She called my name and mewled like a sick cat, but she didn't know I was here, and finally she left."

Kate gave her the bundle of "dog bed" sable, the brown bag of sandwiches, and her valise, hugged her impulsively, and headed for town.

Ordinarily she would favor Atlanta's metropolitan rapid transit system, called MARTA, with her business.

She heartily approved of paying a dollar, finding a seat to her liking, and opening a book and reading all the way to town. Sometimes for the first half of the trip—the bus to Lenox, where she transferred to a swift, clean, musically tooting little train—she exchanged greetings with other passengers. But more often they all sank into their books or newspapers or, in the case of a young woman who was learning to knit, into needlework. Kate liked it that way.

But once or twice a week she felt the need of having her car in town, and this Monday morning errands stretched out endlessly. She needed to check with the medical examiner. What about funeral plans for Garney? She wanted to call Sergeant Alvarez to see what they had found out about the knife-toting man she had felled just short of Kate's back. And she had an unfinished, unsatisfied feeling about old Jenny, to whom she had been talking when he appeared.

Jenny had said she had seen Garney Wilcox down there, and the man with the knife had cut short any other information she might have given about him. Kate decided to go back and see her.

Dr. Asa Reed, the medical examiner, was almost as annoyed with Garney Wilcox as a corpse as were those privileged to have known him in life.

"A mul . . . multiple . . . mess!" he complained to Kate, stuttering a little, as he did when he was rushed. "All that effort to kill the big b-b-big bum when one thing could have finished him off neatly."

"What did kill him?" asked Kate.

"Running some tests," said the doctor, who was bucking for the job of director of the state forensic laboratory. "Would you settle for the old blow on the head until we find out what kind of brew he drank and how many volts that electric wire shot into him?"

"Sure," said Kate. "I'd settle. Do you know what hit him?"

"The usual bl-bl-blunt instrument," said Asa.

"Big and heavy, huh?" persisted Kate, trying to eliminate the possibility that it had been wielded by an old lady.

"Big and heavy," reiterated Asa. "I'll finish up with him and get back to you, Kate. Right now I got a line of folks ahead of old Garney. And, well, who cares . . . ?"

Until they heard from the medical examiner there would be no funeral and, of course, in Fulton County, no coroner's inquest. A hundred and fifty of the state's 159 counties retained coroners, but Fulton and some of the other more densely populated did not. Kate admired the orderly assimilation of testimony at inquests held in the English way, feeling a need to know the things that were set forth about the condition of the body, the scene, the witnesses, who found it, and what they saw and did. This way the medical examiner would report directly to the police, who would report to the D.A., who would go before the grand jury, and it was perfectly possible none of them would tell Kate anything, despite Asa's promise.

She was having a slow day at the office. The Desk was disappointed in her story from the Red Dog raid. They had expected more interviews, drama drenched in pathos. The tone of her story had been casual, as had been the Red Dog raid and the householders who witnessed it. Except for the man with the knife.

She thought about offering that as an excuse for her colorless report. After all, she had been in peril herself. But The Desk didn't look with favor on reporters who got themselves wounded in combat. You were supposed to stay out of the way. During World War II there was a photographer who had been on a ship which was torpedoed in the Pacific, and management's attitude was that he had brought it all on himself. He must have been pushing for a Pulitzer.

She said nothing about the threat to her own backside but offered to go back and see if there were any mop-up stories after the raid.

Riding to the Rose of Sharon housing project in her car in broad daylight seemed ordinary and safe, compared to the dash down there with the Red Dogs the night before. She parked in front of the littered doorway where she had seen the "home boys," as the police called them, gathered the night before, where, indeed, she had seen the knife brandisher coming her way.

An ice cream cart was pulled up near the door and two little black children negotiated with an old man for Eskimo Pies. All seemed quiet until Kate got near the steps. She heard the high keening sound of women weeping.

She rushed past the children and pulled open the hall door. The mournful lament, now louder like a fugue, came from Jenny's room. She pushed her way into the half-open door. Half a dozen women sat around the bed on which the little white-haired woman lay. Kate fell to her knees and took one of the limp little hands between hers.

"Jenny," she whispered. "Jenny . . . ?"

"She going," one of the women said gently.

The woman suddenly picked up the tune of an old spiritual. "Sit down, Lord, have a chair. I cain't stay . . . got to climb that stair."

"She's not gon' die," Kate said. "She's gon' be all right. Did somebody call for an ambulance? What happened?" Kate wanted to do something, to take charge. "What happened?" she repeated desperately. "Is she sick? Did somebody call Grady? We can't let her lie here."

"Back broke," one of the women said. "And her so old and frail. Best not to move her."

At that moment there was the brief peremptory yelp of a siren out front and Grady Hospital's ambulance pulled up. The stretcher crew was gentle with the little body, but Kate didn't think it would make much difference. There didn't seem to be enough life left in it to hurt. She walked to the door and saw Jenny lifted into the ambulance, and then she turned to one of the women picking up a bundle of bloody clothes which had been piled in the corner.

"Whupped," the woman said simply. "Whupped to death."

Kate was torn, wanting to go to the hospital with Jenny but compelled to find out what happened.

"We don't know," the woman with the bloody clothes said stubbornly. "Don' hear nothing. Don' see nothing. This morning I come to bring Miss Jenny some coffee, and there she was on the floor covered with blood."

"Did you call the police?" Kate asked.

"Too late for her. Just in time to git us whupped." She turned to the departing group for confirmation.

They nodded, murmuring assent, and disappeared down the hall.

"Dear God, why?" asked Kate. "Why Jenny? Do you have any idea who did it . . . and why?"

The black face was impassive, the dark head shaking silently from side to side.

Kate followed the woman, determined not to let her abandon the conversation. "You know last night there was a man with a knife coming at her. Or me, I don't know which. But the police got him. He isn't out yet, I know. Do you know who he was? Why would he or anybody hurt Jenny? What has she got to do with those insane criminals?"

The woman shook her head.

"Got to wash Miss Jenny's clothes," she said, opening a door to the basement. "Shame. So bloody."

"No!" cried Kate. "Give them to me. The police might find something to tell us who did it. Not just her blood, maybe his blood or hair or fingernails or something."

The woman looked at her with new interest.

"You a police?" she asked.

Kate shook her head, reaching for the clothes. "I just read a lot of murder mysteries."

* * *

The homicide department accepted Jenny's clothes and sealed them in a plastic bag—without much interest, Kate felt. A prominent northside woman had been throttled that morning as she bent over her camellias. She was the wife of an industrialist and had herself acquired a kind of reverential regard in town for her work with garden clubs and children's hospitals. A little black woman whose claim to fame had been that she had been a wonder at doing fine laundry, what did her beating mean to them?

Kate went to Grady Hospital and lingered in the emergency clinic with mop-up victims of weekend wrecks and shootings and knifings. Babies cried and toddlers tugged impatiently at their mothers, trying to pull them to the candy and Coke machines by the door. An old man in a wheelchair talked to himself, and a young woman, coughing and wheezing, leapt to attention every time a door opened and a nurse or orderly or intern appeared.

"Lordamercy," she said to Kate, moaning. "I know my baby's dead. I couldn't git no breath out of him."

"Don't worry," Kate said. "They're good here. They'll do all they can for him."

She knew it to be true. Old Grady, named for the famed newspaper editor of the 1880s, Henry W. Grady, had seen Atlanta and the adjoining counties through every crisis, and although it was overcrowded and endlessly shabby, she held it close to her heart. Her father, wounded by a holdup man's bullet, had been rushed there, later going back to die. Benjy, sent to a private hospital for his cancer, wished himself in what poor folks called "the Gradys" for the show-down. He missed the familiar movement, the crowds, the coming and going of emergency squads and his brother officers. He had died quietly in ICU with only Kate and a doctor and a nurse standing by—no milling crowds, no singing, praying, coughing, retching fellow townsmen. Benjy missed them.

A few minutes before she knew she had to leave to make first-edition deadline, an intern she knew slightly came out and invited her into a small room adjoining the emergency clinic.

"You're here for Jenny Balcom?" he asked.

Kate nodded.

She had just died of multiple injuries to her head and spine and loss of blood.

It had been a cruel, barbarous beating.

Back at the office Kate wrote a limping, lifeless account, unable to find words for the tears in her eyes and an unaccountable trembling in her hands. It seemed so senseless, so damned outrageously senseless that little Jenny would be wanted dead by anybody.

When her last line of copy was in, she sat awhile looking at the deepening twilight over her town and scrubbing at the brine on her cheeks. Shell, the city editor, came and stood behind her chair, putting a hand on her shoulder.

"Good story, Katy," he said briefly. And then, "You didn't tell us you were in the line of fire yourself last night."

Kate shrugged. How had he found out?

"Police report. Sergeant Alvarez thought that knife might have been meant for you."

"Aw," said Kate listlessly. "Who would want me done in?"

"Beats me," said Shell tiredly, turning away. He had more pressing problems. "Be careful," he said, when he got to the door. "Don't be a casualty yourself."

Or a victim, Kate thought, turning off her computer and picking up her bag.

Her car was parked down under the bridge which criss-crossed back of the building, covering acres where the once-grand Union Station had stood and passenger and freight trains wove in and out endlessly. Now a few trains passed that way, but the great concourse, where presidents and opera stars had arrived and departed and servicemen and -women went forth to war, was a parking lot, hundreds of automobiles lined up like brightly carapaced beetles. The overhead lights were dim and the lot half empty when Kate got there.

She never liked coming there at night. Not that she was afraid, she told herself, fumbling for her keys and checking the little flagon of Mace that Benjy had made her accept. She often left it in another coat pocket, but tonight there was obscure comfort in having it within reach. The parking lot attendant had gone off duty. He was a pleasant, gray-haired former railroad man with whom Kate exchanged weather reports when she happened to drive to work. A security guard was somewhere back there, she suspected, but she didn't see his car.

She walked rapidly over the broken, potholed paving, avoiding the black pondlike puddles from yesterday's rain. Benjy had instructed her in moving rapidly, head up, eyes front, car keys in hand, when she was alone on the street. This evening she had to fight an impulse to run. It was senseless. She hadn't seen or heard anything to alarm her, but suddenly she was terrified. There were eyes in the rafters overhead or footfalls behind her. The whistle of a freight train crawling along the track behind her screamed in anguish, and a merciless cyclops eye of light on its engine swept over her.

She took off running.

Once back of her steering wheel with the doors locked, the engine running, and the headlights on, Kate thought she saw a shadowy figure moving in the line of cars ahead of her, and she revved up the engine and roared out of the parking space toward Foundry Street and the exit.

The trip home, even in rush-hour traffic, was often a time to relax since Benjy had become interested in playing music for the journey. They had inherited her father's old tapes and added to them, and sometimes they had listened to Dixieland, which Benjy had especially liked, or soothed themselves with the measured cadences of a string ensemble or a symphony. Tonight Kate reached for the first tape in the basket on the seat beside her and fitted it into the slot on the dash.

To her amusement it was *Peter and the Wolf,* an old favorite of her childhood. She let the grand full music and the voices of the duck and the birds and the cat and Peter himself and the wolf and grandfather wash over her, delighting as always when the narrator, Sir

Ralph Richardson, said in his precise English voice, "And Pe-terr made a lass-ooh."

Oh, a lass-ooh, thought Kate. Wouldn't it be great if, like Peterr, she could make a lass-ooh and catch a killer more horrible than a Russian wolf or even catch up the odds and ends of what increasingly seemed oddly related violence?

The cabin itself was dark when Kate drove into the yard, but a small light burned in a farm lantern hanging by the driveway in the persimmon tree. Pepper and Sugar waited beside the tree for her, and she saw that their feeding pans had been filled. On the kitchen stove she found a pot of turnip greens, and through the ajar oven door a skillet of corn bread. But no Miss Willie.

Kate checked the bedroom and the bath and wandered back in the yard, looking toward the old Wilcox house, thinking Miss Willie might have gone there. She couldn't see beyond the Shining Waters Subdivision lights, of course, noting absently that the castle seemed to be enjoying a flurry of visitors tonight.

And finally, too weary to eat Miss Willie's offering of turnip greens and cornbread, she put them away and went to bed.

The next morning she realized Miss Willie must have gone back to her own garden to get the turnip greens. Kate had none, and the old woman had no way of getting to market. She hastily donned her running clothes and rushed through the subdivision down the path to the old homestead.

The police department's scene-of-the-crime tapes had been removed. That could only mean they had decided on the cause of Garney's death. Kate kept Pepper by her side and walked carefully, looking for Miss Willie's tracks. She found none, but the turnip patch did show signs of having been visited: cropped stems here and there and holes from which pearly turnip roots had been wrested. Of course, the neighbors, especially the Gandys, had made free with whatever was left in Miss Willie's garden, and they, as well as Kate, were free to harvest the greens. Kate tried the door and on impulse reached under an overturned flowerpot near the house's foundation and found a key. Miss Willie had ever kept it there, and habit was strong.

The rooms were dim and nearly empty. An old Victorian bed with a headboard reaching to the ceiling had apparently been considered too cumbersome to move and was unwanted. It stood catercorner in the front room with a feather tick turned over its footboard. Kitchen and pantry shelves held an assortment of dusty, mouse-invaded boxes and bags and a few jars of what appeared to be Miss Willie's jams and jellies, all cobwebby and with rust-rimmed lids. The electricity was probably off and Kate had no desire to check out the cellar, but she opened the door, thinking to see where Garney had fallen. The stench of vomit rose up to meet her, and she hastily slammed the door and turned back to the front of the house.

There was no sign of Miss Willie or the murder instrument that she could see. Perhaps the police had found something. She paused idly beside the front room mantel and noticed that the tattered fireplace screen Miss Willie had made out of burlap sacks and flour pasted over with movie star pictures stirred a little in the breeze from the open door.

She turned to see the Gardiners, Ron and Valerie, from the castle standing in the doorway.

"Finding anything interesting?" asked Ron, smiling.

Valerie, expressionless as always, said nothing.

"Doesn't seem to be much to see," Kate admitted. "Are you all all right this morning? I thought you must have had company at your place last night. Saw lots of lights."

"Our families," said Valerie coldly.

"Wish you'd have come over," said Ron, turning restlessly and walking through the rooms. "Always glad to have you."

"Aw, thank you," said Kate helplessly. "Guess I'll go. You all want to lock up when you leave?"

"Sure," said Ron. "Not that there's anything anybody would steal."

Valerie moved, and the breeze from the door moved with her, stirring a flour-pasted picture of Marilyn Monroe on Miss Willie's fire screen. Suddenly Kate saw it—what must have been the murder weapon: a three-legged iron pot Miss Willie had used for years for fireplace cooking.

It was buried in ashes and a half-burned log but wedged so tightly under the old buggy-axle firedogs that it seemed to be a part of them, a bulbous, pioneer-sized andirons ornament. The police had not recognized it, but she did, and she had to get it out of there.

Clutching the door key, she walked out on the porch and stood a moment looking toward the river.

"I wonder if there's any watercress left," she said conversationally. "Would you all care to walk down there with me and gather some?"

"*No!*" said Valerie sharply, and Kate thought with amusement that she wanted to say, *Hell, no!*

"Guess not," said Ron, following her. "Guess we'll take our morning canter. Come on, hon."

Kate walked slowly toward the creek, allowing time for the Gardiners to get out of sight, and when she was sure they were gone she hurried back to the house to get the pot. It was not easy. The andirons, made out of slender axles from the Wilcoxes' last buggy, were light, but the old pot itself was heavy and wedged in with wet ashes and smut from rain which had coursed down the chimney. Kate found a kitchen spoon and dug it free and then sat back on her heels wondering what to do with it.

If Miss Willie had wanted a murder weapon, this one was her style. Iron cook pots were the most familiar implements in a lifetime of hard work. She knew how to wield a pot. *But, oh, Lordy, I hope she didn't sling one against Garney's head,* Kate said to herself, trying to fit the pot under her sweatshirt for the walk back to the cabin. If she met the Gardiners it would be difficult to be casual and offhand with an iron pot protruding from her belly. She didn't meet them.

The phone was ringing when she attained her own yard, and she ran to catch it. Voncile.

"Where is she?" shrilled the widow. "What have you done with her?"

"Miss Willie?" asked Kate, as if she didn't know. "What are you talking about, Voncile? Isn't she in the nursing home?"

"You know damned well she's not there!" shouted Voncile, now beside herself. "You're hiding her somewhere. I know it. The police know it!"

"Oh, shut up, Voncile," said Kate, exasperated. "You're talking like an idiot. Why would I hide Miss Willie? I haven't the slightest idea where she is. You and the police want to come out here with a search warrant to make sure? You're welcome."

"Well, I tell you this," Voncile said viciously, "she's not coming to my dear one's funeral. And neither . . . neither are you!" She was crying now, and Kate felt sorry for her in spite of herself.

"I'm so sorry," she said, with a sarcasm she couldn't resist. "I meant to come. Thought I might be of some comfort to you."

"Oh, shit!" cried Voncile, and hung up.

Kate had barely fed the cat and dog and toasted a croissant for herself when a police car pulled up in the yard. Steve Sizemore got out, gaping and stretching in the morning sunshine and looking around the yard before he came to the door.

Pepper, augmented by the guineas, set off the alarm. Kate called and shushed Pepper, but the guineas, swarming grayly toward the shelter of the weigela bush, potracked shrilly.

"Lord, the watchdogs you got!" he said, grinning at Kate. "Couldn't nobody slip up on you."

"Well, I keep the guineas for snakes," teased Kate.

"They scare 'em out of the yard and let me know when they're doing it."

Steve, country-bred, knew the talents of guineas, and he approached the steps smiling. "Now, good morning," he said, when he could make himself heard over the racket. "You got company?"

"Just you," said Kate. "Come in and have a cup of coffee."

"Naw, much obliged," he said. "Bunch of us kinda got a taste for old Bill Johnson's Iron Skillet in Roswell. We meet there for breakfast a lot. You know —grits, country ham, biscuits."

"Oh, my," said Kate, "and I was about to offer you a croissant. Sit down."

He pulled out a chair at the little pine table and tilted back in it, studying the rafters in the ceiling and stealing glances toward the living room.

"You and the major done a lot with this old place," he said. "Looks good. Homey." And then suddenly, "Miss Willie Wilcox with you?"

Kate managed to look surprised. "Miss Willie? No. Why? Isn't she at the nursing home?"

"Took off two nights ago," the policeman said. "They bad to mislay their patients, ain't they?"

Kate laughed. "They probably don't have many, with the go-yonders like Miss Willie. Did you look around town?"

"Yep," he said. "Evvawhere. Knew you was buddies. Thought maybe you'd—" He lifted his head and listened, but it was just Sugar coming down the stair step, his snowy tail lifted high in immense dignity.

"Thought maybe you'd taken her in. You know it's murder."

"Aw, foot!" said Kate. "You know Miss Willie as well as I do. Would she be able to kill anybody, much less that rascally son of hers? Steve, you know how she loves him. Always has. You all better find another perp."

Still he didn't move. The chair swayed a little under his weight and the hardware at his waist—gun, flashlight, handcuffs—clinked musically. He sighed and tilted to his feet.

"Mind if I look around?" He asked diffidently. "Always have wanted to see your cabin."

Kate laughed. "Steve, my house is your house. Make yourself at home. Here, take a cup of coffee with you."

She poured a cup and he took it, grinning sheepishly.

The pot, Kate thought, as he lumbered toward the stairs. *Oh, the iron pot. Suppose he sees that.* She had not had time to hide it. Where on earth would she hide it, anyhow? She had set it down on the hearth next to her money-piece whiskey condenser with no idea what to do next. Now, hearing the policeman's footsteps overhead, she grabbed a bouquet of goldenrod and joe-pye weed from a bucket on the back porch and stuffed it in the iron pot, pushing it back into the shadowed fireplace. *No time to make it a flower arranger's dream,* she thought, eyeing it critically. But it did seem to belong there.

Steve came down the stairs, draining his cup. He

looked around the room, as if expecting to find body-hiding cupboards and closets, but said nothing.

"Got a heap of books, haven't you?" he said, eyeing the shelves, as if they might give up an old lady.

"Not enough," said Kate. "You know, when you live in the country, reading's your best recreation."

"Sure," he said indulgently, handing her the cup. "Well, thanks for your . . . cooperation."

He turned at the door.

"Promise me one thing. If Miss Willie shows, will you give us a call?"

Kate decided enough was enough.

"I might and I might not," she said impudently. "Y'all go find yourselves a real murderer and quit harassing an old lady."

Steve looked startled and then grinned. "Can't harass what you can't find," he said, heading for his car.

Only then did Kate begin to worry about what had happened to Miss Willie. Kate just might get by with hiding an iron pot, but how could you hide an old woman? The answer was that Miss Willie, ever resourceful, would hide herself—but where?

And there was Jenny. What had happened to little old Jenny? Kate decided to go to the Willeo section of Roswell, where Jenny had lived for nearly a century, and see what she could find out.

Willeo, named for a creek that threaded through the pretty little antebellum town, had a handful of small, neat houses belonging to the blacks who were mostly descendants of the slave cadre which arrived from the coast with Roswell's founding planters in the early 1800s. Kate knew and claimed several of them for friends, including a white-haired black man named Otto who served as a sort of majordomo to a law firm downtown. They often rode the MARTA train together, and Kate had been to programs at his church where there was mighty singing and ceremonies honoring his Boy Scout troop.

She suspected that he was somehow related to Jenny, and when she pulled in his driveway he walked across the yard to meet her with grief unmistakably etched on his furrowed dark face.

"Otto," she said helplessly. "Jenny . . . Jenny Balcom . . ."

He ducked his head and swallowed. "My awntee," he said. "My grandma's sister."

"Well, I feel so bad about her," Kate said. "I wish I knew what happened and why."

Otto opened the car door and ushered her to the little porch, where falling leaves starred the floor and steps with scarlet. "Don't make any sense what happened," he said. "Nobody would want to hurt Aunt Jenny. No sense to it. She shouldn't a been there. Some of our people moved to town, and she went along. Thought she might get fine laundry in the city."

He laughed shortly. "Her ninety years old but hating to give up. My cousins couldn't take that public housing, and they moved down south of town, but Aunt Jenny, she stayed on."

He was silent.

"And you don't have any idea why anybody would want to kill her?" Kate asked.

"No reason," he said. "Unless . . ." he lifted his head, "unless they thought she knew something she didn't. Tell me she talked to a newspaper lady Sunday night. That was you, wasn't it?"

Kate gulped and nodded. "But just for a minute, Otto. Not really talk. She said . . ." She was silent, trying to remember. "She said something about having seen Garney Wilcox from Roswell at the housing project one day. That kind of surprised me. Before we could say any more a man came up with a knife and . . . well, I pushed her and myself out of the way and a policewoman disarmed him. And that was all."

He nodded. "And somebody come back that night and—" He couldn't go on. The account of that brutal beating was more than he could think about, more than Kate wanted to remember.

"Oh, Otto," she said, taking his hand, "I'm so sorry! I feel somehow like it was my fault."

"No," he mumbled uncertainly. "No. Maybe it was the Lord's will. She was old but shouldn't . . . shouldn't a gone that way."

They walked together to Kate's car, and as Otto opened the door he said, "Wake tonight at the funeral home, if you want to come. Funeral tomorrow afternoon at the church."

"I'll come to the wake," Kate said. "I'm not sure I can get back in time for the funeral, but I will if I can." She had no desire to brave Voncile's wrath and go to

Garney's funeral, unless she could take Miss Willie, but she would go to Jenny's if possible. And where was Miss Willie? Would she really stay away from her beloved Garney's funeral?

CHAPTER 4

Kate had fed the animals and walked over the yard for her late-day check. The sky in the east seemed to have caught its color from the Michaelmas daisies by the well house—a silken lavender blue—while the sun was painting the western horizon with red and gold. She marveled at the blueness of the daisies and thought of cutting a bouquet for the house. They looked sumptuous in an old rose soup tureen she had picked up at a yard sale.

She paused, wondering if she should get the clippers and idly watching the guineas seeking a roosting place in the maple tree. They chose a different tree every night, fluttering awkwardly and complaining to one another, a sort of rusty cavil. Their droppings were a nuisance if they chose a spot over the swing or the lawn chairs, but Kate was fond of them and willing to transfer guinea manure to a flower bed anytime.

In a moment she would shower and change her clothes and go into Roswell for Jenny's wake. But for a little while she savored the weather and the time of day and the pungent smell of old-fashioned chrysanthemums just coming into bloom along the rock wall at the edge of the yard.

That was when the Gandy girls arrived.

They lugged between them a plastic tote bag from which the leg of a faded blue jean drooped.

"Hi, Miss Kate," they said together with a kind of false cordiality. "We come to spend the night with you!"

"Oh, girls—" Kate began with the futile idea of telling them it was not convenient, but Sheena interrupted.

"Daddy's totaled our new BMW and just about totaled hisself. They took him to the Gradys, and Mommer had to go with him. She said for us to come spend the night with you."

Not *May we?* or *Would you mind?* but a fait accompli. They were there. They would stay. Kate groaned inwardly, but she smiled at the girls, putting an arm around each.

"I'm sorry about the accident," she said. "What happened?"

"Aw, Daddy took on a little too much," said Kim Sue, using the family's euphemism for dead drunkenness. "You know that sharp curve up there on Arnold Mill Road? He took it too fast, I reckon."

"They say our new car, it cain't be fixed," put in Sheena importantly.

"How about your father? Was he badly hurt?"

"Mommer said not to worry, he ain't gon' die."

To these young realists it was enough.

"Well, come in and I'll see about some supper," Kate said.

"We was wondering," said Sheena, "if you being tired from a-working all day, if you might want to take us to McDonald's?"

"It would rest you, maybe," added Kim Sue hopefully.

"Yes, it would," said Kate gravely. "That's what we'll do."

Home cooking had largely fallen out of favor since the fast-food establishments had come to north Fulton County. Kate could certainly understand how families who had toiled long and hard to raise food and then broke their backs butchering and canning and freezing would welcome a chance to bypass the cooking. A hot hamburger and french fries cooked by somebody else and handed out a window seemed a glorious luxury. She couldn't deny it to the Gandy sisters.

But what was she to do with them while she went to Jenny's wake?

She carefully broached the subject. Her friend Jenny had died, and since she couldn't get off to go to the funeral tomorrow she planned to go by the funeral home and speak to the family and pay her respects tonight.

"They gon' wake her tonight?" inquired Kim Sue. "We like to go to wakes. Can we view the body?"

"Aw, now," protested Kate. "I don't think we want to do that."

"We've viewed lots of bodies," said Sheena.

"You ever viewed any bodies?" asked Kim Sue.

"We-ell . . ." Kate floundered. She had, but not with the obvious pleasure it gave these girls. She was personally opposed to body-viewing, but she didn't expect to have much luck swaying Kim Sue and Sheena that way.

"I don't usually . . . well, I don't think," she said uncertainly.

"Oh, you oughter see how they fix up the corpses at them funeral parlors," said Sheena. "They git their best clothes, even new ones, to be buried in and put on makeup and fix their hair. Our grandma looked the prettiest, Mommer said. It was a plumb pleasure to see her a-laying there so peaceful."

Kate winced and then scolded herself. There was a certain comfort for the family of one who had worked hard and done without all her life to see her painted and prinked up, wearing a nice dress and taking her ease.

"Okay," she said. "You can go with me, but you must be very quiet. Stay by my side and don't go wandering off peering in coffins 'viewing' bodies."

The girls seemed willing to forgo body-viewing for McDonald's "party meals," little box lunches filled with the makings of a fast supper for children and with trinkets to entertain. They sat in the car while Kate went in to speak to Otto and his wife and several of Jenny's cousins and old friends. The room was crowded and the scent of floral "arrangements" banked against the coffin was almost overpowering. Among them was a washboard, symbol of Jenny's life's work, with little pink carnations lined up to sim-

ulate the ridges for scrubbing and white chrysanthemums serving as the backboard. There was even a bar
of soap contrived from miniature yellow chrysanthemums resting on the soap shelf above the ridges.

Kate saw it and, marveling at the ingenuity of flo-
rists, regretted that she had not remembered to send
flowers. She went back to Otto and drew him aside.

"I'm sorry I didn't send flowers," she murmured,
"but I'd like to give you a little something toward the
funeral expenses, if it's all right."

Otto nodded. "We appreciate it," he said. "Auntie
paid by the week on her burial insurance for thirty
years, but it's not enough now for the coffin or anything." Turning his back away from the crowd, he accepted the folded bill she pushed into his hand and
said softly, "This is bad business, Miss Kate. There's
going to be others killed or hurt. Are you protecting
yourself? And Miss Willie, where is she?"

"Otto, I don't know," Kate said. "I have no idea.
Do you think anybody would hurt her?"

He shook his head. "I don't know, but then I
didn't think anybody would hurt Aunt Jenny."

He glanced toward the coffin. Kate patted his arm
and whispered "I'm sorry" again before she hurried
toward the door.

She had to go find Miss Willie.

She had just gotten back to her car and was making the Gandys put their food wrappings in the parking lot garbage can when Otto appeared at her side.

"Miss Kate," he said, glancing over his shoulder,
"try Miss Marlowa Walton's." Before Kate could answer, he was gone.

She started the car and sat a moment caught between surprise and amusement. How on earth would Otto know that Miss Marlowa was involved with Miss Willie—except that Roswell, old Roswell not yet taken over completely by newcomers, would retain its small-town network. Otto, a dignified old black gentleman who went about the business of his employers at a downtown law firm all day . . . how would he have any contact with Miss Marlowa up there back of the white columns on the hill? Then she remembered Ida, probably another cousin.

The Gandys protested staying in the car and waiting for her in Miss Marlowa's backyard, but Kate was adamant.

"If you're going to spend the night with me, you have to do as I say," she pointed out. "I won't be but a minute, and I want you stay right here and be quiet. No fighting, you understand?"

"Yes'm," they said together, looking deceptively meek, and Kate left them, assuming that there wasn't much trouble they could get into in the now dark backyard. As an afterthought she turned back and said softly, "Lock the car, girls."

Ida met her at the kitchen door. On impulse Kate didn't ask, she directed.

"Go tell Miss Willie I want to see her, Ida," she said firmly.

"You come to a goat's house looking for wool," said Ida, smiling. "How'm I gon' take messages to somebody ain't here?"

"Well, call Miss Marlowa, then," ordered Kate.

"Miss Marlowa got her . . . her company," Ida said. "She don't let me interrupt."

The tentative use of the word *company* caught Kate's attention. Was Miss Marlowa entertaining company or not? From Ida's attitude she couldn't tell.

She heard music and voices, soft and indistinguishable behind the thick walls of the old house, drifting down from upstairs. Could it be that Miss Marlowa had a beau?

"I believe I'll wait, Ida," Kate said.

"No'm," said Ida. "She don't want that. You best leave."

Ida held the door open. Ida's obvious embarrassment and distress at putting her out touched Kate and rendered her helpless to protest. Whatever was going on with Miss Marlowa, Ida couldn't help it, and she had her orders. No visits, no interruptions.

Kate went outside, but before she started the car she walked to the corner of the house nearest Miss Marlowa's upstairs sitting room and listened. Somebody—a man, she thought—was singing a tune oddly familiar. If she could hear more she would think what it was, but she was interrupted by the Gandy sisters loping down the walk from the barn.

"Where have you been?" she demanded. "I told you to stay in the car! Why don't you mind me?"

Sheena answered. "Aw, Miss Kate, we didn't go nowhere. We thought we saw a light in the barn and we thought you would want us to go see. Ain't you some kind of private eye?"

"No!" said Kate peremptorily. "I'm not a private

eye, and I don't want you all prowling around in the dark. Get in the car!''

Kate saw the girls through the shower, which they loved, sprayed them with cologne, and arrayed them in her best silk nightgowns, the ones she was saving against some calamitous future illness. She tucked them in her bed, kissed them good night, and went to spread a sheet and blanket for herself on the daybed.

''Don't talk now,'' she admonished. ''Sleep. I'm tired.''

Before she lay down she called Grady Hospital for a report on the girls' father, Spurgeon Gandy. ''Stable'' was the word, the only word, she could get, and that wasn't worth relaying to his daughters, who didn't seem much concerned anyhow, but she walked to the foot of the stairs with the idea of calling a bulletin up to them.

She heard Sheena, her normal high-pitched jungle keen muted to a furtive murmur, saying, ''It is so Miss Willie's truck! You don't know a Chivvy from a hole in the ground!''

''I do so!'' cried Kim Sue. ''I just wasn't paying attention to the truck, I was looking at them girls in it!''

So the truck was there and the girls knew about it! Kate sat down heavily on the foot of the daybed. And who were the girls in it? She couldn't think what to do. If she tried to swear Kim Sue and Sheena to secrecy, the whereabouts of Miss Willie's truck would be known to every child in Apple Tree Elementary

School by noon tomorrow—and thence to Roswell and environs. There was nothing they liked better than telling secrets. Perhaps it would be better if she didn't say anything to them, better to let them assume that what they had seen was of no particular interest. And yet one word and Miss Willie would be out her precious truck.

Kate moved restlessly around the room, straightening books on the old pine harvest table, brushing ashes off the hearth into the dark maw of the fireplace, where the goldenrod and joe-pye weed had wilted in Miss Willie's iron pot. In her haste to camouflage it for Steve Sizemore she had forgotten to fill it with water. Now, abstractedly, she drew a pitcher of water and poured it into the pot, hoping it wasn't too late to revive the flowers.

Suddenly she came to a decision. The Gandy sisters had thought she was a private eye. She would make private eyes of them! She climbed the stairs to interrupt squirming and whispering.

"Girls," she said, sitting down in the little rocker by her bed. "We have to talk."

"Omigod," said Kim Sue, automatically reacting as her mother would to unpleasant talk.

"Shut up," said Sheena virtuously. "Don't take the name of the Lord, thy God, in vain. What you want to talk about, Miss Kate?"

Kim Sue reached for the bed lamp and Kate stopped her.

"No lights," she said. "What I have to tell you is better told . . . in darkness."

She had their attention now. They stopped squirming and sat up in bed.

"You asked me if I was a private eye," she said softly. "I'm not, but I am—" she hesitated, seeking a word.

"A agent? A secret agent?" Sheena supplied the word.

"Yes," said Kate gratefully. "A agent. And I need some lieutenants. I wonder if you all have the time to help me and if you can abide by . . . the code." *Boy, I'm going good,* she congratulated herself, wondering at the same time what she was talking about.

"Oh, yes, ma'am, the code," said Sheena eagerly.

"What's the code?" asked Kim Sue.

"Secrecy," Kate said in a deep sepulchral voice. "Total and complete secrecy. There are certain things you don't tell—ever, ever."

"Even if they cut your tongue out," put in Sheena, "or drive splinters under your fingernails. You don't tell."

"Ah, you know, then," said Kate.

"Yes, ma'am, I want to be a lieut—what you said," Kim Sue said, wriggling in delight.

"Well, there's the oath," said Kate. "You have to swear to keep all CIA activities . . . undercover." *There I go again,* she thought, pleased to have detective clichés at hand and to have invoked the CIA.

"Me, too," said Sheena. "When do we start?"

"Now," said Kate decisively. "But first the oath. I'll have to get my paper document and make sure I have it right. I have it locked away, of course, but if you are willing to serve, to make the sacrifice, I'll bring it out. Turn on the light, Kim Sue.''

She went to the little washstand at the head of the stairs and fished out a grocery list that had floated to the top of a mess of letters and bills. Holding it close to her chest, she said, ''Raise your right hands and repeat after me: I, Sheena Gandy, and I, Kim Sue Gandy, committed to serve God and the United States of America, do solemnly swear that in the case of the state of Georgia versus Miss Willie Wilcox and all matters pertaining thereto''—the freckled faces before her were taut with solemnity, the upraised hands stiff with importance—''I will exert every effort to fathom the truth and report it only to my superior . . .'' Kate fumbled for a title, ''Chief Inspector K. K. Mulcay.''

The young voices, almost always shrill and loud, were choky with gravity.

Genius, Kate thought, to have come up with that fine title for herself. And, carried away, she threw in for the finish a little Latin, intoning majestically, ''*Pro bono publico!*''

''*Pro bono,*'' repeated the girls faithfully, stumbling a little over the *publico*.

''What does that mean, Miss Kate?'' asked Sheena.

''Ah.'' Kate was disposed to hang on to the mystery, but she thought better of it. ''You are to be trusted now, so I'll tell you. It means,'' she whispered, ''for the public good.''

The girls were wide-eyed. She started to return the grocery list to the washstand drawer, but decided against it. Any decent secret document deserved to be destroyed, à la Fawn Hall. She produced a match and an ashtray and before the reverent faces of her new lieutenants started a small blaze.

"Now!" she said, returning to the rocker. "Tonight you saw something which could be important. The truck . . . I mean, the *vehicle*"—good police word—"and the subjects therein . . . white females?" More police words.

The girls nodded. "Cheryl Wilcox and Judy Carson," Sheena said.

"Did you see what they were doing?"

"Yes'm, smoking pot and talking," said Kim Sue.

Kate took a deep breath. It was too much that these little girls, hardly more than kindergarten age, recognized pot.

"One of them's pregnant," offered Sheena.

Pot and pregnant. Kate groaned inwardly. *Oh, poor babies!*

"How do you know?" she asked.

"They was talking about what to do," Sheena said. "Abortion or what."

"Did they say which girl is pregnant and who the father is?"

The girls shook their heads.

"You come out of the house too quick," Sheena accused. "We heard you shutting the door and we run."

"I know." Kate sighed and stood up. "Well, you realize all of this is top secret."

They nodded, awed by the enormity of the secret.

"You gon' give us a badge or something?" inquired Kim Sue.

"Aw, shit, you can't wear a badge and be a secret agent," said Sheena scornfully.

But they did need something to remind them of the magnitude of their assignment, Kate realized, and she looked around the room, wondering what would do. Her beeper, a nagging little device Benjy had given her years ago but which she had managed not to wear, lay in her mother's old pin tray on the dresser. She stood up and reached for it.

"This is to keep you in touch," she said. "One of you must wear it when you are on assignment. Meanwhile, keep it hidden in a safe place. I'll explain how it works."

"No need," said Sheena. "We seen them. Is this one a vibrator?"

"A what?" asked Kate.

"You know, instead of beeping it vibrates against your body and nobody hears you got it on you. But you know you got a call. Boy at school's got one and the teacher don't know nothing about it. When he gits a call he just pretends he's got to go to the bathroom and he heads for the telephone."

"I'm afraid it's not a vibrator beeper," Kate said. "I'll ask . . . headquarters . . . if they can supply us with one."

She returned to her daybed, thinking hysterically, *I'm not up to coping with these sophisticated infants. Pot, pregnancy, the boy in Sheena's school who wears a vibrating beeper! How on earth did we come to this? Why?* She should find out the name of the boy and report it to the narcotics squad. Obviously he was serving as a flunky for drug dealers. At the age of nine or ten! And she should find out if, in truth, and which girl was pregnant.

She tossed restlessly on her daybed, fighting for sleep. Sleep came briefly, with sunrise.

The Gandy girls dressed in clean jeans and shirts they had brought in their plastic bag, wolfed down a breakfast of cereal, toast, and eggs, and prepared to walk to the school bus stop up at the crossroads. But before they were out of the yard they came back to hug Kate, who was feeding Pepper and Sugar.

"G'bye, K.K.," Sheena whispered daringly, and lifted her skimpy, sand-colored eyebrows in a meaningful look.

Kim Sue looked surprised at the "K.K." but rallied and said softly, "Thank you for letting us stay all night, Miss K.K."

Impulsively Kate held on to them and hugged them back hard.

"You're sweet girls," she said with a rush of affection, "and you're always welcome. Tell your mother that if you need to, you can spend tonight with me. And if there's anything I can do, tell her to call me. I hope your father's all right."

"And the BMW, too," said Kim Sue. "We sure need that."

Kate nodded and smiled, and in a moment they were in the road and out of sight beyond the low-growing hollies and viburnums she had planted as a screen.

The phone was ringing when she got back to the kitchen. It was the medical examiner's office.

"Want to come by and get the word on your friend, Garney Wilcox?" Ed Snow, a homicide detective assigned to the office, asked. "It's the damnedest thing you ever saw!"

"Tell me," said Kate.

"Naw, the doc wants to explain it to you, but it does look like the blow on his head was what did him in. The poison and the electricity were just extra frills. Why don't you stop by? I think they gon' release the body to the family today and they'll probably go ahead with the funeral. You might want to alert Miss Willie."

Sure, Kate thought, *if I could find her.* She resolved to make one more run to Miss Marlowa's to see if either Miss Willie or the truck was still there.

She drove to the back of the house and parked where she could see the grape arbor without too much maneuvering. The truck's battered and muddy rear end was barely visible from the path. It might have been any piece of discarded farm machinery. At least it indicated that Miss Willie wasn't helling around the countryside behind the wheel, she thought, reassured, and headed for the back door.

To her surprise not Ida but Ida's niece, Canary, so-called because she dyed her hair yellow-bird ochre, answered her knock.

"Hi, Canary," Kate said. "School out today?"

The black girl smiled in greeting and shook her head. "I took a leave day—at Aunt Ida's insistence."

Ida had financed Canary's education, working hard to keep Miss Marlowa and her way of life in the big house going so Canary could go to Spelman College in town and equip herself to teach school. She was said to be a fine teacher and she had repaid her aunt with loving care and money since.

"Ida here?" Kate asked.

"No, that's why I'm here," Canary said. "She went somewhere with Miss Marlowa and her friend and asked me to house-sit and do a little cleaning until they get back."

"Was the friend Miss Willie Wilcox?" Kate asked.

Canary's dark face split into a wide white smile and Kate saw that she had dimples. "They didn't say," she said with what Kate thought was pure evasion.

"Well, do you know where they went?"

Canary shook her head. "I assumed Highlands. You know Miss Marlowa goes up there every year to see the leaves in North Carolina. Aunt Ida goes with her to drive."

"Did they leave a number where they can be reached?"

Canary looked vague. "I reckon. They usually do, but I wasn't here when they left, and I haven't checked. You want to come in and wait a minute, and I'll look?"

Kate followed her into the back hall and stood by the downstairs sitting room door, gazing absently at a pile of papers and tapes on a small cherry spool table.

"Excuse the mess," said Canary. "Miss Marlowa planned to take all this stuff with her, I imagine. I reckon she forgot."

Kate went closer and saw that all the tapes had the same picture on their plastic cases—a smiling man and woman with their heads together in loving propinquity. Jeanette MacDonald and Nelson Eddy!

"Ah, the romantic duo!" she said, smiling at Canary. "I haven't thought of them since I used to play hooky from Girls' High and go to Loew's Grand to see them. I saw *Naughty Marietta* five times."

"Did you?" asked Canary absently, studying a pad by the telephone. "I bet Miss Marlowa can beat your record. She's a real Jeanette-Nelson buff."

She looked up. "Please don't say anything about that. I think she's a closet buff, always looking at their movies and listening to their songs back of closed doors."

Kate shook her head, smiling. "I won't say anything, but I'd love to join her sometime. I wonder if she has *New Moon* and *Maytime?*"

"She has 'em all," said Canary, straightening up. "But I don't have her telephone number in Highlands or an address. I'll keep looking. She usually leaves them. Check back with me, if you want to."

"Do you know how long they'll be gone?"

Again that faint flicker of evasiveness on her young face as Canary shrugged her shoulders.

"Forgot to ask," she said. "Aunt Ida wouldn't have thought it was any of my business. I'll just come and go every day until they turn up."

The pointed suggestion that it might not be any of her business, either, amused Kate. When you come right down to it, she had no business there asking questions. She had better go to work and stop worrying about Miss Willie's whereabouts. Except . . . was her old friend safe? Otto's low-voiced warning worried her. The police's repeated contention that Miss Willie had "confessed" worried her.

Kate stood on the back steps listening to the rumble of a bulldozer beyond the little town square and down the hill near the river. At the edge of the square there was a signpost with the names of all the antebellum houses and gardens which were of tourist interest. One of the loveliest, Laurel Hall, had a line drawn through it. It had burned months ago. Now developers were clearing the site for an apartment complex.

Kate had not joined that fight, but she knew most Roswell citizens were bitter about it. The historical society and the civic association, environmental groups and assorted old families had plans to restore the crumbling mansion and its fine gardens for use as a museum, library, and garden center. The original owners had been distinguished in state history, a couple of governors, a U.S. senator, Confederate generals. One of the women in the family had written novels, seldom read for a century but popular in her day. The gardens covered acres overlooking the Chattahoochee River, with mountain laurel and rhododendron in banks of dark green and deep rose in the spring outlining an avenue to a big rock, which jutted out of the bluff, a lookout since Indian days.

While champions of the museum-library plan fought to raise money, developers were photographing and surveying the land and drawing plans for a multi-unit complex of townhouses and apartments which, as a sop to local history, would be "colonial"—to the extent of white columns ornamenting a hundred doorways. The current owners lived in California and had no interest in the controversy, waiting merely to collect from the highest bidder. The civic association and historical society had gone to court and obtained an injunction to stay the destruction of Laurel Hall and in a great coup had Laurel Hall designated a historic landmark. They had beaten anybody who would destroy the house, they thought, but they had reckoned without fire. One winter night Laurel Hall burned to the ground. The arsonist was never caught. The developers themselves had impeccable alibis and expressed suitable regret that they had won through calamity. Now they were celebrating victory to the tune of whining, droning bulldozers uprooting trees and laurel and rhododendron.

At the time, Garney Wilcox was serving as a flunky to the out-of-state developers and Kate often wondered if he had been, in the classic Atlanta phrase about the Union General Sherman, who burned the town, "kind of careless with matches." She didn't know whether he profited from it, and without profit Garney was immobile. Now, listening on Miss Marlowa's back steps, she wondered if some zealous environmental or history buff had killed him.

It was a happy thought, she decided, as she maneuvered the car out of the driveway and headed for town. Anything to get Miss Willie off the hook.

There was a sheaf of little green telephone messages beside her computer at the office, and Kate shuffled through them. All of them would keep except one "Please call" from Sergeant Alvarez.

Kate picked up the phone.

"Hi, this is Mellie Alvarez," said the voice on the

other end of the line. When she heard it was Kate, she said, "You got time for lunch today? You like barbecue?"

Kate said "Sure" to both questions and agreed to meet her at an old rib shack whimsically renamed Mama's Grease Pit just off the South Expressway. First she had to knock out a column and finish a book review she had started days before. The book was pretty good, the first effort of a local teacher, but she found, as she sought descriptive phrases, that she didn't remember much about it. *Give me a book*, she thought mournfully, *like* Gone With the Wind, *where the most obscure characters had staying power*. Honey Wilkes, she mused. A minor character, but people fought over who should portray her in the movies fifty years ago, and you could still get an argument from fans about her. And here Kate was struggling to remember the names of the hero and heroine in last week's read.

Is it the book or me? she wondered. *Am I getting fuzzy-minded?*

Sergeant Alvarez was already in a booth in the back of the room when she got to Mama's, seated at a slick plastic and chrome table with red plastic curtains at the window above it and bottles of red pepper sauces on the table. The policewoman waved, and Kate was glad. She wasn't sure that she would have recognized Sergeant Alvarez out of uniform, and in a raspberry-colored wool suit with a white silk shirt, pure Neiman-Marcus and probably two hundred and fifty dollars, at that.

"Sergeant," Kate said, inclining her head.

"Call me Mellie," the young woman said, showing her white crooked smile. "I'm off duty. But don't call me—"

"I know," said Kate, laughing, "Melanie Scarlett."

"Right," Sergeant Alvarez said, handing Kate a menu. "You want a beer? It helps to take the fire out of Mama's pork."

Kate skipped the beer in favor of sweet iced tea because it was the middle of a working day and beer might make her sleepy. They settled on sandwiches of pork sliced from the outside of the cut because it would be crusty and smoke-tasting, and they each ordered a cup of Brunswick stew to go with it.

After a languid, slow-moving teenager had written everything down, apparently checking her spelling with the care of one doing a Mensa puzzle, and slouched off kitchenward, Kate said, "What are you working on today?"

Sergeant Alvarez shrugged. "Nothing much. I'm off until tonight and I wanted to see how you're surviving the near attack the other night."

"Thanks to you—" Kate began.

Sergeant Alvarez interrupted. "No thanks. I just did what anybody else would have done. Lucky I walked in from the backyard in time, is all. Knife-toters are my bread and butter, but I don't imagine you get to play victim all that much."

"First time . . . I think," said Kate. "But I can't believe I was the intended victim. I think the man was after Jenny. You know what happened to her after we left?"

Sergeant Alvarez sipped her beer and stared out

113

the window at a moving van groaning up the hill leading to the expressway ramp. "I know," she said in a
low voice, "I saw her."

"Well, doesn't that suggest to you that he was after her and not me?"

"No," said the policewoman, returning her gaze
to Kate's face, her eyes suddenly filling with tears. "It
suggests to me that he was a low-down son of a bitch,
full of heroin, out to kill or mutilate anybody who was
in his way. You or Jenny. You *and* Jenny. It didn't
matter to him. Same thing happened to my mother.
That's why I got in the Marines. That's why I'm policing."

"Oh," said Kate, catching her breath. "Oh, I'm
sorry!"

Sergeant Alvarez returned her eyes to the traffic
on the street.

"He didn't even know her," she said in a low
voice. "She was coming home from market with her
groceries in a basket. He got her in the hall—not a
knife but a broken bottle. From our yard, I think, the
one my mama kept trying to clean up."

Kate couldn't think of anything to say. The waitress returned with their order and they both regarded
it absently, as if it were something beyond their
knowledge or acquaintance.

Sergeant Alvarez was the first to rally.

"Oh, well, that was a long time ago," she said,
"and I don't let myself think about it much. I'm just
glad we got this dreamboat. He's got a record as long as
your arm—a known addict and a toadie to the big
dealers. In his crazy mind he thought you and Jenny

114

were a threat to his bosses. By the way, what were you talking about that could have alarmed him?"

"Nothing, really," said Kate. "I hadn't seen Jenny in years. She moved away from Roswell and we were just greeting one another. She mentioned having seen Garney Wilcox, the man who was murdered the other day near my house. She said he'd been there in the housing project, and that surprised me. I couldn't imagine what he'd be doing at Rose of Sharon—big rich man dedicated to high-cost housing. Unless," she added, "he had figured out some way of razing the place and selling the land for an industrial plant or a condominium or something. That was his specialty."

"Must have been something else," murmured Sergeant Alvarez. "It's not easy to get your hands on a federal housing project. Was he into drugs?"

"I don't know," said Kate slowly. "I hadn't thought of that. Money was his passion."

Sergeant Alvarez nodded and picked up her sandwich. "That," she said, biting into a slice of pork, "is what the drug traffic is all about."

"Maybe a drug dealer killed him," Kate ventured hopefully.

Sergeant Alvarez grinned at her. "Anybody to save your old friend?" she said. "You know we're looking for her, don't you? For questioning, so far. No warrant yet. Are you hiding her out somewhere?"

Kate laughed. "I would if I could. But you don't take charge of Miss Willie. She's her own person. I don't know where she is. Wish I did. I guess they'll do Garney's funeral tomorrow, and I imagine she'll be there."

"You going?" asked Sergeant Alvarez.

"I've been ordered not to by the widow."

The policewoman raised her eyebrows. "You certainly don't have to let that stop you. What if I go with you?"

"You want Miss Willie?"

"Told you," said Sergeant Alvarez, "I'm off duty in the daytime—today and tomorrow." She reflected a moment. "But yes, if I saw her I would call in or set up a meeting with homicide. Wouldn't you?"

"Maybe, if I were a policeman," Kate admitted. "But I lost my badge. I don't for a minute believe Miss Willie capable of murder, and I sure wouldn't want to mess with her at her son's funeral. You don't know how she adored that fool—and him a stepson, at that. From the time he was in diapers her whole life was centered on him. Why would she kill him?"

"Why would she tell everybody that she did it?" countered Sergeant Alvarez.

"Well, you know," said Kate, "there are always people who come out of the woodwork to claim they committed crimes they were nowhere near. You know that. Nuts."

"Are you saying Mrs. Wilcox is nuts?"

Kate decided to level with this friendly woman.

"She's the steadiest, most sensible, most honest person I know. There's not an ounce of pretension in her. But . . ." Kate hesitated and then blurted it out: "But she would grapple with bears or alligators or rattlesnakes for somebody she cared about!"

Sergeant Alvarez's brown face was pensive. "Question is, who does she care about?"

"Garney, first. And after that his daughter, Cheri. I don't think it would be possible for her to love Voncile, but she would be loyal and protective if it was needful."

"This granddaughter . . . what's she like?"

"I don't really know her," Kate said. "They moved to town when she was a little girl. But she's very pretty, long blond hair, one of those fantastic sixteen-year-old bodies."

She paused, not knowing how much to tell and how much to withhold and if any of it really mattered. She decided that in the absence of Benjy to hash things over with, Mellie Alvarez might do.

"My operatives tell me it's possible she is pregnant, either her or her best friend, Judy Carson. So the poor child probably has problems she can't handle. I can't see Voncile being supportive. She'd consider it betrayal aimed at her personally and probably insist on a wedding—the biggest and gaudiest that she could buy. If it's too late for an abortion."

"Does she know?"

Kate shook her head. "I don't know. I just heard last night. It's possible it isn't true. But it's also likely, I'm afraid."

"Maybe I can help there," Sergeant Alvarez said. "If she needs a refuge, I know a couple of good foster homes. I don't know how I can make the offer, though. You look for a chance. How far along is she?"

Suddenly Kate remembered Judy Carson's cryptic message for Miss Willie: Four months.

"I'm guessing four months."

Sergeant Alvarez sighed. "Well, they certainly

aren't by themselves, these young girls. There's a lot of teenage pregnancy going around. Did this best friend tell you?"

"Not exactly. She gave me a message for Miss Willie. I didn't understand it at the time, and I forgot . . . or rather, I never got around to getting it to Miss Willie. She said, 'Tell her four months.' "

"Then the grandmother knows?" Sergeant Alvarez said.

"I suppose," said Kate tiredly, wondering if any of this was relevant.

"Four months," mused Sergeant Alvarez. "Getting late. Most Atlanta clinics won't take you after three months. However, there is one that will go up to six months. You have to check into their hospital and spend two or three days. I wonder if they know that."

Kate couldn't imagine Voncile coming to her for counsel, and she couldn't think of any way she could get Sergeant Alvarez's obvious desire to be of help through to Cheri. She shrugged.

"I don't know. I just hope Miss Willie doesn't know any of this. She has enough to worry about with those ominous words 'The police want to talk to you' hanging over her head." She smiled ruefully at Sergeant Alvarez. "To somebody of her age and upbringing, illegitimate pregnancy would be about the worst thing that could happen to a girl."

"A Victorian, is she?"

Kate laughed and shook her head. "Nothing so prudish and prissy as that. She's a plain country woman with a stringent set of morals and . . . well,

118

sort of innocent and chaste, if you can imagine that in an octogenarian.''

"You do love her, don't you?'' Sergeant Alvarez said thoughtfully. "And you're afraid she's guilty—so you'll do *anything* to protect her.''

Kate swallowed hard. The excellent barbecue seemed lodged in her chest. She tried to look indignant but found she couldn't pull it off with this thin, brown Puerto Rican Red Dog.

"I do *not* think she's guilty,'' she finally said, and then with an effort she grinned. "Sure, I'd do almost anything to help her. Why don't you come with me to see what the medical examiner found out?''

"Okay,'' said Sergeant Alvarez, reaching for the check. "Postman's holiday, but what the hell?''

What the medical examiner found out was not going to be immediately available to a newspaper reporter. The doctor himself and several of Kate's old friends from homicide who assisted him had gone to a shooting at a mall where three bodies had been spread over the lunchroom floor by a killer whose only reason so far was that he was unhappy and disillusioned with life. The invitation to her to drop by and see the report had not been relayed to the middle-aged woman at the desk. She admitted that a report had been made. She herself had typed it. But she wasn't authorized to show it to anybody.

Sergeant Alvarez showed her badge. "I'd like to see it,'' she said gently.

The receptionist looked at the elegant suit, the gold earrings, the single-strand gold chain, and back at the badge.

"Please," Sergeant Alvarez said.

Kate was glad the Red Dog sergeant was along to interpret the medical examiner's report. Two yellow pages of facts and figures—all the statistics of Garney's life, really—were enough to wade through, but the coroner's report on the location of death, the injury, the manner of death, the cause of death, the time of death, the contents of the stomach, and all the rest of it took more time than she had to give. She got to the line "Killed by another" and handed the report back to Sergeant Alvarez.

"He had poison—enough to cause digestive upset and sleepiness. Cardiac glycosides insufficient to cause death," Sergeant Alvarez read. "Burns from an electric wire. Immediate cause head trauma due to or as a consequence of a blow with a blunt instrument."

"Oh, good," said Kate before she thought.

Sergeant Alvarez and the blue-eyed woman back of the counter looked at her reprovingly.

"Well, I mean . . . it must have been a quick and easy way to go," Kate floundered.

"I know what you mean," said Sergeant Alvarez, grinning.

The Gandy sisters were in residence when Kate got home. Kim Sue was picking scuppernongs, the very ones Kate was saving for wine. And Sheena was playing Miss Willie's parlor organ.

"Well, girls . . ." Kate greeted them uncertainly, wondering if or when she was ever to have her little house to herself again. "What's going on?"

"That beeper didn't work!" Kim Sue said accusingly. "We thought there was something ailing it, and we asked Troy Haskins—he's the boy with the vibrating beeper—whatcha did if one didn't work. He said you gotta have bat-ries. You got any bat-ries?"

"Oh, I don't know," Kate said tiredly. "I'll see. Benjy used to keep them in the refrigerator."

"Ha!" hooted Kim Sue. "Like they was good to eat!"

Sheena merely waved her hand and went on pumping the old organ with legs that barely reached the pedals but moved like fat jean-sheathed pistons. "Look, I got it!" she cried. "I can play 'Cain't Git No Satisfaction'! Listen!"

The old organ from a lifelong association with church hymns and folk songs wheezed and protested, but Sheena got some rackety semblance of a tune out of it, finishing with a whomping bass finale.

"I ought to take music, oughtn't I?" she said, whirling the piano stool around to face Kate.

"You got a piano at your house now?" Kate asked, wondering if proceeds from their grandpa's cornfield had stretched that far.

"Aw, no," Sheena said disgustedly. "But I could practice here, huh?"

Kate shuddered, but looking at the hopeful young face with the greenish spattering of freckles on nose and cheeks and the ambitious light in the blue eyes, she found herself unable to say anything but, "Sure. All right."

There was no likelihood that the Gandys would have money for lessons or would spend money for music lessons if they did have it. And maybe Sheena, fat chance, did have talent. Kate couldn't find it in her heart to discourage a child who wanted to learn—even if the sum total of her accomplishment was "Cain't Git No Satisfaction."

She couldn't always be sure if it was a thirst for knowledge or a mischievous catlike curiosity that motivated these girls, but then Sheena, following her to the kitchen, said, "Miss Kate, them foreign words you said to us last night, bony something, what language was they?" She lowered her voice and looked at the back window and the open kitchen door. "Would they be secret agent language?"

Enough of this deceitful charade, Kate said to herself. She felt scroungy fooling her eager young assistants. But still she had to keep the whereabouts of Miss Willie's truck secret until she knew the whereabouts of Miss Willie. She temporized.

"They are Latin, honey," she said, putting an arm around Sheena's shoulders. "It used to be a language everybody learned in school. They don't teach it much anymore, except to doctors and lawyers."

"Good," said Sheena with satisfaction. "That makes it real secret."

Kate smiled at her. "Not real secret—just sort of semi-secret. I had some Latin in Girls' High, and, of course, I have run into it in court. It's kind of fun because so much of English we use every day comes from it."

"Would you learn me some?" asked Sheena.

"Teach," Kate automatically corrected her. "Sometime, honey, but not now. I need a shower and to feed the animals and round up something for supper."

"Don't worry about us," put in Kim Sue, bringing a basket of scuppernongs and setting it down on the back porch. "Mommer's cooking spareribs and rice tonight, and we got to go home. They bringing Daddy home, and she wanted to have something good for him. Here your scuppernongs. I picked them for you."

And I thought she was eating them as she picked, Kate reproached herself.

"Why don't you take them home with you?" she said in a rush of generosity, surprising to herself and summarily quashing her plan to make wine. "Maybe your mother and father would like some."

"Oh, yes, ma'am," accepted Kim Sue enthusiastically. "They do love scuppernongs. And Miss Kate, Troy Haskins wanted to see our beeper but we wouldn't show it to him. He said we could buy bat-ries for it almost anywhere. If you don't have any in the Frigidaire, you want to give us money to buy some?"

Kate couldn't make a "bat-ry" decision because she suddenly realized that they were giving her the name of the boy whose beeper activity seemed awfully suspicious.

"Do you know where Troy got his beeper?" she asked.

The girls shook their heads.

"Do you know who calls him on it?"

They shook their heads again.

"Leave me our beeper," she said, "and I'll get proper—official—batteries for it tomorrow." She guided them toward the door.

"Your mail's on the table," Sheena said, divesting herself of the beeper, which was in the bosom of her T-shirt. "We brung in the stuff you got. Didn't look like much."

It was time once more to chide them for touching her mail or, for that matter, taking possession of her cabin when she was absent, Kate thought, but there was something endearing about their eagerness to help and she would take up the matter of invasion of privacy when she wasn't so tired. Or she would lock the doors, breaking with precedent. Nobody in the Cove ever locked a door, and if they did it was a matter for concern—and alarm—to everybody else in the settlement.

She stood on the porch, watching the girls with the basket of scuppernongs between them head toward their special path through the woods. Suddenly, at a signal from Sheena, they turned and lifted their grubby paws and said together in a cryptic but carrying whisper: "Bony!"

Oh, bless their hearts, Kate thought chokily. "Bony!" she called after them. It was fully as good as *pro bono publico.* Tomorrow she would teach them *amo, amas, amat.* They deserved to know "I love; you love; he, she, or it loves."

She poured herself a glass of sherry, picked up the mail, and took it to the kitchen rocker by the window. Sheena was right. It looked like "nothing much" except for a lumpy little package which had no return address, no stamps, and was addressed simply to "Kate." Her old neighbors had often dropped off little gifts, packages of seeds and jars of honey or preserves, putting them in the mailbox rather than coming to the door with them because they were usually on their way to the store over on Arnold Mill Road and the mailbox was handy.

The script forming her name wasn't enough for her to recognize anybody's handwriting. She fumbled with the string and brown paper and found a cassette tape carefully enveloped in a linen handkerchief. A Jeanette MacDonald-Nelson Eddy collection of songs!

Had Miss Marlowa brought it? Kate thought in astonishment. And when? How did she know that Kate would be interested? Did it mean that she had talked with Canary or been back home since Kate's early morning visit?

Kate put the tape on the table and looked up the number at the Marlowa Walton mansion. Canary answered.

She had been there all day cleaning, Canary said, and she had not seen or heard from Miss Marlowa. Nor had she found her usual note with a telephone number or address where she might be reached if the house burned down, a constant fear with the old lady.

"She's awful old, and I reckon she forgot," Canary said. "But I'm surprised at Aunt Ida. She usually catches up the loose ends Miss Marlowa leaves trailing."

"Funny," said Kate, "and you still don't know who the friend is who went with them?"

Canary hesitated. "I don't *know* anything. I'd be guessing, that's all."

"Well, for the Lord's sake, *guess!*" implored Kate. "The police are looking for Miss Willie Wilcox, and it's important that I find her. Hiding just makes it look like she's guilty, and of course she's not. Do you think it's possible she went with Miss Marlowa and Ida?"

"That the old lady who used to sell butter and eggs?" asked Canary. "Lived out in the country?"

"That's right," said Kate eagerly.

Canary cogitated. Finally she said, "I don't know. I was guessing it was Miss Fenwick, a white-haired lady used to come out from town to spend weekends. One I saw here the other day was white-haired and stylish. That wouldn't be Mrs. Wilcox, would it?"

"No," Kate admitted reluctantly. "Miss Willie's got gray hair well mixed with brown. And she never laid claim to being stylish. The Mother Hubbards she wore when she was young, as they say, cover everything and touch nothing. She still wears them."

She reminded Canary to call her if she heard from the travelers and went back to the mail and the mystery tape.

She hadn't heard the romantic songs of Jeanette MacDonald and Nelson Eddy since her high school years, and she thought it might be fun to light the fire and pour herself a drink and listen, for a change, to real love songs, as compared to "Cain't Git No Satisfaction." On the other hand, without Benjy what did she care about love songs? They would just make her sad and lonely, and she didn't need that. If she heard "Must We Say Farewell to Dreams?" or "Wanting You," she would have to go to bed and bawl.

Instead she needed to call Mellie Alvarez about Troy Haskins. Sergeant Alvarez would know which members of the narc squad would handle a little fifth grader with care. She dialed the number Sergeant Alvarez had given her and was holding the line listening to it ring when Pepper barked, heralding a visitor in the yard. Kate stretched the telephone cord to the window over the sink and saw Ron Gardiner coming up the path. He was alone for once and not dressed in his habitual running suit but tennis shorts and shoes and a knitted shirt with something—Kate never could read them—embroidered on the front to indicate that it was expensive.

"Hail, neighbor!" he cried when he saw Kate at the window.

"Hi!" said Kate. "Come in." And then into Sergeant Alvarez's answering machine, "This is Kate. Please call me tonight."

"Oh, you're lonesome tonight, too," said Ron from the back steps. "Val's gone to Miami for a few days, and I thought since you're alone and I'm alone . . ."

Oh, nuts, thought Kate. *He's coming to sit and talk, and I'd hoped it was to borrow a cup of sugar or something and get out.*

As if reading her thoughts, he said in his jovial, I'm-such-a-card way, "Thought I might borrow a cup of scotch. Then I decided, why not borrow it in a glass with ice and soda and enjoy it with a neighbor?"

"Why, yes," said Kate, "that's a good idea . . . if I have any scotch. I don't stock much hard liquor—just beer and a little wine."

"Anything will do," said Ron, flopping down in the kitchen rocker. "Whatever you're having."

"Well, it was sherry," said Kate helplessly. "But I'm afraid I drank the last. Will a beer do?"

"Aw, I could run home and get a bottle," said Ron. "I was kidding about borrowing scotch. I may not be the subdivision's brains, but I don't let my booze run out. I always have some. How about that?"

"No, I'm afraid I haven't much time," Kate said. "I've some stuff I must write tonight. But I'll be glad to get you a beer."

Ron accepted the beer, declined one of Kate's frosted mugs from the freezer, tilted the bottle to his lips, and half emptied it, his wide-eyed, ingenuous gaze on Kate.

"You know, we ought to see more of each other," he said. "I always heard that you southerners were neighborly, big on hospitality and all. I apologize for not visiting more. Matter of fact, you don't visit much, either, do you?"

"No," Kate said. "I'm sorry, but I always seem busy."

"Val's noticed that," he said. "She's from Jersey, and she thought moving here would be more friendly-like. Kind of hurts her feelings that the neighbors don't run in and out much, you know."

"That's a shame. I'm sorry she's hurt," Kate said automatically, positive that Val didn't give a hoot in hell for neighbors and resenting Ron's effort to make her feel guilty. "If I didn't have to go to work every day I'd probably be more neighborly, but probably not. There's so much I need to do here. You know most of the people in Shining Waters Subdivision are from other sections of the country. They must be sociable."

"Aw, Yankees," said Ron, enjoying his little joke, which took into account that he himself came from New Jersey. "I'm talking about old settlers like yourself. Ho! Don't get me wrong—I don't mean old in age, I mean old in living here. You're still a mighty good-looking woman and as active as Val and me, if not more so."

Kate gritted her teeth and turned toward the refrigerator. She might as well have a beer if she had to put up with his exposition on hospitality and his gratuitous comments on her age and vigor.

"Southern hospitality," she said with more heat than she intended, "is a stereotype—about half myth. It might have started in the old days when distances between houses were great and there wasn't much to do except to entertain and be entertained by one's friends and relatives. It was pretty usual to have houseguests who came for a day and stayed for weeks and months. Now everybody's busy, and unless they really like you, southerners are no more inclined than anybody to spend time with you."

It sounded curt and she hadn't meant it to, but she hated his aggressive friendliness. She wouldn't blame it on the northern section of the country from which he came. Actually she didn't know any man from the South or anyplace else who would come barging in without advance notice or a specific invitation unless he was an old friend.

Ron rocked the chair a little and let his eyes travel over the rough rafters in the ceiling and into the main room. He assessed the wide time-stained boards which made up ceiling and floor, the rock chimney and the blue checked sofa and chairs grouped around it. His eyes rested on the hearth, and Kate gulped. Did he see the iron skillet?

"Looks like a nifty fireplace you got there," he said. "What do you say I run home and get a bottle and we build a fire? These shorts are not the warmest things I ever wore, and it seems to be getting chilly. Come on, be neighborly!"

Kate stood up.

"Sorry, neighbor," she said coolly. "I'll have to ask you to make it another time. Come back when Val gets home and I'm not so busy. Right now I'm bogged down."

"You sure?" he asked, standing up and moving closer to her.

Good heavens, Kate thought to herself, *he's about to put his hands on me! The jerk!*

She moved quickly to the door and stepped out on the porch and then into the yard. There seemed to be nothing for him to do but follow. He stood around by the back steps looking uncertain and, Kate suddenly realized, a little drunk. Anger seemed to descend on him from somewhere. His rosy, pursed mouth thinned into a slit, his wide, childlike blue eyes were gray as ice on a winter pond.

"Miss Nicey Nice," he said lopsidedly, like one trying to sneer but missing. "Don't flatter yourself I was going to try to sleep with you. I hear you only sleep with cops."

Kate picked up a hoe and, grasping the middle of the handle, shook it at him.

"Get the hell out of my yard!" she said in a low voice.

Pepper, sensing her anger from his pad on the porch, plunged to her side, growling.

Ron waved a threatening fist at the dog and Pepper leapt forward, his teeth bared only inches from the man's hairy calves.

"No, Pepper," said Kate, grabbing his collar. "Not this time. You'd better go, Ron," she said with a return to calmness. "We'll see each other at some better time."

"Guess so," he mumbled, turning toward the front yard. His anger had apparently dissipated as rapidly as it had gathered. He glanced nervously at the hoe, which Kate still held, and at Pepper, restrained by her other hand, mumbled "See you," and left.

Oh, what a silly encounter, Kate thought as she poured food into Pepper's bowl. She should have handled it with more tact. An ugly episode with the neighbors was the last thing she wanted. She hadn't realized at once that he was drunk, but she should have known and eased him out with humor and diplomacy, instead of a hoe and a watchdog. She smiled ruefully at Pepper and gave him an extra measure of dog food.

Mellie Alvarez returned Kate's call close to midnight, just as Kate stopped struggling with a magazine piece she was writing and prepared to go to bed. Mellie said it had been only a so-so evening for the Red Dogs —two dope peddlers at the same housing project—but they had lucked into the crack just as a kid attempted to shove it into the sewer. One of the dogs deserved the credit.

"Congratulations," Kate said. "My dog was the hero here this evening. He rose up to protect me and help me get rid of a drunken neighbor."

"Ah, a fine fellow," said Sergeant Alvarez. "I'm glad you got him if you're going to live in some godforsaken rural place."

"We're pretty uptown now," Kate said. "Half-million-dollar houses all around and, I'm afraid, drugs in the school."

She told Sergeant Alvarez about Troy Haskins and his beeper. Having a beeper itself wasn't any more suspicious than the walkie-talkies all the kids had taken up a few years ago. But having a vibrating beeper and leaving the classroom to make phone calls did suggest drugs, didn't it?

"Sure does," said the sergeant. "Gimme the name of the kid and the school and I'll get somebody to look into it."

They rang off, and Kate went up to bed, taking care to fold Miss Willie's mother's old quilt over the foot and to put her starched pillow shams with their red turkey work script on a chair to keep from rumpling them. Miss Willie had given them to her—one pillow embroidered with a glamorous reclining lady and the words, "I slept and dreamt that life was beauty" and the other showing a disheveled old frump with the legend, "I awoke and found that life was duty."

"Selah," said Kate piously, turning back the cover.

Ron Gardiner's slur came back to her: "You only sleep with cops." It was true. Not cops. One cop, and some nights going to bed without him, without him ever again, seemed insupportable.

With the funeral in prospect—and Sergeant Alvarez had thought it important that Kate go—Kate had to go in early and get her work at the newspaper out of the way. Her absorption in Garney Wilcox's murder seemed to have detached her from the run of daily news. There were always plenty more interesting ones, if she opted for murder. She read about a new "drive-by" in one of the old seedy apartment complexes. A child, napping on a sofa, had been sprayed with bullets from a speeding car and died instantly. There was a rape-murder in the woods back of a pleasant middle-class subdivision, and a man meeting his wife at the MARTA station at Candler Park had been shot to death as he sat in his car. No robbery, but the teenage assailant had taken his car, tumbled him out on the parking lot, and left him lying there to bleed to death.

It reminded Kate of a little box the paper used to run on an inside page headed MEETINGS TODAY. Nowadays MURDERS TODAY would seem appropriate. And here she was, hung up on an old last week's murder of a man she didn't even like.

She riffled through a folder she had labeled COLUMN IDEAS with letters and clippings she planned to follow up. But everything seemed to need more time and thought than she had. She remembered the Jeanette MacDonald and Nelson Eddy tape and decided to do a quick, cheerful nostalgia piece, confessing to her own adoration of the singers and wondering why their fame and their following weren't as durable as that of Elvis Presley, for instance.

Before serious music had come into the lives of the average teenager, MacDonald and Eddy had introduced them to gloriously listenable opera and especially operettas by Victor Herbert and Sigmund Romberg. Would anybody who heard it ever forget Jeanette singing "Ave Maria" on a hill overlooking rubble and ruin the day after the 1906 San Francisco earthquake and fire in the movie *San Francisco?*

It was a quick and easy column, she thought, what an old editor denounced as a "thumb-sucker." She wished, as she headed for the parking lot, that she had given it more time, had in fact listened to the tape she had found in her mailbox. But between the Gandy's visit and that of Ron Gardiner and work on the magazine piece, she had forgotten all about it.

Garney's funeral was held at Patterson's Springhill, of course, the old Spring Street establishment which affluent Atlantans had elected to handle their dead since 1881, when Hyatt M. Patterson joined forces with a local undertaker and advertised "a full line of metallic and wood caskets and coffins, burial robes and fine hearses and carriages at reasonable prices." Voncile would not know it or care, but as Kate walked through the rose garden adjoining the English country house-style mortuary, which had been built in the twenties, she thought of all the famous citizens who had departed from Patterson's—governors and congressmen and, of course, author Margaret Mitchell and editor Ralph McGill. "Little Alec" Stephens, who served as vice president of the Confederacy despite his friendship with President Abraham Lincoln, had been one of Patterson's more famous customers, with a funeral which a newspaper reporter at the time called "the most successfully managed large funeral ever known to Atlanta." Well, Garney's didn't promise to be a large funeral, Kate thought, looking at half a dozen cars in the parking lot.

There was no police car. Sergeant Alvarez, waiting for her at the front door, must have come in an unmarked car.

She was out of uniform again, wearing today a smart navy-blue suit, piped in red, with a white pique blouse with a bow knot at the throat and high-heeled navy pumps.

She smiled tentatively at Kate. "Where do we go from here? I have buried the dead on the battlefield, but I don't know what to expect here. You lead the way."

"It's customary to go by the room where the family gathers and speak to the bereaved," Kate said. "But since Voncile ordered me to stay away, I guess we should skip that. I'll just peep in and see if Miss Willie is there, and if she isn't we'll go on into the chapel."

Only a few people, most of them strangers to Kate and not the old neighbors from north Fulton—and certainly not Miss Willie—stood around the room where Garney's casket, banked with flowers, seemed to be holding court. She did not have to worry about being seen by Voncile because the widow, spectacular in old-fashioned midnight black "weeds" with a hat and veil copied from Jacqueline Kennedy's costume on her day of mourning, knelt on a little bench beside the coffin, weeping loudly. Her daughter Cheri, also in black, stood by her side, patting her plump shoulders ineffectually.

Cheri looked up as Kate started to withdraw and mouthed a single word: *Wait.*

Puzzled, Kate stood a moment and then backed into the hall, showing a baffled face to Sergeant Alvarez.

Suddenly Cheri was at her side.

"I need to talk to you," the girl whispered. "Do you know where Grandma is?"

Kate shook her head. "No, do you?"

Cheri ducked and Kate thought she was trying to manage feelings of grief for her father, but when she lifted her face her eyes were dry and her pretty young lips firm with resolution.

"I've got to see Grandma. They're going to put her in jail, Mom says, and maybe electrocute her. And that's not right. What she did was for me. He tried to kill me, Kate."

In the room Voncile's grief had reached a crescendo and Cheri looked nervously over her shoulder. "I better get back in there. But when this is over, would you talk to me?"

"Of course I will," said Kate warmly, putting an arm around the soft young shoulders. "Anytime you say. Call me or come by."

Cheri hurried back into the room, where Voncile was now blowing her nose into a black-edged handkerchief—*where do you get those?* Kate wondered—and asking for "my baby girl."

136

"Did you hear that?" Kate asked Sergeant Alvarez. "He tried to kill her."

Sergeant Alvarez nodded. "I heard. Are you now thinking about switching your defense from not guilty to justifiable homicide?"

Kate looked guilty. "Well, if he did . . . whatever she did . . . Oh, shoot! I'm so one-track. I am concerned about whatever happened to that child. But she looks healthy, doesn't she?"

Sergeant Alvarez grinned. "Beautiful. A real beautiful girl."

They followed a small group of people into the chapel, where the sun poured through the tall colonial windows and the organ softly played "Abide With Me." To be less conspicuous Kate chose seats on the back pew, but she needn't have bothered. The family seemed sequestered offstage in a room to the left of the platform, podium, and casket.

The minister had apparently been recruited from a city church instead of the weathered old clapboard primitive Baptist church where Miss Willie had taken Garney to Sunday school and church as long as she had any control over him. He made a brief eulogy, referring to Garney as a "real country gentleman" cherished by his neighbors, to whom he was an ever-present help in time of trouble.

Kate nudged Sergeant Alvarez. "We must be at the wrong funeral," she whispered, grinning.

The service for the dead was read, another hymn was played over the PA system, and the little flock of funeral-goers stood while the coffin was wheeled out the side door to the hearse, followed by Voncile and

Cheri and a couple of men Kate took to be Voncile's brothers. No Miss Willie.

"You going to the cemetery?" Sergeant Alvarez asked.

"If it's the family graveyard in the Cove I'll go," Kate said. "But if it's one of the new 'memorial gardens,' I don't think so."

She paused to ask a funeral home man. As she suspected, Voncile had chosen a new cemetery instead of the weedy little plot in a grove of cedar trees where Garney's father and several of his ancestors were buried.

"No point in going," she said to Sergeant Alvarez. "Miss Willie might have been at a grave in the country in a spot she knew and loved, but I don't think she'd go to a 'memorial garden.' "

Sergeant Alvarez was scrutinizing the faces of the departing funeral congregation and did not answer.

CHAPTER 5

"Oh, Kate," Shell called after her as she started for the elevator. "Fellow here's been wanting to meet you."

Kate turned inquiringly.

"Hey, Bax!" Shell called across the newsroom. "Here's the lady herself, Katherine the Great of Coon Holler!"

Kate made a face at him. It was one of their most frazzled jokes since she moved to the country. The newsroom consensus was that she had gone bucolic with a vengeance. Everybody had a joke to contribute from time to time and she took them with what grace she could muster.

But the good-looking stranger walking toward the city desk clearly wasn't rising to the Coon Holler gambit. He looked at her almost shyly and held out his hand in a tentative manner that touched her, like he wanted to shake hands but suddenly realized the proper way was for her to offer her hand first.

Kate smiled at him.

"Bax?" she tried the name curiously, extending a not too clean hand.

"Yes, ma'am, Baxter Winters," he said. "I just got hired last week and I told Mr. Shelnutt one of the reasons I wanted to work here was because of you. I've admired your work a long time."

"Well, aren't you nice?" Kate said, pleased. "Where are you from and what are you going to be doing here?"

"He's from everywhere," Shell said over his shoulder, turning back to his computer. *"Times, Post,* Paris, Iran, *evva-where!* And he's going to write a column. Bear in mind that when a fellow compliments you like that he might be fattening you up for the kill. Your space on the front of the feature section—you could be replaced!"

The young man gulped and looked at Shell's back in consternation. "I assure you, Miss Kincaid . . . ! Mr. Shelnutt has to be—"

Kate laughed and said lightly, "Well, somebody is going to replace me sooner or later, and it might as well be you."

"Oh, yeah," said Shell, swiveling back toward them. "I forgot to say he's also from *Hah-vud.*"

Baxter Winters decided to take charge of the conversation.

"I'm not *from* Harvard, Miss Kincaid. I'd like to be. I was a Neiman Fellow. I'm really from Middleton,

Mississippi. My grandfather and my mother had the paper there."

He glared at Shell's back before he turned a gentle, whimsical smile on Kate. "If you have time . . . may I buy you a drink?"

"Aw, I'm sorry. I've got to get home," Kate said out of habit. She hardly ever lingered after work for the beer-joint sociability which occupied the younger members of the staff. Going home to Benjy was all she had wanted to do for years. They'd had projects and they enjoyed being together, and then there was his illness. Now she wasn't sure why, but the pattern survived. She went home after work.

Suddenly she wanted very much to have a drink with this pleasant young man, but he had apparently accepted no for an answer.

"Another time, then," he said, walking with her toward the elevator. "Or maybe lunch? Are you free tomorrow?"

"Yes!" said Kate eagerly. "I think so. I'm not sure about a couple of things, but let's see in the morning. Okay?"

"Fine," said the young man. "I'll come and find you. It's really true"—he glanced toward Shell—"that I am excited about meeting you."

"Pooh," said Kate as the elevator opened. But as the door closed behind her she wished she had thought of something gracious, if not witty, to say. She wished, she thought in self-amusement, that she had combed her hair and put on some lipstick and maybe worn a more becoming dress. Baxter Winters, standing there seeing her off, was so attractive-looking. He wore a navy jacket over dark gray trousers with a blue button-down shirt snugly anchored with a tie—unusual in the newsroom at near deadline time. Only his dark red hair looked disheveled, as if he had been combing it with his fingers while he searched for a lead. He had nice brown eyes and a good smile, she decided.

A lot of young reporters came to see Kate, and she wondered as she drove home why she kept thinking about him. He was not as young, maybe, as most of them, but he *was* young—thirty-five or forty. Was he tall? She couldn't remember. He seemed taller than her five feet ten inches. And why, for goodness' sake, did she care?

She turned on the cassette player and made a mental list for the grocery store. She'd have to get pet food, of course. There was always that.

Mahler's "Romantic Music for Strings" filled the dusty little car, reminding Kate that she still hadn't played the Jeanette MacDonald-Nelson Eddy tape that somebody had put in her mailbox. She would take a look at it before bedtime.

A vintage Ford touring car all glittering under a coat of bright blue paint stood in the driveway as Kate drove into the yard. She sat a moment admiring it before she turned off the switch and gathered her grocery bags. Her father had owned such a car in her childhood but it was serviceable black, never the glorious equipage that this one was in its cerulean blue paint. What fun to have one, she thought, all open with a top that let down and probably side curtains for winter weather. She didn't know whose it was, but she might ask to take a ride in it.

The owner appeared to be a young man who sat on her back steps. He stood up as she approached the house and offered to take the grocery bags from her.

"Oh, thank you," said Kate, "but the heavy ones are the cans of cat and dog food and a case of beer still in the car. If you don't mind, I'd love to have you bring them. By the way, I'm Kate Mulcay. Can I help you?"

"I'm sorry, Miss Kate," the young man said. "I've met you before, but I guess I was a lot younger and you wouldn't recognize me. I'm Wayne Simmons. Cheri Wilcox is my girlfriend."

"I'm glad to see you," said Kate, setting down a bottle of milk and taking his hand. "Come on in. Where's Cheri?"

"She's in your kitchen, using your phone," he said. "Is that all right?"

"Oh, sure," said Kate.

For a long time hers was the only telephone within a couple of miles, and she was glad to have her country neighbors make use of it. Calls to Atlanta in those days had cost fifteen cents each, and sometimes her bill for long-distance tolls ran as high as a dollar a month—small cost for the sociability she enjoyed. Her friends, innocent of the knowledge of Southern Bell's many costs and increases, didn't know it cost anything and they never paid. But Kate hadn't minded.

Cheri turned from the phone as Kate entered the kitchen, her face crumpled and wet with tears.

"Miss Kate," she whispered, putting a hand over

the mouthpiece, "I'm making myself at home. Did you meet Wayne?" She spoke again into the phone in a low voice and hung it up.

"I told her we were going to a movie," she told Wayne as he came in with the rest of Kate's groceries. She lifted the tail of the outsized sweatshirt she wore and mopped her eyes.

Kate put down her packages and held out her arms to the girl. *Such a pretty girl*, she thought, *so full of woe*.

"I sure did meet Wayne," she said cheerfully, "and he's just saved me a big backache, hauling in my stuff. Why don't you run upstairs and throw some cold water on your face, and we'll have something cool to drink out under the tree."

Cheri smiled at her gratefully and moved to obey. Kate put up her groceries and rummaged in the refrigerator for Cokes. She might have a beer herself and her guests would probably have been glad of the same, but she knew they were under drinking age, and besides, would she want to put that pretty blue treasure in the driveway at risk when they started home?

Cheri came down the stairs looking somewhat better. She had apparently run a brush through her long, fair hair and applied some pale pink lipstick. She smiled at Kate and held out a hand to Wayne, who put a skinny sun-browned arm around her shoulders.

"You said I could come and talk to you," she reminded Kate. "I guess I thought I needed help the most, but Wayne is going to marry me, so that's all right. I'm really the most worried over Grandma. Could they really send her to the electric chair?"

"Of course not!" Kate said sturdily with more conviction than she felt. "They don't electrocute many really bad people anymore. And an old woman in her eighties . . . aw, no. Besides, why would they? What has Miss Willie done?"

Cheri looked at Wayne, who took her hand and squeezed it. He was blond, too—white, cotton-haired blond, not the deep broomsedge gold that made Cheri's hair spectacular. The summer sun may have bleached his, or maybe he belonged to that tribe of country people who worked in the old textile mills and were called "lint-heads" whether they had lint in their hair or not. They owed their coloring to their mountain ancestors, who came to the southern hills from Scotland and Wales.

Now Wayne's blue eyes rested adoringly on Cheri. He couldn't have been much older than the girl—sixteen or seventeen.

"Now, tell me why you think your grandmother killed your father," Kate said, passing them soft drinks and cheese and crackers and pulling up a chair beside the swing under the maple tree.

"It's my fault," the girl said, looking as if she might cry again. "I shouldn't have told her about Daddy. For years—since I was a little girl . . ." She gulped, unable to continue.

Kate waited.

"Since I was a little girl," Cheri went on after a long silence, "he has been after me. You know, putting his hands on me, pushing his you-know up against me."

She bit her lips and looked at Wayne, who seemed

to have detached himself from the account. His eyes followed the progress of a blue jay at the bird feeder. His young neck was flushed a deep red.

"And then . . ." Cheri gulped and tried again. "And then one night when Mama was gone to one of her clubs, he . . . he raped me!"

Her voice broke, and a sob rose up in her throat. She put her hands over her face to hide the tears which seeped out through her fingers.

"Oh, honey," cried Kate helplessly, reaching out to hold the girl. But Cheri wasn't done. She lifted her eyes to Kate's face in an agony of shame and grief.

"It made me pregnant!" she said in a low, tortured voice.

Kate sighed. She had known it, but she had hoped it wasn't true.

"I didn't know what to do," Cheri went on after a bit. "I couldn't tell Mama . . . you know how she is. So I told Daddy. I thought he might know where I could go, what I could do. He was awful. At first he acted nice. He said he would get an apartment for me and we'd get an abortion and I could live there and be his . . . mistress! He said a lot of men kept girlfriends in apartments and bought them lots of beautiful clothes and cars and things, and he would do that for me if I'd be sweet and let him . . ."

"Have sex with you anytime he wanted to!" Kate put in angrily.

Cheri nodded dumbly.

Wayne's freckled, knobby young hands clenched and unclenched convulsively, but he kept his eyes averted.

"So what did you tell him?" Kate asked.

"I told him a story," Cheri said. "I told him he couldn't have anything to do with me or my baby because it wasn't his. It was—" she looked guiltily at Wayne, "it was Wayne's."

Wayne swallowed, his Adam's apple working jerkily. His pale blue eyes were full of tears.

"That made Daddy real mad," Cheri went on. "He started hitting me and calling me bad names. Whore and stuff like that. He knocked me down on the floor and was crawling on top of me . . . I reckon to rape me again. But then Mama came back. I didn't want her to see me and I was scared to stay in the house, scared of Daddy or both of them. So I went to the nursing home to see Grandma, and she made them put up a cot in her room for me. She told them she needed me to take care of her, but it was the other way around. I was pretty bad hurt."

"When you told her about your father . . ." Kate prompted.

"She said she'd kill him," Cheri said simply.

"Yes," said Kate. "Yes, I think she would."

They sat in silence for a long time. Birds were making last-minute forays to the feeder; Pepper and Sugar had taken up their posts close to Kate's feet. The guineas had flapped noisily up to a roost over the corncrib.

"I heard her crying in the night," Cheri said after a moment.

I'll die, Kate thought miserably. *I'll die. This child . . . abused, pregnant. Poor Miss Willie crying in the night. What, oh, what have we come to?*

"In about two days Daddy was dead," Cheri said.

"He deserved it," said Wayne, speaking for the first time.

Kate nodded. "Yes, but the law doesn't let us decide. Have you told this to anybody?" she asked Cheri.

The girl shook her head. "A little of it to Judy Carson, my best friend, but not all. I was ashamed. All those times Daddy was doing things to me I thought it might be my fault—something I did wrong or something. And the rape . . . !"

She started crying again, and Wayne put his arm around her and pulled her close.

Kate sighed and stood up. "Let me think what to do. Do either of you have any idea where Miss Willie went?"

"Mama says she's running from the cops," Cheri said. "And she's gon' hire some big-name detective agency to help them find her. If they don't electrocute Grandma they'll put her in the crazy house and Mama can claim what's left of her land and house and all. Being called crazy would be better, I reckon, but it's not Grandma's fault, and I wanted to ask you if I should tell the law. Would having them know about Daddy . . . and what happened to me . . . make Grandma feel worse than to be put in jail?"

Kate considered. "It might. But don't do anything right now, Cheri. Let me see if I can't figure out something. First, I want to find Miss Willie and talk to her."

The young couple stood up.

Kate took Cheri's hand and walked with them toward the car.

"You can come and stay with me, honey, anytime you want to."

Cheri shook her head. "Mama would kill me. She wants me right there with her. She was mad because I told her I was going to the movies with Wayne. She said on the day of Daddy's funeral it was a sacrilege for me to go to the movies." Her young mouth curved in a bitter smile.

Kate laughed and changed the subject.

"I love your car, Wayne. Did you restore it yourself?"

"Yes, ma'am, every lick," he said proudly. "I got it out of my grandpa's barn, and I've been working on it a little bit at a time since I was about ten years old."

"It's a beauty," said Kate. "My father had one I wish was still around. Original black paint—and a lot of rust. Not beautiful like this."

Wayne helped Cheri to the front seat through a door which seemed to be stuck. He was grinning happily, but suddenly his young face sobered.

"Would you like to buy this one, Miss Kate?"

"Aw, you wouldn't sell it!" objected Kate.

He looked at Cheri and lowered his voice. "We gon' need the money getting married and the baby and all."

"On, no!" Kate protested automatically. But then she thought, *They will do what they have to do.* "Wait, Wayne," she urged. "Wait a few days and let's see. Don't do anything drastic."

They nodded obediently and the blue car rattled to life and bore them majestically out of the drive.

* * *

Kate moved restlessly around the cabin, not hungry and unable to settle down to work at her desk or at small domestic chores. She finally picked up a sweater, called Pepper, and went out into the twilight. The gravel road which Benjy had once measured off into one-mile increments when they were walking or jogging for their health was now too busy for a leisurely stroll in the failing light. She no longer ran or jogged as she did when Benjy was at the peak of his push for physical fitness. She might walk briskly for half a mile and then veer off into the woods or the old pasture to inspect a plant or gather a wildflower. At this time of day she would simply stroll and wait for the therapeutic effects of being out-of-doors in the autumn darkness. The anguish of her friend Miss Willie was unimaginable, and she racked her brain for sources of professional help for young Cheri.

Incest and rape were hideous, life-warping experiences, soul-searing crimes. She knew more about them than she wanted to from having interviewed victims through the years. How practical was marriage between two sixteen-year-olds? And what about a baby that would be the girl's own half-brother or -sister?

On impulse Kate turned through Shining Waters Subdivision and headed for the old Wilcox house. The Gardiners' house seemed scantily lit for the number of cars in the driveway. Kate counted four before she passed the gateway and walked on to the rock wall, which cut off her view. There seemed to be one dim light in the foyer and maybe one in the upstairs hall, but otherwise the castle was in darkness.

The path through the woods to Miss Willie's was also dark, and Kate was glad to have Pepper run interference for her with snakes. Luminous light from the sky lingered in the yard around the old house, but there was none inside the house. Kate had not expected that there would be. She knew somehow that Miss Willie wouldn't be there. It was just a destination for a walk, and she crossed the yard thinking she might walk along the creek a little way when a car without headlights turned into the driveway. *Cheri and Wayne,* she thought, *seeking privacy,* and started to wave and call out to let them know she was there. Some instinct kept her silent. Instead of calling out, she sat down on the ground back of an elderberry bush thick with shriveling purple berries. The vehicle was not the racy blue touring car but something new and long and quiet—a van. It drew up in front of the old buggy house and Kate could make out the silhouettes of two men bringing something out of the structure—small suitcase-sized packages—and loading them into the van. She was about to stand for a better view when Pepper, coming back from a sortie down the riverbank, saw that he was behind with his watchdogging and raced forward, barking ferociously.

One of the men threw a rock at him, which really incensed Pepper and instead of stopping him propelled him forward, growling ominously. The men scrambled into the van and backed out, swerving the rear end into the yard to make the turn, and Kate could see the one in the right seat craning his neck and peering into the woods.

"The Mulcay woman's dog," he said, and to Kate the inference was clear. The Mulcay woman herself must be somewhere nearby. She later wondered whether it might have been better if she had stood up and spoken to them.

When the van was out of sight and sound, Kate crawled cautiously out of the elderberry thicket and started home. She was tempted to check out the buggy house, but darkness had deepened and she decided that whatever had been stored there was now traveling somewhere in the van. She would be glad to get back to her own house and lock the doors.

Sometime around midnight Kate gave up trying to sleep. The books stacked up by her bedside, reliable opiates usually, only served to make her impatient and restless. They ran to picture-pretty gardens, and what did that have to do with the pain and confusion which engulfed her part of the world? The Bible often helped, and she opened it to a psalm and her eye fell on the verse beginning, "Why art thou cast down, O my soul? And why art thou disquieted within me?"

Cast down, disquieted, right on. She closed the book.

The night was cool, and she pulled her old terrycloth robe around her, found her slippers, and wandered downstairs. A cup of cocoa and two aspirin, and old friend once told her, would bring on sleep. She'd give it a try.

While she waited for the chocolate to heat she sorted through the little pile of mail the Gandy sisters had brought in. There was the Jeanette MacDonald-

Nelson Eddy tape. She might as well listen to it as to anything. She hadn't heard the glamorous singing movie stars since her high school days, and she wondered if it might be sad and disillusioning to hear them now. Critics in the years between had taken to calling them excruciatingly sentimental and ridiculing their films as campy. She remembered a line in some review which called their operettas "arch and archaic."

Well, the songs were pretty, and they might be soothing and sleep-inducing. She put the tape on her player, adjusted the volume, and settled herself with a cup of cocoa to listen. Immediately the opulent voice of Nelson Eddy filled the room.

"Ah, sweet mystery of life," he sang, "at last I've found thee. At last I know the secret of it all. All the longing, seeking, striving, waiting, yearning, the idle hopes, the joy, the tears that fall . . ."

Um, lovely. Kate sighed, sipping her cocoa. Not camp, but a song for the times. She prepared to hum along with Mr. Eddy, but suddenly she stopped singing. There was a break in the tape, the scratchy sound of a reel in trouble. She got up to check it just as Jeanette MacDonald hit "The Italian Street Song." The torrent of high C's poured out with words Kate had trouble understanding until the soprano hit the theme: "Napoli, Napoli, Napoli!" It wasn't her favorite, although she remembered it from that lovely fragrant curio of the past, *Maytime*. She listened to it for a few seconds before there was another break, more scratching, and Nelson Eddy back with the hearty, booming "Tramp, tramp, tramp along the highway!"

She prepared herself to hear that break down, and

it did when Mr. Eddy sang that he had "heard the wolf calling when nighttime was falling" and waded up to his knees in blood.

Kate turned off the player and put her cup in the sink. She didn't know where the tape came from, unless Miss Marlowa Walton had somehow heard of her enthusiasm for MacDonald and Eddy and dropped off one of her rejects. Maybe the Gandy sisters had tampered with it. Maybe they had dropped it in the yard and Pepper had chewed it up.

Shame, she thought, *such nice music messed up*. She went back to bed.

CHAPTER 6

News was in the doldrums at the office. Kate fiddled with a column, answered some mail, talked to three women who were enthusiastic about her mention of Jeanette MacDonald and Nelson Eddy a couple of days earlier. And worried.

As Sergeant Alvarez had suggested, Miss Willie, without even knowing of the rape, could claim justifiable homicide if she killed Garney. But Kate couldn't see her either killing him or exposing to the world Cheri and the hideous thing that had happened to her. Kate was sick and tired of all the puzzling things which kept happening—Miss Willie's disappearance, the death of Jenny, nighttime excursions of strangers who had the effrontery to invade Miss Willie's buggy house. What were they up to, and why did she have the creepy feeling that she should care? It was none of her business. She wished for something pleasant and normal to happen to her, and suddenly it did.

She had forgotten her luncheon date with Baxter Winters. He stood at the door smiling at her.

"You remember?" he asked. "Baxter Winters. We were going to have lunch."

"Oh, yes!" said Kate, punching the STORE key on her computer and standing up. "I'm glad you remembered. I'm starved."

She reached for her bag and wished once again that she had had the foresight to wear something different from her dull gray suit and had combed her hair and put on some lipstick. Now she fumbled ineffectually in her handbag for the elusive compact and then decided against finding out how she really looked. The way he was smiling at her made her feel that it didn't really matter, she looked fine.

They walked through the newsroom, which seemed to Kate to be supernaturally quiet these days. No teletypes clattering, no rackety typewriters, just the say-nothing sound of word processors. Even the telephones were whiners or purrers instead of honest clangers with the urgent forthright blare of bells. Row after row of reporters and editors leaned toward flickering screens like pilgrims doing obeisance at holy shrines. They were young and almost uniformly good-looking. Kate knew that they were generally better educated and brighter than the reporters and editors of her youth. But she often missed the colorful and disreputable crew which had inhabited the newsroom when she came there as a kid. Where were the chain smokers, the drunks, and the young, lighthearted, and irreverent geniuses?

Baxter Winters stood aside to let her go ahead.

"Where are we going?" she asked.

"I hope you don't think it's pretentious," he said, "but I thought the Ritz Carlton."

"I think it's lovely," said Kate. "But are you on expense account?"

He shook his dark red head, now freshly combed and smooth.

"No, but I think I can manage."

"*Ho!*" said Kate. "No penurious newspaperman for me today!"

He grinned and took her elbow to guide her into the elevator. (He was taller than she!) "I come from a semi-rich family," he said modestly.

The waiter at the Ritz welcomed them by name and steered them to a secluded table in the rear of the restaurant. Kate knew he probably recognized her from her picture in the paper with her column. But Baxter Winters was a newcomer to town, and his name was probably known because he ate there often.

Wine was mentioned, and he looked inquiringly at her.

"Yes!" said Kate. "I feel a need for wild self-indulgence today!"

He nodded and smiled, showing perfect teeth. He and the waiter settled the matter of a white wine after some impressive—to Kate—discussion, and then Baxter turned to her with a warming show of attention.

"Why do you need 'wild self-indulgence' today?"

Kate found she wanted to tell him about Miss Willie and Garney and Cheri and old Jenny and the strangers in the dark van. The wine came and she bent to her story, working in irony and a bit of self-mockery to avoid being heavy-handed and boring with squalor and grief and pain.

This young man seemed too well born and civil for lunchtime regaling of drug shoot-outs and incest. But his attention was flawless. He was clearly concentrating on her every word. Only when she came to the end and drained her wineglass did he speak. Then he instructed the waiter to bring the wine bottle and reached for the menu.

Kate studied his face as he studied the menu.

What a lovely thing is man, she thought. His long-fingered hands, his strong face, the broad shoulders, the auburn hair rising above bright brown eyes, the laugh lines like parentheses at the corners of his mouth, the quiet, resonant voice. *I do love a man,* Kate thought.

Baxter inquired into her interest in salad and soup and entrées, and Kate found she was beyond decision —hungry but not up to settling on anything.

"You choose," she said, accepting another glass of wine. "I don't need the full agenda—just the entrée, if that's all right."

He quirked an auburn eyebrow. "Just what I was thinking," he said, and quietly and competently settled the whole thing with the waiter.

"Now your time," said Kate. "I've done all the talking. Tell me what you're about."

"I'm not sure yet," he said. "You write what I wish I could write but I never could because I don't have your sensitivity, intuitiveness. And, of course, there's that invaluable experience. You know, I've never covered police. I don't even know where the cop shop is. I know nothing about Georgia politics, and as for writing about human feelings and human suffering . . ."

"You'd be embarrassed!" accused Kate, laughing. "I bet you think I'm the cornball queen!"

He regarded her solemnly, wordlessly, for a long moment.

"I think you're wonderful," he said quietly.

Kate knew she should say something modest and deprecating, but she wanted to say, *Do you honestly? Tell me how. Let's count the ways!* Instead, she looked at Baxter, who was gazing across the room almost as if he were talking to himself.

She said nothing, and in a moment he picked up the thread of conversation where they had dropped it.

"I was in Europe for the *New York Times* when my wife died. We have a son, Clay, he's eight years old. I decided I should come back to the South to raise him. I still have family around here and in Mississippi. I applied here . . . and here I am."

"Your little boy," interposed Kate, "what's he like?"

"Skinny, anxious," said Baxter. "His mother was sick a long time. I think it's harder on him than he lets me see."

"Can you spend time with him?" Kate asked, concern for the skinny, anxious little boy welling up in her.

"I try to," he said. "He's a good little kid and

doesn't object when I have to go out of town and leave him with the housekeeper. I work at making it up to him on weekends."

"Why don't you bring him to the country some Saturday? I have a neighbor who has a donkey he could ride, and there are two terrible little girls down the road who would love to take him fishing and muscadine picking."

Baxter smiled at her gratefully. "He'd like that. Don't be surprised if we show up."

The waiter arrived with their food, and Kate and Baxter happily tucked into their lunches. When she had finished, Kate put down her fork and looked up. "When does your column start running?" She grinned. "When do I have to brace myself to be supplanted?"

"That's a terrible joke Mr. Shelnutt—Shell—indulged in," Baxter said, his dark eyes suddenly merry. "He's a nice fellow, isn't he? I've worked for a lot of city editors around and about, and he's one of the best. He's told me to take my time, and I've puttered a bit, I'm afraid. They say they want me to write 'off the news,' whatever that means, and I'm in the Middle East so far—at least in two or three sample columns I have ahead. Now I suppose I'm ready to get into Georgia politics. I go out with some of the candidates next week."

"It's a great way to get acquainted with the state," Kate said. "At least it used to be, when you went to factory gates and packinghouses and fish fries and barbecues with the candidate and sat up late in some little country hotel listening to old stories. Now I'm afraid the hustings consist mostly of going from television station to television station. But politicians are fair Georgia samples, and you'll have fun.''

He smiled. ''I've had fun today—more than in a long time.''

Kate bobbed her head enthusiastically. ''Me, too.''

The waiter was disappointed that they didn't want dessert, but he consoled himself that they were interested in after-dinner drinks. Kate listened to his musical recital of the various liqueurs and was about to decline, but Baxter said, ''How about some calvados?''

''Oh, yes!'' cried Kate. ''Applejack. Ernest Hemingway in Paris. Or was it Ingrid Bergman and Humphrey Bogart?''

Baxter laughed. ''I'm not sure, but I remember that American applejack is French calvados and both are delicious. Let's have some.''

The autumn sun was hot when they left the Ritz, and they carefully picked shady sidewalks for the trip back to the office.

''I think I'm drunk,'' Kate said as they attained the building.

''Nice, isn't it?'' murmured Baxter.

Kate found it difficult to settle down to work when she got back to her desk, and the problem of the Wilcoxes seemed to have floated away. She kept thinking about Baxter Winters. Young—thirty-five, forty, forty-five? Too young for the lingering attention she was lavishing in that direction. *I would like to keep him,* she thought, not out of any sexual attraction. She hadn't noticed that, if it existed. The masculinity, the mindfulness of her wants, the deep-voiced attentiveness . . . it only came with a man. A special man.

One lunch, she thought, jeering at herself, *and I'm acting as sappy as a girl in love, which I'll never be again. Nor want to be. There just should be some room in every life for a balanced mixture of men and women.* Although she approved of the women's rightsers in principle and occasionally contributed a few dollars to their cause, her heart had not chosen up sides in the conflict. She had been treated well by the men she knew: her father, who reared her singlehandedly; Benjy, who loved and cherished her; the men at the office with whom she worked; the policemen who were friends of her father's and Benjy's. She knew of the inequities and she deplored them, but they had not oppressed her personally. She had always been allowed to do work that she loved, and if men were paid more, she only begrudged them fleetingly, knowing too well the struggles of the men she knew to support families. Benjy had laughed at her quick sympathy for even men she didn't know but saw on the streets starting out to work in the morning, their hair hopefully combed, their shoes hopefully shined. They looked brave, she thought, and vulnerable.

"You just think women are stronger, don't you?" Benjy had asked her seriously more than once.

She denied it even as she wondered if it were true.

Toward late afternoon the phone rang with another Jeanette-Nelson fan call, and Kate, thinking about the swelling tide of traffic on the road home, hoped to get rid of the caller fast. It was not to be.

"I just love you for loving Jeanette and Nelson!" the woman caroled. "And I wanted to invite you to go to California with me to the reunion. You know about that, don't you?"

Kate did not know, and the woman was pleased to enlighten her. Since 1936, fans of Jeanette had staged an annual get-together called the Clan Clave—a name suggested by Jeanette herself because it had a Scottish ring and she was, of course, of Scottish ancestry. Scores of people of all ages from all parts of the country met and spent a week looking at the twenty-eight films Miss MacDonald made (half a dozen with Nelson Eddy), hearing her records, visiting with her husband, Gene Raymond, now a gentleman in his eighties, and attending ceremonies at her grave in Forest Lawn Cemetery.

"Why don't you plan to go? We'll have a ball!" the woman on the phone assured her.

"Ah, I wish I could," Kate said. "Maybe next year I'll be able to get away. Is that the only meeting of its kind?"

"No, honey, it's just the best. Almost every state in the union has a Mac-Ed club. In England they concentrate on Nelson, who lived there until his death in 1967, two years after Jeanette passed in California. Ah, that was a sad time! I cry when I think about it."

"A lot of people feel the same?" inquired Kate.

"Loads," said the woman. "Not like Elvis Presley, I reckon, but it's more intellectual. Opera, you know."

"Um-m," said Kate. "That makes a difference."

"Damn right," said the woman cheerfully. "Well, you think about going, sugar. Don't mess with that crowd up in New Jersey that puts out scandal on Jeanette and Nelson. They hint at a lot of stuff to make money on scandal sheets, but Jeanette was the purest, finest girl in the world and her widower didn't get married again for five years after she died. Couldn't bring himself to!"

"My!" said Kate admiringly.

"Well, I just thought I'd let you know about the Clan Clave," said the caller. "But go to any of them if you can. I'm sending you a tape I pirated off the VCR. *Maytime*. You like it?"

"Love it," said Kate, thanking her and hanging up. *I hope it turns out better than the poor thing somebody left in my mailbox,* she added silently.

Sergeant Alvarez called as Kate was getting ready to leave the office. "In a hurry," she said breathlessly, "but I thought I'd better tell you one of the mourners at the Wilcox funeral was a drug dealer. Funny, isn't it, how people like that go to funerals? We've had him in a couple of times, but he manages to beat the rap every time. He's out now."

"Listen," said Kate quickly, "I saw some men taking something out of the buggy house at the old Wilcox place late yesterday. Does that tie in? I couldn't see what it was, and of course . . ." she paused, "you all had it roped off with scene-of-the-crime tapes until a day or so ago. Would anybody dare try to hide drugs there, with you all looking on?"

"If we took down the tapes, we're not looking

on," the sergeant said. "It would seem to be the safest place in the world for dope."

"That makes sense," said Kate slowly. "The police have come and gone over the place with a fine-toothed comb and wouldn't see any reason to go back."

"Exactly," said Sergeant Alvarez. "I've gotta run, but look, be careful, won't you? These kids play rough, and you're mighty close to the situation. Have you found Mrs. Wilcox yet?"

"No, but I'm looking," said Kate, knowing it for an exaggeration. Where was she looking?

"You better," said the sergeant, and hung up.

Kate looked over the newsroom as she left, really hoping for a glimpse of Baxter Winters. She told herself it was merely to thank him again for a pleasant lunch, but she was uncomfortably aware that it was a silly girlish desire to see him and talk to him once more. Although she walked the length of the room, between rows of desks to the ladies' room, she didn't see him.

Confronting the big mirror over the lavatory was shudderingly depressing. She hadn't had on lipstick since early morning and her entire reflection was cast in gray and sag. Her skin was gray crape. There seemed to be more gray in her hair than she had noticed before. Where had the color gone? Once there had been brightness in her hair, pink in firm cheeks and chin. Once her eyes were clear and expressive. Now they lurked murkily behind horn-rimmed glasses.

She sighed and turned away. On the MARTA train

she decided she didn't really like Baxter Winters. He had been everywhere, worked in all the glamorous places, and he was still young enough to start over and would most certainly ascend to a position of power on her newspaper. He was probably rich. (Lunching at the Ritz, wasn't he? And knowing all about wine!) His family owned one newspaper at least, and probably several more. They came in chains these days. And he was probably even now at the Piedmont Driving Club having a drink by the pool or swimming with his little boy. Or, face it, asking some debutante he would probably marry next year to have dinner with him.

When she got home and changed her clothes and went through the evening routine of chores, Kate took a cup of coffee and sat by the cold and empty fireplace. Coffee was better than a drink. It was absolutely decadent consuming wine and calvados in the middle of the day and rightly left one feeling peckish. The unlit fire, the ashes, the wilted flowers in Miss Willie's iron pot suited her mood so precisely she got up and turned on WABE, the classical music station, hoping bleakly that they were playing one of the requiems, preferably Mozart with eternal rest on his mind.

She had accidentally punched the tape button instead of the radio. She had never gotten the hang of the contraption. It had been Benjy's toy. The Eddy-MacDonald tape was still lodged in the machine, and before she had the energy to get up and change it, Nelson Eddy's voice came sweeping out, all mellow and ardent about love.

"Nuts," Kate muttered to herself. "Love, shmove. What's a grown man carrying on about love for?

Doesn't he have any decent work to do?'' Why wasn't he writing a column or solving a crime? Why wasn't *she* solving a crime?

She sat on, letting the scratchy tape with the blank spots play itself out. What was there wasn't bad. She would really enjoy hearing the whole songs instead of these patchy pieces, though. She might even pick up some new tapes at the mall. And the first thing anybody knew, she would be like those other old ladies, trekking around to Clan Claves, worshiping at the shrine of long-dead movie stars, wallowing in nostalgia and sentimentality. They said people of all ages went to those reunions, but she'd bet Pepper and Sugar the fans ran to old ladies whose Maytime coincided with Jeanette's fifty years ago.

Like Miss Marlowa Walton, she thought suddenly, and sat up so fast she spilled cold coffee on her jeans. Miss Marlowa, Canary had said, was a closet Mac-Ed fan. Would she come out of the closet for a reunion? Would she take Miss Willie with her? ''Oh, what am I thinking?'' Kate asked herself. ''Miss Marlowa has more sense than that!''

But she might have sent the tape. It was worth a call to Canary, anyway. Kate went to the phone and called.

Miss Marlowa still wasn't back. No, Canary didn't have any idea where she had gone. No, she still didn't have a clue as to the friend who accompanied her.

Did she know if Miss Marlowa fiddled with tapes, making copies?

''Well, I expect so,'' said Canary. ''Everybody else

does. Only I don't see why she would want to. She can buy new ones right down the street at Turtle's.''

Kate hung up. Canary was right. Miss Marlowa could buy new tapes—unless she wanted to edit an old one, for some reason. Slicing into Nelson's and Jeanette's songs sure smacked of on-purpose tampering. She went back to the cassette and played it again.

"Ah, sweet mystery of life,'' sang Nelson. Mystery was the key word, all right—what we've got plenty of. There was all that ''longing, seeking, striving, waiting, yearning, the idle hopes, the joys and tears,'' which, God knows, Kate had personally experienced.

Hot ziggety, thought Kate gleefully. Miss Marlowa was telling her something. "Wanting you . . . nothing else in the world will do.'' *Who, me?* Kate asked herself, and answered gaily, *Sure, me.*

Then there was Nelson again with ''Tramp, tramp, tramp along the highway.'' It meant a trip, of course. But where to? Jeanette sang ''Beyond the Blue Horizon'' and Kate wanted to hit her. The blue horizon is everywhere you look. *Get to the point, songbird*, she thought impudently. *I know there's a rising sun due most days. You don't have to tell me about it. Just tell me where.*

She played the whole thing again, backing up the ''Italian Street Song'' to hear Nelson mention once more that he had ''heard the wolf calling when nighttime was falling'' and had—oh, gruesome thought—waded up to his knees in blood.

Kate glanced out the cabin window and saw that night had just about fallen. For some reason she felt impelled to get up and lock the door. She turned off the tape and sat in the darkness awhile to think about it. The only excuse for the "Italian Street Song" that she could see was that it might be a tip that Miss Marlowa and her guest had gone to Italy, and somehow she didn't think that was likely. It would require passports and planning beyond the time the old lady probably had.

If she thought hard and constructively she might figure it out, but Pepper sounded the approach of the Gandy girls and she gave up and went to the door. Before she could turn on the light and open the door wide, the two youngsters squeezed by her and stood in the kitchen, breathing fast.

She reached for the switch to turn on the tin-shaded light over the table, and Sheena stopped her.

"No light, K.K.!" she said urgently. "We're being followed!"

"You are?" Kate murmured, ready to laugh.

"Yes'm, the God's truth," whispered Kim Sue. "Lock the door!"

Kate obeyed and then pulled out a chair and sat down.

"Tell me about it," she ordered.

"Troy Haskins is gone," Sheena said. "He left school day before yesterday and didn't come back, and even his mommer don't know where he's at. She come up to the school to talk to the teachers and all of us. I didn't tell her, but I reckon me and Kim Sue was the last ones to see him. He was showing us how to use his vibrating beeper."

"Where did that happen?" Kate asked quickly.

"In the play yard in the corner where some bushes are."

"Did anybody see you?"

"No'm. The bell had rung and everybody was heading back inside."

"There was a man setting in a car outside the fence," interrupted Kim Sue. "But he wasn't paying no attention, just setting there reading a newspaper."

"We run to git in before the last bell," said Sheena, "and we didn't see Troy no more."

Kate took a deep breath.

"What made you think you are being followed?"

"There was this black van that stuck close to our school bus. Kind of *oozed* along behind us, making evva stop our bus made," Kim Sue said.

"Most drivers have to do that on our road," Kate suggested in an effort at reasonableness. "It's hard to pass a bus on so many curves and hills."

"He coulda passed." Sheena was implacable. "But he didn't, and me and Kim decided not to git off at our stop. It's too much of a run up the hill to the house. We stayed on down to our aunt's, which is right by the road."

"Smart girls," approved Kate. "What happened to the man in the van?"

"He speeded up and *then* he passed the bus and went on toward Marietta. But he was back today. Parked down there on the gravel road right across from our house. Mommer had to go back to the Gradys with Daddy. So we waited in the house till dark to come down here."

"Did the man see you?"

"We run through the woods," said Kim Sue. "I

170

think he knowed he couldn't ketch us in the woods. We're pretty fast.''

"Aw, he didn't see us!" said Sheena. "We eased through the woods, like ghosts.''

"Yes, he did!" proclaimed Kim Sue.

Before further argument could erupt, Kate put a finger to her lips to silence them and stood by the door, listening hard. Pepper would have sounded the alarm if anybody came in the yard, but she thought she heard a car engine idling somewhere out front. She picked up the phone and called Sergeant Alvarez.

To divert the girls, she waved them toward the refrigerator and then jerked a thumb toward the upstairs bedroom and television. They nodded and obeyed, making their way toward the stairs carrying chocolate ice cream Brown Cows on sticks, and Cokes.

Kate shuddered and turned back to the phone.

"Look, Mellie," she whispered when Sergeant Alvarez answered, "the little Haskins boy has disappeared. You know the one?''

"With the vibrating beeper, sure," said the sergeant. "I got the narc boys interested. Somebody has probably already been out to see him.''

"He's not at school or at home, I'm afraid," Kate said. "Vanished two afternoons ago after somebody saw him showing my little Gandy friends his beeper. The girls have been asking him questions because I let them use mine. Since then they think somebody's been following them. I feel awful. They're here now." She tried to laugh. "Maybe imagination. I'm afraid I've psyched them up for cloak and dagger. But I don't want to risk it.''

"Don't risk it," Sergeant Alvarez said briefly. "I'm going to send one of the county boys out to make sure you and the girls are all right. Keep them there."

"No choice," said Kate. "Their parents are not at home, as it's easy for anybody to see. The precious BMW is not in the yard."

Kate checked on the girls, who were sitting on her bed watching television, apparently having forgotten that they were in peril. Kate hadn't forgotten, and she didn't turn on the light until a north Fulton police car with a brightly whirling blue dome light pulled in the driveway. She recognized Steve Sizemore as he came across the yard with the headlights backlighting him. He walked fast, and he was breathless when he reached the door.

Kate had it open for him.

"You okay, Kate?" he asked.

"Fine," she said, smiling weakly.

"Them little Gandys, are they all right?"

"Fine," said Kate. "Upstairs watching television."

He let out a long, deep sigh, sat down, and pulled out a handkerchief and started mopping his sweaty face.

"Well, I got bad news," he said after he caught his breath. "That little Haskins kid is near 'bout chewed to death. Happened a couple of hours ago at the edge of his folks' farm. A pit bull got after him."

"Oh, dear God." Kate moaned, collapsing into a chair. "Whose dog was it? How did it happen?"

"The dog is dead," the policeman said, "so we might never know where he came from. A neighbor of the Haskinses was coming back from hunting rabbits in the woods, and he saw the kid running down the lane. He didn't see the dog at first for the tall weeds, but the kid stumbled and fell and the dog was right on him. Fellow said it happened so fast he liked to have not seen the dog until he heard the kid scream. Going for the throat, the dog was. Fellow shot him, but it may have been too late. The child's at North Fulton Hospital.''

Kate cupped her face in shaking hands, and tears slid down her cheeks and drenched them.

''Yeah, bad,'' the policeman said, sighing. He put out an awkward hand and patted her shoulder. ''You were friends with the Haskinses?''

Kate shook her head and picked up a checked napkin and wiped her face. ''I didn't know them. But a child, Steve, a little kid. . . . I can't stand it! It's depraved!''

She swallowed hard and stood up. ''I better call the office. Can you stay and look after the Gandy girls if I have to go see the Haskinses?''

''Sure,'' said Steve. ''I'm here to protect you all. You got any coffee?''

CHAPTER 7

Kate had to pass through a convocation of neighbors and friends of the Haskinses, who in the old-time custom of the country hunkered down under trees or sat on the steps and in the halls of the new hospital. They belonged to rural Georgia, where a trip to the hospital was generally believed to be a death sentence. They had heard with horror of the dog's attack on Troy, and knowing few of the details, they had come out of neighbors' or blood-kin's duty but probably also out of love and compassion for the Haskinses.

Kate's heart went out to them and to the parents, who waited outside the emergency room for doctors and nurses to finish working over their torn and bleeding child and let them back in.

Sam Haskins, the father, was still wearing the worn, earth-stained overalls he had been working in.

May, her tortured face now pinched with fear and anxiety, had just gotten home from searching for Troy and changed to a shapeless shift and cloth bedroom shoes, which she still wore. She automatically hugged Kate, not caring that she didn't know her but accepting her as a sympathy-giver.

"How is he?" Kate whispered.

"We don't know," Sam Haskins said gruffly.

"He's gon' die," May quavered. "I know it."

"Aw, Mrs. Haskins, they can do so much now—wonder drugs and great surgery."

"He's gon' die," May Haskins repeated.

"They ain't said that, May," the father contradicted her. "They'd tell us if that was so."

"They don't know. I'm his mother. I know!"

"Let's not give up hope," the father said. "Like this newspaperwoman said, they can do so much now."

"Cain't put his arm back on!" the mother wailed, bursting into tears.

"His arm?" whispered Kate, looking at the father.

He nodded. "I think it's off."

The Haskinses didn't know anything about the dog or where it came from. They didn't know of any pit bulls in north Fulton County since a woman in Decatur had been killed and so many owners of dogs of that breed had voluntarily taken their pets in to the dog control center to be put down.

"We got bird dogs," Sam Haskins said. "Troy helps to raise them, and he ain't scared of dogs. He may have stopped to pet that pit bull."

"No!" cried the mother. "He was running, a-running for his life! Joe Bettis saw him!"

Kate clutched her pencil numbly. She couldn't move. The most pitiful words she'd ever heard: "a-running for his life."

"How old is Troy?" Kate asked after a moment, hoping to divert the mother from some of the horror.

"Twelve," said the mother. "And the best young'un in the world. He worked all the time to help out at home. We got three children younger than him, and Troy wanted them to have."

To "have," Kate thought bitterly, at what cost?

"Where did he work?"

May Haskins looked at her husband.

"You know, for some of them new people moved out here," he supplied uneasily. "Cutting grass and helping out in their gardens and like that."

"Can you give me their names?"

He looked at May.

She shook her head. "There was so many . . . I don't know . . . I cain't think right now." She twisted her hands together and looked piteously toward the emergency room door.

"Troy had been missing for a couple of days, hadn't he?" Kate asked.

"He had," Mrs. Haskins said. "Didn't come home from school on Tuesday, it was. We thought he mighta been in a accident or something. We looked—"

"You know how kids are," Sam Haskins put in. "Musta gone home with a friend and forgot to call us."

"Was that something Troy might have done?"

"No, never!" cried May. "He never would have

done that. He was never a minute's trouble or worry. Now, you know that's the truth, Sam."

Sam looked up and down the corridor and swallowed hard. "He's a good boy, all right."

Kate found Joe Bettis, who had shot the dog, at the center of a crowd which included television photographers and enough lights to make his neat brick bungalow a movie set. He sat in a plastic chair on the front porch and told the story again and again for all comers. It was pretty much the same story Steve Sizemore had told her. He was coming through the woods from rabbit hunting ("Didn't get a one"), had seen Troy Haskins running down the dirt road that led to his house. Then he had seen him fall and heard him scream, "and I knew something was up and I ran over there."

"As luck would have it," he reported with satisfaction, "my rifle was still loaded. I fired—I don't know how many times. The beast fell over dead."

"Took pretty good shooting to miss the kid," one of the photographers said admiringly.

"Well . . ." Bettis was obviously pleased, "I made sharpshooter in the Army."

The police had turned the body of the dog over to the animal control unit, presumably to test for rabies.

"But I've seen a mad dog once," said Bettis, "and this one wasn't rabid. Just one of them naturally mean killer dogs."

Kate listened to Bettis's interview wind down, then left to look for a telephone. She dictated the story from a pay station at the Roswell Market Mall. When she had finished she called Sergeant Alvarez.

"Yeah, I heard," the sergeant said. "The counties are looking for the owner of the dog. So far no luck. He wasn't wearing a tag and nobody in the neighborhood ever saw him before. It looks like he was brought in."

"Brought in and sicced on a little boy," Kate said.

"I told you they play rough," Sergeant Alvarez said. "Incidentally, Patrolman Sizemore took your little Gandy friends home. Their mother called. She was back looking for them. Thought they'd be with you."

"He warned her about the man who was following them, I hope," Kate said.

"I don't think so," Sergeant Alvarez said. "Didn't want to scare the lady. Looks like her husband is not doing too well, and she and the girls are there by themselves. Steve is staking out the house. If anybody tries to bother them, he's there. For you, too," she added after a moment.

"Not me," said Kate. "I'm all right. Just tired."

"Well, get some rest, and by the way, have you got a line on Mrs. Wilcox yet?"

Kate sighed. "That again! After all that's happened, you all aren't still looking for her, are you?"

"I'm not," Sergeant Alvarez said. "Homicide is. Don't you think all this is connected?"

"Killer dogs and Miss Willie? Don't be silly!" Kate said briskly, and hung up.

But after she got home and in bed Kate got to wondering if there was a connection. She got up and went downstairs in her nightgown and without turning on a light punched the PLAY button on the tape deck.

This time she listened hard to the words, refusing to allow herself to be beguiled by the music.

She heard it through once and then turned on her desk light and got a pencil and paper. She punched REWIND and played it again.

"Ah, sweet mystery," she wrote. "Wanting you, nothing else in the world will do . . . Tramp, tramp, tramp down the highway . . . heard the wolf calling when nighttime was falling . . . up to our knees in blood . . . Beyond the blue horizon, and then, inexplicably, 'Italian Street Song.' "

That Jeanette, she decided, turning off the player and taking her pencil and paper up to bed, that Jeanette was a tease. Just singing away there to confuse her. Why on earth would Miss Marlowa or anybody fool around messing up a tape when a phone call or a note would be simple and direct?

Kate put the paper and pencil on the table and turned out the light. She was too tired to think, and she decided that Miss Marlowa in her purple pants suit and high-heeled sandals was a victim of senility or old-age foolishness and contrariness with her dark, deep-laid plans.

Kate said the words over to herself—"dark, deep-laid plans." Who was she quoting? she wondered. Not Jeanette and Nelson. Suddenly she knew.

She padded back downstairs and pulled a book off the shelf by her desk. The *Portable Mark Twain*, bought at a used book sale and often read. There it was, a chapter heading, "Dark, Deep-Laid Plans," and she knew what they were. Tom Sawyer, in order to conform to all the literary pictures he admired, had made Huck Finn participate in an idiotically complicated scheme to save the black slave Jim, when they could have simply opened the door and let him out of his crude cabin prison.

Kate had hated Tom's complications when she was a child, but as she got older she had been amused to reread the story. Huck had pointed out that they could free Jim by wrenching off a board, and Tom had protested that they had to find a more complicated way than that. They stole a sheet to make him a ladder he didn't need and a shirt for him to keep a journal on, using his own blood for ink, although Jim couldn't write. They tried to dig him out with case knives because Tom thought that more literary than the old picks and shovels which were stored nearby.

Huck had rightly called it one of the "most jackass ideas" he ever saw, but Tom said there was a *right* way and he insisted on pursuing it, despite the delay in freeing Jim. He wanted Jim's escape to be as stylish as that of prisoners in the bottom of a dungeon in the harbor of Marseilles.

Miss Marlowa all over, I bet. Just like Zelda Fitzgerald. Anything done in moderation is not worth doing. Whatever her scheme, whatever dumb secret she was cosseting in her bony old bosom, she wasn't going to make it easy for Kate. Once more Kate turned off the light, rather cheerfully because she was remembering Tom's prose and the message he dictated for poor Jim to leave behind:

"Here a captive heart busted . . . Here perished a noble stranger, natural son of Louis XIV."

It would be so nice for Kate if Miss Marlowa could have worked Louis XIV in on whatever her jackass plan was, Kate decided.

Early the next morning with her first cup of coffee, Kate played the MacDonald-Eddy tape again. This time she suffered through the "Italian Street Song" twice. Much of it she couldn't understand. After all, it must have been recorded forty years ago, and Jeanette's operatic enunciation wasn't exactly Kenny Rogers country. The word that came out loud and clear was "Napoli" trilled over and over.

Kate got another cup of coffee, leaving the tape on, and called the hospital to check on Troy Haskins. He was in critical condition but holding his own. She called the Gandys, fortuitously awakening them in time for them to get ready for school. Officer Sizemore was going to take them hisself in a police car, Sheena reported.

Just as she hung up, "Napoli" came belting out loud and clear, and she understood it.

Naples, of course, she thought. *How could I have been so stupid?* The name of the song was "Italian." Any fool should know that the city was Naples.

She turned off the tape and grabbed the big atlas she kept, for lack of space, under her desk. Was there a Naples in Georgia? There wasn't. She knew of a Naples, Florida, but somehow that didn't seem right. She looked at Alabama and Tennessee. There, not too far from the North Carolina line and Dolly Parton's Dollywood and Conway Twitty's Twitty City, was Naples, Tennessee.

Kate dialed information for the Naples Chamber of Commerce. There was none. Tourist bureau, she decided. Every mountain town had tourist bureaus going at autumn leaf time. It was too early in the day, not open yet.

She hurried into the shower and into her gray suit —again—pausing to feed Pepper and Sugar on the way out and then hurrying back to lock the door. Pepper would fault her for that. He liked to push the kitchen door open and nap in the shadows when the midday sun grew hot.

But she needed him outside to bite strangers, she decided.

Ten miles down the road near Canton, Kate stopped for gas and the telephone. The office made no objection to her taking the day off to follow a wild goose, as she explained. The Naples tourist bureau was open and glad to give her a rundown on the season's attractions.

"Do you have a meeting of a Jeanette MacDonald-Nelson Eddy fan club?" Kate interrupted to ask.

"Oh, yes, ma'am," said the young tourist person. "That's our biggest attraction. We already got two hundred fans in town and more coming. The motels are full. Were you gon' be wanting a room?"

"I don't know," said Kate. "Don't worry about it. I'll sleep on the street if I have to."

The girl giggled. "That's more like our summer rock festival. Nearly *all* of them sleep in the street."

Driving through the hill country in the fall brought memories of Benjy back. He had loved the bright foliage and the mountain views and often planned weekends, even a vacation or two, for them to spend at Gatlinburg or Asheville or traveling along the Blue Ridge Parkway. The way the earth was put together in these places and bedecked with gold and scarlet and all the range of color in between filled him with awe and a kind of reverence. With such beauty richly, profligately given, how could you believe in the evils of the world?

What, oh, what would you do about Garney Wilcox's legacy of evil? Kate asked him silently. She had not done anything to help poor little Cheri, and she didn't know what to do. She couldn't even call to offer comfort and encouragement because it was too likely Voncile would answer the phone. The girl's major concern had not been for herself but for her grandmother, Kate conceded. If she could find Miss Willie, maybe that would be a start on working things out.

The little town of Naples nestled in a valley. Kate saw it as the road rounded a hill brilliant with maples and poplars and descended in a deep curve. She could not, in fact, miss it because the sky above it and the blue mountains beyond it were blotted out with a giant billboard carrying a full-color likeness of Jeanette and Nelson, nose to nose.

WELCOME TO SWEETHEART TOWN! a ground-level sign heralded.

Kate slowed down at the city limits and heard the music piped from somewhere at full volume: "Sweetheart, sweetheart, sweetheart!"

She almost stopped and gave way to the giggles. *Take that, Victor Herbert! Was your famous waltz wrought for this?*

She parked beside the biggest motel in a row of motels. Whatever its real architecture, it was now a castle complete with balconies and battlements worked out in pink plywood. A sign wreathed in painted roses announced that it was festival headquarters.

Kate went in the lobby and found the young woman she had talked to on the telephone back of a desk shaped like a piano with notes she suspected spelled out LOVE across its backside.

"Do the festival visitors register with you?" she asked. "I'm looking for some ladies from Georgia."

The girl shook her head.

"You'll have to try the motels," she said. "We don't keep a list of attendees, just a mailing list."

Kate felt sure Miss Marlowa was on the mailing list, but she wanted Miss Marlowa in person. She asked at the motel desk, which mercifully looked like a desk. No Miss Walton registered. She walked out into the declining sunshine and looked over the other motels.

The mountains, which she could now see, were ablaze with color, although the sun was hovering at the rim of the ridge in the west, ready to set. The air was cool and fresh but the traffic, moving at a snail's pace, was terrible.

Kate tried three motels with no luck. No Miss Marlowa registered at any of them. She picked up a program of festival events.

New Moon, the movie, was showing that night at the high school auditorium, to be followed by a concert starring Lisa Bentley and Leander Jones, soloists in the high school glee club. They would sing—Kate's mind reeled—"Indian Love Call," "Rose-Marie," "Will You Remember," and "I'm Falling in Love with Someone." For an encore, Kate speculated, how about the duet from the "Sweetheart Waltz," the town's theme song?

There was a tearoom where she could get dinner before the show, said the kid at the high school box office, where she went to buy a ticket. Kate found it, tucked back of a neatly trimmed hemlock hedge, named Rose Marie's. Kate wondered if it retained that name all year or changed to whatever the latest country or rock heroine was called in those seasons.

The food was good, fresh country vegetables, hot rolls of a fine feathery lightness, and a choice of fruit cobblers for dessert. Kate was torn between strawberry, peach, apple, and blackberry, and finally settled for a cup of coffee.

The waitress, a pretty college girl named Mavis from the state university, was relieved. It suited her fine to finish serving early. She was meeting her boyfriend, who was going to take her home to change to her hoop skirt for the dance, which would follow the concert.

"Waltz?" Kate asked.

"Oh, yes, ma'am," the girl said enthusiastically. "Waltz, polka, reel, all of it. We do the dances that were in all the movies. You're coming to the high school gym, aren't you?"

Kate assured her that she wouldn't think of missing it. "I'm really looking for some old friends, a couple of elderly ladies and their maid. Have they been in here?"

The girl giggled. "Just about all the ladies who come in here are seniors," she said. "But a lot of the kids in my age group are getting interested. I'm a music major, and I think light opera is neat. Did you know that the Jeanette and Nelson operettas prepared the American public for opera and all the Broadway musicals that are still popular? And Oscar Hammerstein, before he wrote so many wonderful show tunes, collaborated with Sigmund Romberg on 'Lover Come Back to Me,'" she showed off proudly.

"My goodness," said Kate. "I'll look forward to seeing you dance tonight."

"Oh, don't just come to look on," said Mavis. "Put on your long dress and bring your boyfriend and *dance!* Everybody does."

Kate doubted that Miss Marlowa and Ida would dance. She did not see them in the auditorium when she arrived early for the show. Not registered at a motel, not signed up for the movie, the concert, or the dance—she began to worry. Maybe she had guessed wrong. Maybe the tapes weren't Miss Marlowa's jackassy, Tom Sawyer directions for making things complicated. She had misunderstood.

The movie *New Moon* was still charming, almost as heartthrobbing as Kate remembered it from her high school days. The stars were handsome, the songs romantic. "Lover Come Back to Me" had to be poignant to anybody who ever loved and lost. "Remembering all the little things you used to do./ Every road I walk along I've walked along with you./ I'm so lonely!/ The night is cold/ And Love is old./ This heart of mine is seeking./ Lover, where can you be?''

It made Kate so sad she gave up looking over her shoulder for Miss Marlowa and just sat, tired and discouraged and feeling a bit sorry for herself.

At intermission, when the high school glee club took over, she slipped out and went to try her hand at getting a motel room for the night. It was after nine o'clock and she figured there might be one they were saving for late arrivals. There was one at the Maytime Motor Court. Kate reserved it and went back to the auditorium in time to hear Lisa Bentley, a plump teen-ager whose young bosom threatened to overflow the bodice of a ball gown right out of the court of Versailles, and Leander Jones, a lanky, pimply-faced young fellow whose voice had not finished changing, hit "Will You Remember?''

They did the "Sweetheart Waltz" encore, as Kate had anticipated, and led the school band, playing it brassily, into the gym where costumed couples were already lined up for a polonaise.

Kate looked for young Mavis and found her in a white lace dress which billowed out cloudlike. The girl was pink-faced and smiling as she gave her hand to a young fellow who seemed to be wearing a mixed bag from Napoléon's court. Over tight military-school wool uniform trousers he had a nipped-in Nehru jacket with a high stiff collar.

The couple pointed their toes and arched their backs and took off, leading the set. And following them—Kate blinked and looked, took off her glasses and wiped them and looked again—an apparition in lavender brocade over hoops with velvet panniers front and back and creamy lace at the wrists and throat! The face was half covered by a satin mask, and the hair, a blond pompadour with a single coquettish curl bouncing on the shoulder, was like nothing Kate had seen outside the most rococo movie spectacle. There was something about the figure, something about the movement of the lady dipping in a not quite steady curtsy to the young man who was her partner.

"Good lord in Zion!" breathed Kate. "Miss Marlowa Walton!"

Kate moved closer on the hard bleacher seat. She couldn't take her eyes off the couple. There was no doubt about it, the old girl was one of the best dancers on the floor. She even made her partner, probably a 4-H Club boy who excelled at raising pigs, look good.

Many of the young dancers seemed to be watching Miss Marlowa and her partner and following their lead. They did a minuet and something Kate supposed was a gavotte and a polka and went back to the waltz. It was nearing midnight and, tired herself, Kate knew the old hoofer must be dead on her feet. Miss Marlowa gave no sign of exhaustion until the floor cleared, the band struck up a country dance, and a covey of young cloggers in gingham and denim came running out.

The Mac-Ed memoir seemed to be over.

Kate climbed off her bleacher seat and went down on the floor to meet the slightly wilted apparition in lavender, who had released her young man and was making her way—slowly, slowly—toward the door.

"Miss Marlowa," Kate said tentatively, wondering if the mask was intended to render the old lady incognito.

"Well, it's about time!" said Miss Marlowa sharply, flapping an ivory and lace fan to cool her painted face. "We've been waiting for you. Didn't you get my message?"

"I got a tape," said Kate. "I wasn't quite sure what the message was, but I took a chance and came here."

"Dense," grumbled the belle of the ball. "Took your time. I thought surely a journalist would catch on."

Kate decided to take a more ingratiating tack.

"Oh, I would have been here sooner just to see you dance if I could have made it. Miss Marlowa, you're wonderful—and your dress! Where on earth did you find it?"

It worked. Miss Marlowa stopped flapping her fan and lifted it coyly before her face. "Thank you," she murmured demurely. "I have always enjoyed the dance. And I try to stay in shape. The dress, of course, was in a trunk in the attic."

"What a triumph!" exclaimed Kate, dead set on her course of flattery. "And now please tell me where Miss Willie is."

"Oh, Willie Wilcox!" said Miss Marlowa scornfully. "She sits back in the motel grieving. I have to leave Ida with her to keep her from wandering off. I vow she'd start walking back to Roswell and give herself up to the police if I didn't take precautions. I brought her here to keep her out of trouble and to show her a little fun, but she doesn't know how to have a good time.''

Kate bit her lips to keep from laughing aloud at a mental picture of Miss Willie decked out in flounces whirling and curtsying in a seventeenth-century dance.

''Which motel?'' she asked. ''I didn't find you registered.''

''Well, of course not,'' said Miss Marlowa. ''We are incognito. I am registered as Miss Melissa Warwick and party of Savannah at the Maytime.''

''Oh, good,'' said Kate. ''I'm at the Maytime, too. Shall we go? I'm beat.''

Miss Marlowa, who certainly looked beat, smiled smugly. ''My dear, you should take better care of yourself. Daily exercise and cold baths I have always found to be salubrious.''

But she leaned on Kate going down the auditorium steps, and she grew short of breath before they reached the door of her room. Kate took her key and unlocked the door.

Ida, fully dressed in a white nurse's uniform, lay on the double bed closest to the door. Miss Willie, still clad in one of her grayish old housedresses with a shawl over her shoulders and her hair skewered into a knot on the back of her head, sat in an orange plastic motel armchair by the window. She looked up when they entered the room and her sad, shriveled old face lit up.

''Kate! Lordamercy, young'un, I'm glad to see you! You've come to git me, ain't you?''

''I don't know,'' Kate said, going forward to hug

her and wave a hand at Ida, who got up from the bed and went to help Miss Marlowa out of her finery. "I've come to see what mischief you're up to."

Miss Willie grinned wryly. "I reckon I done all the mischief I ever will."

Miss Marlowa was the one who changed the sleeping arrangements. Miss Willie should share Kate's room, she said, where there were also two double beds. Miss Willie had been stubborn about not letting Ida sleep on the maid's rollaway bed the motel had provided, holding that she herself was used to a hard, thin nursing home-type mattress and would be more comfortable on it than Ida would.

It was embarrassing to both Ida and Miss Marlowa, but Miss Willie had prevailed.

Kate helped Miss Willie get her nightgown and slippers and led her outside and down the walk past the swimming pool to her room. She noticed for the first time that the Maytime Motor Court's slogan, blinking on and off, was A MOTEL OF NOTE, and there was a neon sign which said WE'RE WANTING YOU! all framed in notes which undoubtedly spelled out the tune of the song.

When Kate had seen Miss Willie into one of the two double beds and undressed herself, she pushed two pillows on the edge of her bed closest to the old lady and propped up, prepared to talk. But Miss Willie had fallen asleep and was snoring lightly with her mouth open.

"Reckon talk will keep," Kate said philosophically and, thumping a pillow, closed her eyes.

But sleep eluded her. The idea that Miss Willie

would get up and walk away crossed her mind, although the old lady didn't seem strong enough for any such feat. Kate kept waking up and checking the bed next to her. About dawn she fell into a deep sleep, and when she awakened an hour or so later Miss Willie's bed was empty.

She jerked her foggy brain and tired body into instant wakefulness, sitting bolt upright in bed.

Miss Willie spoke from the bathroom.

"Good morning to you, Kate. I'm a-going to that machine I seen down in the hall and git you and me a cup of coffee."

"Here," said Kate, fumbling for her pocketbook. "Let me give you some money. It'll probably be fifty cents a cup, and I have change."

"If that ain't the beat!" cried Miss Willie, standing stock still in the middle of the room. "Four bits, you say? I'd druther do without, wouldn't you?"

"Un-uh," said Kate. "I'd rather have my coffee."

Reluctantly Miss Willie accepted the "four bits" and left, bringing back coffee which she held gingerly as befit such a high-costing substance. Kate sat up in bed and drank half of hers before she opened the subject of murder, incest, and rape.

"Garney was the sweetest little feller," Miss Willie said. "I reckon I spiled him. But I never believed he'd do nothing bad. Yet he ruint his own little girl. Ruint her, Kate!"

"I know," said Kate. "She told me."

"That's ugly, ugly evil, and God don't love ugly!"

"Did you see him and talk to him about it?"

Miss Willie nodded. "I had to do that. I called him

and he come to the home. He tried to tell me there was nothing wrong with what he done. There's plenty of sich in the Bible, he said. Then he got mad and told me to mind my own business, I was just a crazy, mean old country woman without no sense."

She paused and stared out the window at the sun striking the swimming pool.

"I wisht it was so. I wisht I didn't have sense enough to know what he done to that child and what I done."

She was silent and Kate saw tears were filling her eyes and sliding down her furrowed old cheeks.

"What did you do?" Kate asked.

"I asked him to drive me to the old house and let me set a spell on my own gallery. It might ease my mind, I told him, and help me to see things in a clarer light. He didn't want to, but I let on that my persimmon beer had likely made, and I hated to see it go to waste. I knowed he loved my persimmon beer and he might go for that. He railed around a good bit, but finally he said all right, we'd go."

"How did you get there?"

"We took the truck. Garney didn't want to. Since he growed up he thinks he's too good for the truck. Got to drive one of them big cars. Some feller come out to Roswell with him and went off somers—to be right back, he said. Garney told Lulu at the home where we'd be at and for him to come on there if he got back before we did. We wouldn't stay but a few minutes, he said."

The old lady was silent, looking out the motel window.

"Did you give him the persimmon beer?"

"Wasn't none there. I knowed that. He was put out. But I told him I reckoned some of them had throwed it out when they come to clare out my house. He said 'Voncile' and called her a name and I said maybe there was some white whiskey left in the cellar.

"It wasn't just white whiskey, Kate. It was pizen whiskey. I mixed some herbs in it a long time back, thinking to use it to treat dropsy and a swelling in the legs. But it got too strong with them foxglove leaves in it, and I set it back, thinking to try it on Japanese beetles that was so bad last year."

She gulped and bowed her head, looking at her wrinkled and spotted old hands, which she was twisting in her lap.

"Didn't git to plant no tomaters this year."

Kate nodded. Probably for the first time since she was a child, Miss Willie had not had a garden of her own.

"So then what?"

"I told him whur to look in a fruit jar back of some beans I had put up. Nobody seemed to want my beans and just left them there, though they was about the best white half-runners I ever growed. The white whiskey was amongst them. Garney found it all right and brought it up to the gallery, and we set out there on the steps. He said it tasted f-funny!"

Miss Willie was crying now, and the words came out in a long, wracking sob.

"But he downed most of it and follered it with well water. He laid his head back on the floor like he was a-going to sleep, but I figgered he was dying. I didn't want him to die there by hisself even if he had done a foul deed."

She put her hands over her face and trembled in a paroxysm of grief.

"Ah, Miss Willie, ah, don't cry," Kate said, patting her shoulder. "You did what you felt you had to do."

"Vengeance is mine, saith the Lord," quoted Miss Willie. "But, Kate, I warn't a-looking for vengeance. I was after stopping Garney's wickedness. I knowed if I didn't do it nobody would, and there was no telling what ruin and ravagement he'd be up to next. He as good as told me he wouldn't change."

"I know," said Kate sadly.

"I set there till almost dark a-watching him. He didn't say nothing, just laid quiet. I figgered he was near 'bout a corpse. I talked to him some about the old days when he was a little boy and I told him what he done was a sin agin God and man and I'd pray to the Lord to forgive him. I sung a old song he loved to have me sing when he was little, and then I went out and started the truck and drove on back to town."

The room was very quiet after the stirrings of guests upstairs and the creaking of the cleaning woman's cart going by. "'Twas foolish of me, warn't it, to sing him a lull song?" the old lady asked.

"What lull song?"

"A old one I knowed as a child back in the mountains. He used to beg me to sing it."

Miss Willie's cracked old voice rose surprisingly soft and sweet in the stereotyped motel room:

"Hushaby lil' boy child,
Sleep, sleep, sleep!
The lambs air a-bed in the silver wood,
The cows air gone to the broom.
Shades of night air creepin'
My sweet lil' child is sleeping.
Ooom, ooom, oomh!"

The incongruity of the old lady sitting on the splintery steps singing a "lull" song to that hulking child molester and rapist she thought was dying suddenly was more than Kate could bear. *Love, oh, terrible love*, she thought. *What a trap.*

"Was that all, Miss Willie?" Kate asked at last. "You didn't hit him with anything or push him into that raw electric wire on the cellar steps?"

Miss Willie was honestly astonished.

"No, no, I didn't do that! You mean that electric w'ar come loose agin? Oh, Kate, did he git agin that? I knowed I didn't do such a good job of electrifying my house. That w'ar hung loose a lot of times but I taped it up and pushed it back and was gon' tie it up good until I had to leave. Did he touch that thing?"

Kate nodded.

"And hit, who hit him?"

"I don't know, Miss Willie, but that's what killed him, not your poison liquor. That just made him sick."

Miss Willie let out a long sigh, and for the first time in weeks she smiled. "Thank you, Lord," she said simply. "Thank you."

Kate couldn't bring herself to say any more about the Wilcox family's tragedies. There would be time enough to worry about Cheri's plight when they got back to Georgia.

Meanwhile, she thought of breakfast.

"Yes'm, I'd be obliged," Miss Willie said with country courtesy when Kate asked her.

Kate expected to meet Miss Marlowa and Ida in the coffee shop, but only Ida was present. She had finished her breakfast and was waiting for a tray to take to her employer when Kate and Miss Willie joined her at a table by the window.

Miss Marlowa was still asleep, she said, but there was going to be a memorial service at noon for the "dynamic duo" and she knew Miss Marlowa wouldn't want to miss that.

"You gon' back to Roswell and miss it?" she asked Miss Willie.

Miss Willie looked almost serene as she nodded.

"I'm proud to say I am," she said. "Kate's a-carry-ing me home."

"You ain't exactly hoodooed by Jeanette and Nel-son, is you?"

"Oh, they all right. They fine," said Miss Willie graciously. "Sing pretty and all. But I got more things on my mind than that."

"Lord, I wish you'd git Miss Marlowa interested in something else. When this hurrah's over she want to go on to Dollywood and Twitty City. She found out she can still dance and she don't care if the music ain't to her taste. Calls Mr. Twitty and Miss Dolly's singing 'common,' not elevating like these people over here at Sweetheart Town. But she be bound to go anyhow, and me with her."

Ida made a face at the foibles of an old lady.

"She certainly was kicking up her heels last night," said Kate, looking up from the menu. "She really shakes a leg."

"And more," said Ida. "Sometimes I believe she think she still a girl and they tuning up the fiddles at Walton Hall."

Kate smiled. Balls at Walton Hall must have been a far cry from a whomped-up PR festival with its pink plywood and high school heavy-on-the-tuba band. But you couldn't tell it from the way Miss Marlowa flung herself into the dance the night before. Even the dress, which must have been a hundred years old, seemed to fit right in.

The waitress brought a plastic carton of breakfast for Miss Marlowa, and Ida stood up to go. She would bring out Miss Willie's things, she said.

"And Ida," said Miss Willie, grinning, "you can have that white wig Marlowa bought for me."

Kate sent her thanks to Miss Marlowa for hers and Ida's kindness to Miss Willie. "Tell her I have to get back to work and Miss Willie wants to get in touch with the authorities."

Miss Willie looked up from the sourwood honey on her plate, which she was sopping with a bit of biscuit.

"What authorities?" she asked suspiciously. "I thought you said I had come clare."

Kate was loath to tell Miss Willie she was not "clare," because she wasn't sure. She didn't want to frighten her and put her on the run again—but suppose they clapped her in jail? Dollywood and Twitty

City looked pretty appealing at that moment. Kate believed the old lady's story with a sweeping sense of relief. But they still had to convince the police. And until they found the person who rearranged the live wire and walloped Garney on the head with a blunt instrument, they might suspect Miss Willie.

"Just a formality, Miss Willie," she said. "We have to tell them what happened."

CHAPTER 8

ate called Officer Steve Sizemore from her cabin. She told him Miss Willie was with her and would be around if he or anybody in the department wished to talk to her. She said it casually, ignoring the fact that the old lady was a suspect. She hurried on to ask about the condition of Troy Haskins.

Steve skipped Troy Haskins's condition and went straight to the question of Miss Willie's whereabouts the last few days.

"Where in God's name has that old lady been hiding out?"

"Hiding?" Kate repeated with a touch of hauteur. "My goodness, Steve, Miss Willie wasn't hiding anywhere. She just went up to the mountains with Miss Marlowa Walton for a little R and R. She's surprised that anybody was looking for her—except maybe the nursing home crew."

"Well, they not looking anymore," said Steve. "They told us they had packed up her gear and would turn it over to anybody who wanted it. They don't want to be in the position of harboring a criminal."

"Harboring a criminal!" Kate sputtered in disbelief. "They are a fine bunch of jerks! They should be honored to have a woman like Miss Willie stay in their old firetrap fleabag. She doesn't need them."

"Not if there's room in the Fulton County jail," muttered Steve.

"Now, really," Kate said severely, "I don't want you to talk like that to Miss Willie. She's suffering enough from the loss of that scoundrel son of hers, and I won't have you all coming around threatening her with jail. You hear me?"

"Kate, I don't make the law," Steve said. "Mrs. Wilcox *said* she killed Garney. Now is she backtracking?"

"Oh, Steve!" protested Kate. "You know how an old lady's mind works. She probably thinks it was her cooking that did it, or something like that. You don't believe everybody who comes forward and 'confesses' to a crime, now, do you?"

Steve ignored the question.

"Keep her there," he said. "Somebody from homicide will be out to see her."

He prepared to hang up.

"Steve!" Kate called quickly. "What about Troy Haskins?"

"Died this morning," the policeman said.

Kate sat by the telephone staring into the woods back of the cabin. She knew, whether homicide believed it or not, that the boy's death was no accident. He wasn't attacked by a stray dog. He was attacked by a killer turned loose on him when he started home after a day and a night's unexplained absence. "A-running for his life," his mother had said.

Kate choked back tears and called the office. She had initiated the story of the attack, and the desk wanted her to follow through. She said she would be in after she had checked the hospital and seen Troy's parents.

Miss Willie came down the stairs with some clothes she planned to wash.

"You got to go to your job?" she asked.

Kate nodded. "Little Troy Haskins was killed by a dog."

"Lord God, what next?" Miss Willie asked prayerfully. "What next air these pore humans got to suffer?"

Kate stood up. "You want to go with me? You could sit in the car while I work."

The old woman shook her head.

"I'm kinda done in by all the traipsing around Marlowa Walton had me a-doing. I'll just stay here and rest, and I might walk over to the old home place for a spell. You got any cornbread and buttermilk? I got a kinda hankering for some."

"Milk, yes, and meal, I think. But Miss Willie, you be careful. Strangers have taken to poking around over there, and they might make trouble for you."

Miss Willie smiled. "That's my own stay-place. 'Twill be all right."

Kate quickly showered and donned a tweed skirt,

a cotton shirt, and the Irish fisherman's sweater Benjy had brought her from Ireland. She considered her black medium-heeled pumps and put them in a tote bag with her library books and tapes, which were days past due. She didn't see much chance of returning books and tapes today, but it didn't hurt to have them along in case there was a moment for dropping by the library. And she always took along what she called her "serious" shoes to change to when her favorite loafers were too disreputable for the occasion. She never knew how much walking the day would involve, and the loafers were reliably comfortable.

She paused beside Miss Willie in the kitchen, considering kissing her on the cheek, but in a day when perfect strangers hugged and kissed on meeting, Miss Willie was oddly reticent. She didn't distribute hugs and kisses freely. Kate settled for touching her lightly on the shoulder and lifting a hand in farewell.

Before she reached her car, Kate saw Ron Gardiner coming through the woods from his house. On impulse she walked to meet him. He had a stick in his hand and was hitting the bushes in a way that annoyed Kate. Why did he have to bruise and beat up on growing things that weren't bothering him? What did he know about them, which ones would grow into shade trees, which ones would become flowering shrubs?

"Hi, neighbor!" he said jovially. "You okay this morning?"

Kate nodded but ignored the question. "I believe you said you used to raise dogs. Maybe you can help me with some information. Do you know anybody around this end of the county who raises pit bulls?"

His eyes narrowed.

"Why do you ask?"

"Because one killed a little boy the other day, and I'd like to talk to its owner."

He snorted. "You think somebody's gon' come forward and volunteer that their dog did that?"

"If they were innocent of evil intent I'd think they'd come forward and try to make amends to the child's parents," Kate said.

Ron shrugged and hit at a sweetshrub with his stick. "As you know, I raise cockers. I know you hear them barking, but I keep them penned up."

Kate did not know that he had dogs. She had never seen him out walking one, and she did not know that the barking she heard occasionally came from his house. But she let it go.

"I just thought you might know somebody. Kennel Club people usually know other Kennel Club people."

He looked over his shoulder at Valerie, who was coming through the stone gates from the castle in her running suit.

"Well, we're not very active in the Kennel Club, but I could ask around."

"Please do," said Kate. "I'd like to talk to the owner, and I'm sure the police would, unless, of course, they've already found him."

"Did they ever find the old woman?"

Kate knew perfectly well that he meant Miss Willie, but she didn't like his tone. It lacked respect.

"What old woman?" she asked.

"You know." He jerked his head backward toward Miss Willie's house. "The one that did in her son."

"I don't think Miss Willie was ever lost. She rested a couple of days with a friend, and I think you should be careful about accusing her of killing her son."

"Oh-ho," said Ron, hitting a lick at a stand of goldenrod. "Got her defense all ready, I presume."

Valerie, beautiful and blank-faced as usual, said, "Let's go, Ron," and they struck out for the road and their morning canter without even the formality of a good-bye.

That's the last I'm likely to hear from them about dogs, Kate thought, and she was puzzled that overexuberant, overfriendly Ron had exhibited a touch of hostility.

She pulled into the rocky, littered driveway by the Gandys' house to check on Sheena and Kim Sue, but the BMW was missing and the house seemed closed up and unoccupied. Steve Sizemore could be counted on to work out some safe way for the girls to go to and from school, she decided, and turned toward the Haskinses' house over by Alpharetta.

The lane down which young Troy had come "a-running for his life" was now filled with cars and trucks parked on the weedy shoulder. The house, a post-World War II bungalow covered with a grayish asbestos siding, seemed to be teeming with people, and Kate thought of the Emily Dickinson line about the stir death makes in a house.

The menfolk, as usual in the country, had gathered in a small quiet cluster of whittlers and tobacco-chewers under a shade tree at the edge of the porch. The rockers on the porch were occupied by children. The women would be in the kitchen bustling about with food, making coffee. *Offering comfort in the only way most of us know*, Kate thought. She asked for Mrs. Haskins, and a plump woman in an apron said May was a-laying down, exhausted from sitting up at the hospital, and she didn't like to disturb her.

"Mr. Haskins—" Kate started to inquire, but the woman shook her head.

"Sam ain't seeing any of us," another woman put in. "He just walks around like somebody dead. I think he's gone out of his mind with grief."

Kate got the hour of the funeral and a list of the survivors, grandparents, and little sisters and brother, and took her leave. Hers was the last car down the lane, and she started toward it when she saw Mr. Haskins sitting on an overturned cow feed bin in the open doorway of the barn. He had a shotgun between his knees.

She walked toward him, timidly because she did not know what the shotgun was for or how disturbed the man was. He looked at her empty-eyed and expressionless and said nothing.

"Mr. Haskins, I'm so sorry about Troy," she said. "Do you know where the dog came from?"

He didn't answer but gazed intently at something beyond her in the yard. She glanced over her shoulder and saw a liver-spotted hound followed by a litter of frisky puppies, the ones Troy was helping to raise. Suddenly an explosion rocked the barn and reverberated in its rafters. The hound dog fell, torn to bloody pieces.

There was another shot and the puppies, yowling in terror, fell.

"Godalmighty!" cried somebody, and there was a rush of men to the barn.

"You hurt, lady?" one of them asked while the others surrounded Sam Haskins and took the shotgun out of his hand.

Kate shook her head.

"Sam, now, Sam," an older man said gently. "You come on in the house. May needs you. It's a bad time, and you should be together."

A younger man, pausing beside the bloody remnants of the family's pets, shook his head in disgust.

"No need for him to do that. Good beasts, hurting nobody."

"Git a shovel, son," the old man said.

Sam Haskins, his shoulders sagging, his head in its frayed straw sunhat bowed, walked docilely toward the house with two men holding his arms.

Kate sat in the car long moments before she had the strength to start it. Sam Haskins was what the psalmist called a bruised reed, she thought, without even the strength of the broken and dying. *And I'm one, too, not up to the madness which surrounds us.*

When she had driven through the country roads and was on the expressway, Kate reached automatically for a tape. It was a mindless habit, this playing of music in the car, reading of books on MARTA train and bus. It kept her from thinking. In happier times she called the library and the MARTA system her good companions, making her travels to and from town, dull by some standards, agreeable and enriching for her. Today she inserted a tape in the slot because she always did and it might ease the day.

She had borrowed it from the library for one side, Dvorak's Ninth Symphony, because the largo section was so touching. She associated it forever with a picture a photographer friend had taken of a black accordionist named Graham Jackson, who followed the funeral cortege of President Roosevelt from the Little White House to the Warm Springs railroad station. It had been known to the President as "Going Home," and as Graham played it tears poured down his dark cheeks. The picture hangs in the Little White House Museum.

Today Kate knew she couldn't bear to hear it. She carefully turned the tape to the other side, Brahms waltzes and presumably soothing and cheerful.

There was a spirited march and a waltz and then, as Kate steered into the exit lane for Atlanta, the famous cradle song poured out.

"Oh, God, not a lullaby!" she cried aloud, and hit the OFF button sharply. "I can't stand another thing."

Kate made her way through the newsroom, barely aware for once of the fresh early day smell of clean new papers, unsullied, unread, stacked by the mailbox. She stopped by Shell's desk and learned there had been no news from police reporters on the search for the dog's owners. She called Reference for the file on pit bull dogs.

Halfway through the story her phone rang and a

soft girlish voice said tentatively, "Kate . . . Miss Kate?"

It was Cheri.

"I wanted to ask you," the girl said shyly, "if you ever found Grandma?"

"I'm glad you called, honey. Yes, yes, I did," Kate said. "She's at my house and you don't have to worry. She didn't kill your father." *Only tried to,* Kate added to herself.

"Could I go and see her?" Cheri asked. "I didn't go to school this morning. If it's all right, I'll get Wayne to give me a ride out there . . . ?"

"Sure, go ahead," Kate said. "I wouldn't say anything to anybody else about it."

"No, ma'am," the girl said bleakly. "There's not really anybody except Judy Carson, and she already knows. I haven't got anybody to tell."

"I guess I was thinking of your mother. She is very angry at your grandmother and might make trouble for her. Miss Willie doesn't need that."

"I'm not at home anymore," Cheri said. "Mama found out about . . . you know, the baby and all, and she made me get out of the house. Said she never wanted to see me again."

"Oh, for goodness' sake!" snapped Kate. And then softening—the girl probably loved her mother—she added, "She was probably just shocked, honey. When she gets used to the idea she'll be different."

"No, she called me bad names. Said I was you know, like a whore and I enticed my daddy to do all those things. She said I could sleep in the gutter 'cause that's where I belong!"

"Well, she's wrong," said Kate. "Don't let her get you down. You're a good girl and you certainly don't have to sleep in the gutter. We'll find better places."

When Cheri hung up, Kate turned back to her story, but she had trouble remembering what she was writing. Voncile's attitude wasn't all that strange. In many of the cases of incest she had covered the mother was more protective of the father than of the daughter. She couldn't imagine why, but it must be a way of coping with rejection, of avoiding the knowledge that she had been replaced by a younger female. It must be that way with animals when the males go for the new crop of females, ignoring the old. It was terrible that incest and other sexual abuse were so much in the news now, but it did mean that women and girls who lacked the courage to report it before were at least able to tell the police about it. Obviously Voncile had not reached that point.

The fifth time the telephone rang, mostly with calls from Jeanette MacDonald—Nelson Eddy fans, whose names suddenly appeared to be legion, it was Steve Sizemore, calling from her cabin.

"Kate, you promised me Mrs. Wilcox would be here, and she's not!" he said accusingly.

"Oh, Steve, I forgot." She sighed. "I've been so busy, and I just forgot. Look upstairs, she may be taking a nap."

In a moment he came back on the line. "Nope, she's not there. Any other suggestions?"

Somehow Kate felt reluctant to mention that Miss Willie might be in her own house eating cornbread and drinking buttermilk. The old lady deserved some privacy, and Kate wasn't sure what Steve meant to do, anyhow. She wanted to be there when he talked to Miss Willie.

"Look, some old friend or neighbor probably came to take her for a ride or home with them for dinner or something. Or"—this was sudden inspiration—"I bet she's gone to the cemetery."

The policeman grumbled, but he seemed resigned. "I hope she hasn't run again, Kate. This is serious."

"I know it's serious," Kate said to placate him. "I'll bring her in when she comes back. And Steve"—to change the subject and put him on the defensive—"what did you do about protecting the Gandy girls?"

"They okay," he said. "That fellow they thought was following them was following his wife. I went up to him and asked him point-blank what he was up to. Took his tag number and checked his driver's license. He seem kind of shame-faced to admit it, but his wife is shacked up with some fellow over there in Shining Waters Subdivision, he thinks."

"And he's going to school and following the school bus?" Kate asked.

"Well, yeah," Steve said sheepishly. "I didn't ask him about that. Maybe—" hopefully, "maybe he's got kids?"

"Steve!" Kate cried in exasperation. "Those girls are in danger. You know what happened to Troy Haskins. Are you gon' let some gangster-dope dealer murder Sheena and Kim Sue?"

"How do you know it was a dope dealer?" Steve asked suspiciously.

"I don't know, but Troy was working for some-body who called him at school on a beeper. Who could that possibly be? And when he was seen showing his beeper to Sheena and Kim Sue, he disappeared—to turn up two days later running from a killer dog. What does that sound like to you?"

Steve Sizemore was a plain cop, getting close to retirement after having started out with the city of At-lanta. He put in a stint there and transferred to the peaceful county force, in the days when the county was peaceful. He was tired, and modern crime with druggies loose in the world gave him the bewildered feeling that life was somehow not playing fair.

He preferred it when Roswell had a one-man po-lice force, and just as he had hopes of being picked for that job the place started going wild with developers and shopping centers and ten thousand more people flocking in to build the kind of homes that attracted burglars. They didn't hire Steve; they put on twenty-five sleek, shiny-shoed young fellows. It had been lei-surely, policing in Roswell in the old days, largely checking the doors of stores on the one business street and dropping by the drugstore at closing time for a cup of bitter leftover coffee and maybe a dish of chocolate ice cream with Doc.

Steve mused morosely. Now Major Mulcay's widow was accusing him of letting little children get murdered and harassing an old lady who had been friends with his own grandparents years ago. He knew there was something he had to do about it, but Steve was tired and, as he told himself, he hated crime.

Kate hated crime, too. She was ready—more than

ready—for time in her yard and books she wanted to read. The tote bag beside her desk was lumpy with books that had to be returned, some of them before she finished them. Where did the time go? The weather was its October loveliest and it wouldn't last forever. Chrysanthemums needed staking. The flower heads were heavy and toppling the plants. The last of her tomatoes reproached her from the vines, awaiting decision. Should she gather the green ones and make her regular Christmas gifts of green tomato, apple, and pepper relish? Or should she leave them on the vines for the first frost to catch them?

She looked out across the newsroom and at Baxter Winters taking off his coat and hanging it over the back of his chair. He seemed smaller than she had thought—narrower of shoulder and of hips. She couldn't remember why she had thought him so dazzlingly attractive two or three days ago. All that wine and the irresistible compliment of his attention, she thought in self-embarrassment. He seemed absorbed in some notes beside his computer. He would write something and it would be good today and forgotten tomorrow. He was just another hoping, striving, erring newspaperman and probably as subject as lesser human beings to sinus trouble and diarrhea and ingrown toenails. She was glad, she thought without shame, that she didn't have to hear him complain that he couldn't eat roast pork because it gave him the greasy belches in the night.

Shell was standing over her with a printout of her story on Troy in his hands.

"You planning on going to the funeral, I hope."

"Sure, I'll go," she said.

She didn't want to go. She was tired of funerals, first Jennie's and then Garney's and now that of a little boy whose death seemed to have drained her of all energy and all feeling. She didn't want any more of grief and trying to sort out people and evidence to find out who was causing it all. She just wanted to go home and sit in the backyard.

Baxter Winters saw her pick up her things and head for the elevator, and he followed her.

"Kate," he said hesitantly. "Haven't seen you in a couple of days. Everything okay?"

He looked really concerned, Kate thought in surprise, and his half smile was very nice.

She shook her head. "Not okay. A mess of trouble."

The half smile vanished. The bright brown eyes were watchful. "Can I help?"

She shook her head. "It's not actually my trouble —and yet it is. But thank you, there's nothing you can do."

The elevator came and she smiled at him. "I'll tell you all the gory details later."

As the door closed she saw his hand was lifted in a wave and the expression of concern was still on his face, intensified.

Miss Willie and Cheri were sitting in the kitchen when Kate got home. Cheri had heated up a can of soup and warmed the rest of the cornbread Miss Willie had made for her lunch, and they were eating. Sugar slept contentedly on top of the refrigerator and Pepper lay at Miss Willie's feet, occasionally putting a paw on her knee to remind her to pat him.

It was a pleasant little scene of domesticity, Kate thought, hugging Cheri and blowing Miss Willie a kiss. The sound of a car on the road interrupted.

Steve Sizemore.

"Quick, Miss Willie, go get in the bed!" Kate said.

The old lady, Kate blessed her, responded immediately with no questions, no foot-dragging. She walked as quickly as her age and infirmities permitted to the stairs, and Cheri followed. Kate and Pepper went out to meet the policeman.

"Come in, Steve!" Kate hoped her gushing hospitality wasn't overdone. "Have a seat here on the porch. Can I get you something to drink? Coke, coffee, beer?"

"Kate, I've come about Mrs. Wilcox," the officer said heavily.

"She's here!" Kate said brightly. "Lying down for a bit of a rest, but you can go up and talk to her. She wants to see you, I know. She remembers your grandparents so fondly."

Steve looked uncomfortable.

"Kate, I don't like to do this, but if I don't, homicide will be here—and that'd be worse."

"You're right," said Kate, adding a touch of chauvinism: "Strangers. They don't even know any of the good old settlers around here. I'm glad it's you, Steve, instead of one of *them*. You *understand*."

Steve took off his cap and mopped his brow.

"Does she still say she killed Garney?"

"Oh, that." Kate dismissed it lightly. "She said she was with him when he drank some white lightning that she had doctored up with herbs to kill beetles in her garden. Blames herself for that. She should have known better and stopped him, and that's about to break her heart."

"The electric wire?" Steve asked.

Kate shook her head in disgust. "You know Miss Willie wired that house herself. A few years ago there was nothing she couldn't do if she put her mind to it. She strung wires all around so she had a drop cord in every room. The one that went down to the root cellar was loose and she said she taped that up, but apparently it came unstrung and Garney fell on it or something."

Kate regretted the "fell." It could be taken that the white lightning caused the fall. She rushed on, hoping Steve had not noticed.

"I asked her if she hit Garney with anything, and Steve, you should have seen her face! She hadn't even hit him with a peachtree switch when he was a bad little young'un. So she couldn't conceive of anybody bopping him on the head with a blunt instrument."

Steve laughed. "That coffee made?" he asked.

"Of course not!" cried Kate flirtatiously. "Do you think I'd offer an officer of the law stale coffee? I was just gon' put on the pot. Won't take a minute."

"Well, I'll go up and see the lady," Steve said.

Kate hurried rinsing out the coffee maker and measuring fresh water and grounds. She didn't want to miss the interview. She reached the bottom of the stairs in time to hear Miss Willie's old voice saying haltingly, "So you're little Stevie Sizemore! I knowed you when you was a shirttail young'un not knee high!"

"Yes, ma'am," said the policeman, determined not to be distracted from his duty. "I am inquiring as to the death of your stepson, Garney Wilcox."

"He was a good boy, warn't he?" Miss Willie asked. "You recollect how fast he memorized Bible verses over at Shiloh Union Sunday school? You was in that group, wasn't you?"

"No, ma'am," said Steve uncomfortably. "My folks took us to Lebanon."

"Well, Garney was a bright scholar," Miss Willie went on, and then she paused and sighed, turning her gray head restlessly on the pillow. "I kilt him, Steve. Sure's the gun's iron, I kilt my boy."

Kate knew what Steve's next question would be, and he didn't disappoint her.

"Well did you *go* to do it, Miss Willie?"

"Grandma!" murmured Cheri, rising from the little rocker at the side of the bed. "Grandma . . ."

Kate knew that Cheri was hoping to deter Miss Willie from giving her reasons for wanting to kill Garney, but Steve interpreted it as an effort to protect the old lady from more painful questions.

"Don't worry, young lady," he said. "I'm not gon' press your grandmother any more today. We might have to talk to her later. Now, Miss Willie, you all"—nodding to Cheri and Kate—"take it easy."

He turned at the stairs, and Miss Willie abruptly sat up in bed and called after him: "Stevie, I done it. I kilt Garney with that poisoned whiskey! As God is my witness, I kilt him!"

"No, ma'am," the policeman said, shaking his head. "It took more'n that and I know you didn't *go* to do it."

Like a fish on a crow, Kate, suddenly cheerful, thought to herself as she followed him down the stairs toward the coffeepot.

Later Miss Willie came down the stairs and Kate, having seen Officer Sizemore off, returned to her coffee. She saw the old lady and burst out laughing.

"You sly old cooter!" she said. "You wrapped him around your little finger."

Miss Willie poured herself a cup of coffee and tilted some of it into a saucer to cool it.

"I didn't tell no falsehood," she said sternly, but her lips quirked at the corners.

" 'So you're little Stevie Sizemore!' " Kate mimicked her.

Miss Willie looked across the table at Cheri, who had Sugar in her lap and was stroking his white fur.

"It don't do to tell all, you know. Me and Cheri have been making plans, and they don't allow for stringing up the family washing for the Fulton County Police to look at."

"Very sound," said Kate, "but what plans? What are you two up to now?"

The old lady and the girl exchanged smiles, and Miss Willie explained. She was going to move back into her house and Cheri was going to live with her.

"And Wayne?" asked Kate.

Miss Willie looked at Cheri. "You tell her."

"Grandma thinks we ought not put the burden of the baby-having and all on Wayne, and I know that's right. At least not until he's older. He's sweet and would marry me, all right, but Grandma says he's too young to make that decision and take on such a load. Not yet out of high school. Grandma says he can come and see me and maybe someday we'll get married. But she says she doesn't like 'have-to' marriages."

Miss Willie nodded. "It ain't like it used to be when I was a gal and you had a woods colt. People are decenter now. They don't brand young girls and their babies. I hear tell there's women now that have babies on purpose without tying up a man to father them."

"That's right," said Kate. "But you're the last person I'd expect to approve."

Miss Willie laughed. "Sometimes, Kate, I think you don't know this old woman at all."

"Sometimes, Miss Willie, I agree."

"Well," said the old woman, getting up and collecting the cups, "me and Cheri gon' have this baby, and he's gon' be a fine one. You wait and see. Tomorrow Cheri's going to take the truck and transfer to the school out here. We ain't gon' let this baby grow up amongst ignoramuses. And I'm going over yonder and sweep out the house and maybe do some scrubbing."

There was no reason for creeping euphoria, Kate knew. Nothing much had changed. But suddenly she felt better. She went out to feed the cat and dog and wildly potracking guineas and stayed out, walking around the yard just to feel the cool breeze and her feet shuffling through copper and scarlet leaves. Tomorrow she would let her mind hack away at the details. Was Miss Willie clear with the police? Could an old woman and a girl manage by themselves? Where was the money coming from? Where was the furniture that had been hauled away when Miss Willie was herself hauled away to the nursing home?

And tomorrow was Troy Haskins's funeral.

CHAPTER 9

The entire Apple Tree Elementary School turned out for the services, which were held in one of the last little white clapboard steepled churches in the area. Two preachers sermonized for an hour each. A tall cadaverous woman with somber black eyes and a powerful soprano voice led the singing of "Near the Cross" and "Jesus Wants Me for a Sunbeam." Troy's little brother and sisters, dressed in their Sunday best, had been assigned to the front pew with their parents, but they squirmed around and faced the congregation, big-eyed and curious at first, their chins on the back of the bench. Growing restless, they slid their hands along the splintery pew and the little boy finally put his head on the seat and hung his feet over the back. Their mother, who had been crying softly but audibly, jerked him up and turned him around, walloping him on the bottom.

The father, dressed in a worn black coat over old army khaki trousers, sat beside her, hands linked between his knees, staring stonily at the little coffin in front of the pulpit.

During the singing of the first hymn, Mellie Alvarez slipped in and stood by Kate, taking the seat next to her when the people closest to her sat down and edged over to make room.

"Your office said you'd be here," she whispered.

"Glad you came," said Kate, offering her a hymn-book. "Funerals seem to be getting to be a habit with us."

"I came with some of the boys from homicide. They're waiting outside. Want to talk to the Haskinses and some of the neighbors afterwards, if it is all right."

"That's good," said Kate. "I hoped they would. But there'll be a service at the graveside after this and then usually some friend or member of the family asks everybody to the house for food. Mr. and Mrs. Haskins will be there, I know, and maybe she'll want to talk about it. I don't know about him. Mellie, he looks like he's dead inside."

Sergeant Alvarez nodded. "I don't wonder. It's a terrible thing."

The service was over and the congregation milled around outside, watching the undertaker's men steady Troy's coffin on a rolling cart and begin the descent down the rocky, dry hill through old headstones to the graveside. The father stumbled after it, his head bent. Kate noticed that he was wearing his old work shoes, scarred and dusty. Somebody had to have gotten him into a shirt with a tie, but he must have drawn the line at new shoes. Mrs. Haskins followed him. She was dressed in a full-skirted navy-blue polyester dress with matching blue shoes and hat. The beginning of recovery, Kate thought. That's what funerals do for the family—make them pull themselves together and move along with material concerns as if their lives weren't split by a great gaping bloody hole.

Mrs. Haskins grabbed the hand of the obstreperous little boy and nudged him along with her knee. The two little girls followed docilely.

The interment service was brief. A chill wind had sprung up, and those who did not linger to speak to the Haskinses clutched their hats and jackets and hurried to their cars. They had either been with them the night before at the wake or would be with them later for the funeral foods.

Kate felt a tug on her tweed jacket and looked around to find the Gandy sisters beside her.

"K.K.," whispered Sheena, "yonder's the man that was follering us."

Before she thought, Kate turned to look, and so did Mellie Alvarez. In a second she realized that they shouldn't have been so quick to show interest, because he was looking at them. A medium-sized man with light brown hair in a blow-dry ruffle across his forehead and before his ears, he was conspicuously well dressed in a crowd of country mourners: dark suit, snowy shirt, polished loafers.

Sergeant Alvarez promptly turned away, forgoing her scrutiny to indicate a lack of interest. Kate followed her example but only a second before the man disappeared in the cluster of mourners with whom he had stood. Cars were starting up all along the road and in the grassy churchyard, and Kate couldn't tell which one was his.

"Which car, girls?" she asked quickly. "Which car does he drive?"

The Gandys looked carefully, but they couldn't decide.

"I think he changes it every day," offered Sheena.

"I bet you're right," said Sergeant Alvarez. "Makes sense, doesn't it?"

The girls studied her with interest as Kate said, "Mellie, these are my good neighbors, Sheena and Kim Sue Gandy. Girls, this is Miss Alvarez, a friend of mine."

"Ain't you a police?" asked Kim Sue in a carrying voice.

Sergeant Alvarez winked at her and said nothing.

Kim Sue was content. "I thought so," she said.

"Shut your mouth, dumb-dumb," said Sheena. "You don't have to tell the world."

The girls returned to their school group, Sergeant Alvarez went off to join her colleagues, who waited in an unmarked police car, and Kate went to catch the MARTA bus to town. She had no reason that she could think of for taking her car all the way into town, and it would be restful to turn herself over to bus and train, go over her notes, and think.

The story took longer than she had expected. She kept thinking of Sam Haskins's haunted face. A few lines of type in the computer couldn't tell the depth of his tragedy, and she was undecided about how much or how little to write. The family members, and especially the father, were entitled to their private grief. Trying to write it down to tell a million subscribers how it felt to have your son torn to shreds by a murderous dog was indecent. The world of newspaper readers, thousands of whom would turn the page with only a cursory glance at the story, wasn't entitled to know. Kate kept thinking of a little boy, trying to help out at home, "a-running for his life."

She bent her head over the keyboard and leafed aimlessly without interest or purpose through the dictionary which lay on the edge of her desk, wishing wanly that she or it had enough words to tell the story.

There was a light tap at her open door, and she turned to see Baxter Winters.

"The word," he said, noting the dictionary, "is ubiquitous—that's u-b-i-q-u-i-t-o-u-s. Me, I'm omnipresent. And how are you today?"

"Aw, I don't know," said Kate. "I've been to such a spate of funerals I'm beginning to feel there's no life, not just *beyond* the grave, but this side of it. Today it was the little Haskins boy."

"I know," said Baxter soberly. "The worst of all the troubles that have been piling up at your door. If I could help . . ."

Kate shook her head. "I think something absolutely awful is going on, but it's beyond my ken. I just hope the police are going to bring it to an end."

Somebody in the newsroom yelled, "Bax! Telephone!"

He turned to acknowledge it with a wave and said quickly, "You mentioned bringing my kid Clay out to the country. Would this weekend, say either Saturday or Sunday, be all right?''

"Sure," said Kate. "I'll give you directions."

"We'll talk," he said, and turned to take his phone call.

It was 5:30 before Kate finished her story, wrote a column, and returned a phone call or two. She looked at the bus schedule and made sure there would be two more leaving the train station for Roswell before the last express at 7:02 P.M. That gave her time to walk up to the library and drop off her overdue books and tapes.

She called home to check on Miss Willie and Cheri.

"Child," exulted Miss Willie, "we been having a high-heel time this day! Me and Cheri and Wayne been helling around in the truck picking up my house fixings in barns and plunder rooms where neighbors and friends have been a-keeping them for me. With the one that's already over there we got enough beds, the stove's there and a chair or two. What more can a body ask for?"

"That's wonderful," said Kate. "I'll help you when I get home, but that'll be a while. I'm going by the library. Can you all fix something for your supper?"

Miss Willie snickered and lowered her voice. "That Wayne, he wants to treat us. He has phoned up a pizza place in Roswell, and Kate, they gon' *deliver*, bring it to your very door! Did you know sich as that went on?"

"No," said Kate. "I'm like you. I belong to the time when we raised most of the vittles we ate and cooked them all ourselves. I'm glad to hear our Shining Waters neighbors brought a new kind of service to the country. But, Miss Willie, do you *like* pizza?"

"Lord, I don't know," Miss Willie whispered. "It'll be my chance to find out."

Kate put the phone down, smiling. Miss Willie was getting a course in modern living from the young people—pizza, and delivered, yet! So, for that matter, was she. She didn't know it went on at the Cove.

She walked up Forsyth Street to the big, blocky, unlovely-looking but satisfyingly functional library, feeling subtly cheered. A sign at the corner marked the street as Margaret Mitchell Square, but the austere concrete building looked nothing like the old Carnegie where Peggy Mitchell had done much of her *Gone with the Wind* research. Nor was it the cozy place where Kate had grown up, reading afternoons away in the children's department, where colorful tiles depicting Joel Chandler Harris's Uncle Remus characters, Brer Fox and Brer Rabbit, ornamented a wonderful fireplace. Now it was a big institutional-looking building, but light-filled and book-filled, and Kate had respect and affection for the staff, which continued to be knowledgeable and unfailingly obliging.

A friend at the desk took her books and tapes, fiddled with a computer for a minute, and gave her the bill for the overdue items, $2.80.

"You're not checking out anything today?" she asked as Kate paid.

"I'm stocked up right now," Kate explained. "Besides, I think I'll stop by Macy's and pick up a cake to take home. That'll be enough to manage on the MARTA train without a sack of books and tapes."

The bake shop in the big store had a five-layer cake with whirls and chunks of fudge clumped in the center. Looking at it, Kate realized she had skipped both breakfast and lunch. She watched hungrily as the saleswoman swathed it in tissue paper and lowered it gently into a cardboard carrying case. They'd have a party when she got home, to celebrate Miss Willie's return to the Cove.

She held the cake carefully as she crossed the street and headed for the Peachtree Center Station. Remembering when Atlanta had no subterranean commuter system, Kate had an affectionate, proprietary interest in MARTA. She felt especially proud of Peachtree Center Station. It didn't have the artwork some stations exhibited, but even better, it had wondrous granite walls towering from the depths of the earth where the tracks were, a hundred and ninety feet to the street. Workmen tunneling for the MARTA rails had had a tough job here, drilling through a solid vein of Stone Mountain granite. Kate regarded it as one of nature's most awesome gifts to Atlanta, and she felt a stir of excitement every time she boarded what had to be one of the tallest escalators in the world—at least the tallest in the Southeast—to descend to the station platform.

Today she balanced her cake on one hand and

grasped the escalator's rail with the other, looking around at the granite walls with pleasure. There was no more beautiful shade of gray than the mica-starred Stone Mountain granite, she thought, no more interesting texture, and it delighted her that Atlanta graffiti experts had never had the effrontery to lay a line on it. Perhaps they remembered, as she did, that the workmen who drilled this tunnel daily spent thirty minutes compressing or decompressing when entering or leaving.

There were few people on the escalator. It was late for commuters. Kate was midway the descent when somebody above her yelled, "Look out! Look out! Somebody, quick, stop the escalator!"

She jerked around in time to see a heavy metal suitcase hurtling toward her.

Three people on the street level watched helplessly as the thing banged and bounced its way over the escalator steps, heading straight for Kate. A fourth walked rapidly through the door to the street. Kate dropped her cake and grabbed the rail with both hands.

There was no room to get out of the path and there was no place to climb to even if she had time. If she could hang on to the rails and lift her body high enough . . . She tried. Miraculously the suitcase swept under her, grazing her feet and landing with a crash on the station floor fifty feet below.

Kate collapsed on the last three steps of the escalator before they disappeared into whatever dark passage escalator steps travel. She was immediately surrounded by people, who lifted her up and helped her to a bench.

"Are you hurt, honey?" a blond woman in a plaid pants suit asked.

"I don't think so," Kate said shakily. "Just . . . who . . . I don't know!"

"Woman, you could have been killed!" a man said accusingly, as if it had been her fault.

"Whose suitcase?" Kate asked, looking at the metal-ribbed, tin-covered box which lay on its side in the center of the platform, undistinguished and innocuous.

"Aw, it was a accident," a woman said, "and the person who dropped that suitcase is probably scared to come and claim it. Scared you were bad hurt, broken legs or cracked backbone or something."

A man went over and pushed at the box with his toe, looking for identifying stickers. There were none. He was obviously considering opening it when a MARTA policeman showed up.

"Don't touch it!" the policeman cried. "Might be a bomb! Wait!" And he called on his radio for help.

Kate got to her feet, unsteady but unhurt.

"You all take care of the bomb," she said to a bystander. "I don't want to miss that last bus to Roswell!"

Always bombs, she thought wryly when she was seated on the train. She did not believe for a moment that the suitcase contained a bomb. She was inclined to agree with the woman who thought it was an accident.

Getting to where you can't even get a surprise package

anymore without the bomb squad wanting to take over, she thought. *Some surprise package, too.*

Her arms ached a little from the unaccustomed exercise of holding her body suspended, and she wondered a little about the man she saw leaving the station in a hurry as the suitcase started its downward path. Maybe it wasn't an accident.

CHAPTER 10

The cabin was quiet when she drove into the yard. Miss Willie's truck was missing and so was Wayne's bright blue Ford. They might be over at Miss Willie's old house. She decided to sit a moment in the twilight before changing her clothes and looking for something to eat. She eased off her shoes and took a beer to a chair in the living room, wondering belatedly what had happened to the chocolate cake.

It was then she heard the tinkle of the music box.

"Sheena! Kim Sue!" she called. "You up there? Stay out of my jewelry box!"

They came to the top of the stairs and peered over at her, one of them wearing Kate's mother's little watch on a heavy gold chain, the other wearing a silver butterfly on a silver chain. It had been given to her for Christmas years ago by Mr. Ben Fortson, who served as Georgia's secretary of state for quarter of a century. He gave all his young women friends the same when word got out that it wasn't safe on city streets at night. The butterfly was a whistle, but the sound it made was minimal. Kate loved it as she had loved the old gentleman who gave it to her, but she didn't think of it as a protective device. Now it swung around Kim Sue's fair young neck.

"We was waiting for you," said Sheena, as if Kate's delay had inconvenienced them.

"We decided to try on," Kim Sue explained unnecessarily.

Kate was too tired for the lecture they deserved. She had no valuable jewelry, except a small string of pearls Benjy had given her years ago, and that was too modest to interest the girls. The contraption that tinkled a tune when the box was opened was what they couldn't resist.

"Well, put my things up and don't bother them again without permission," Kate directed tiredly, slumping into the wing chair by the cold fireplace.

In a little while the Gandys came down the stairs, looking suitably subdued.

"We had something to tell you," Sheena ventured after a while.

"Tell me," said Kate.

"We was selling Girl Scout cookies over in Shining Waters," Sheena said, "and we looked in the Gardiners' house, and K.K., they've hardly got any furnitoor at all!"

"What on earth were you doing in their house?"

demanded Kate. "Were they at home? Did they invite you in?"

"No'm," said Kim Sue humbly. "We just wanted to see."

"The back door . . ."

"Was open?" prodded Kate.

Sheena shook her head guiltily. "It wasn't to say locked good. I just kinda poked at it with my knife blade."

"When nobody come to buy our cookies," said Kim Sue, "we thought we might just leave off some samples so they'd really want to buy theirselves some when we come back that way."

"A likely story," said Kate. "You just wanted to get in that house and prowl around like you do mine."

The girls looked hurt.

"But you're our friend," said Kim Sue.

"Friend, enemy . . . it doesn't matter," said Kate crossly. "You don't *prowl*. That's—" she fumbled for the name of the crime, "that's trespassing."

The girls meekly sat on the sofa and said nothing. Their freckled faces weren't exactly clean. They had been sampling the Girl Scout cookies, obviously the chocolate ones. Kim Sue waggled a foot in a dirty sneaker and looked anxiously at Kate. Sheena picked up a book which was on the little wooden trunk Kate used for a coffee table.

"Okay," said Kate, relenting. "Tell me what you saw."

Both dirty faces brightened.

"Beds," said Sheena. "That's most of what they

got. They ain't even got a eating table and chairs, and no pitchers on the walls.''

"They got a rug and a sofa and chairs in the living room and a great big TV,'' said Kim Sue.

"Yeah,'' said Sheena. "The living room looks nice, real nice, all gold and pink and drapes and everything.''

"Where else did you look?'' asked Kate.

"Shoot, we ain't going in nobody's basement,'' Sheena said.

"Naw,'' said Kim Sue, "we didn't do nothing but open the door and look down there.''

"And?'' prompted Kate.

"Boxes, nothing but boxes.''

"That explains why the house is still kind of bare,'' said Kate. "They probably haven't finished unpacking. And maybe they are like a lot of folks who take their time choosing furniture—just to be sure they have exactly what they want.''

"Yeah,'' said Sheena doubtfully. "I reckon. Anyhow, there wasn't any groceries much in the kitchen, so we left 'em two boxes of Girl Scout cookies.''

"That was nice,'' Kate said, and then caught herself. Now the Gardiners would know the girls had been in their house, and that might not be nice. Still, they were children, and they didn't take anything. How could anybody really mind? She minded when the shoe was on the other foot—but not much, and only briefly.

"Come on,'' she said, pulling herself up out of the chair and picking up her glass. "You can help me make some sandwiches. Sheena, how about feeding Pepper and Sugar for me? And Kim Sue, get out the cheese grater and open that can of pimentos. You do like pimento cheese sandwiches, don't you?"

"They okay," said Kim Sue without much enthusiasm. "We could go to McDonald's."

"We could not," said Kate. "I'm tired. It's been a long day."

"That's what Mommer said," Sheena reported, squatting down to fill the dog and cat pans. "She always lays down when she gits home. Her and daddy are both laying down now."

"Oh, your daddy's home from the hospital?"

"Yeah," said Kim Sue, "but he ain't a-doing too good. Kind of dreened feeling, he said."

"Well, I'm glad he's home. I know your mother feels good to have him in the house at night."

"Yeah," the girls agreed without interest. "She got kind of flustrated when that man was a-follering us. But he's stopped now."

"We didn't see him no more after Mr. Sizemore got on his case," said Sheena. "I reckon when you know the law's a-watching you, you don't git in much devilment."

"I reckon not," said Kate, checking to be sure she had ice cream in the freezer to take the onus off pimento cheese.

When the girls had finished eating, topping off the sandwiches with vanilla ice cream, which in turn was topped with chocolate syrup—and how did they know where she kept that?—they said they'd better go home, and Kate reluctantly decided to walk them to their door. If the man who "follered" them had in truth "give up on devilment," it wasn't necessary. But still, she'd feel better to see them safely home.

Kate was back in the cabin and was on the phone checking the bomb squad when she saw Wayne in his bright blue chariot coming up the driveway.

"Kate, the feller who threw that suitcase at you knew what you needed!" chortled Officer Frank Higgins. "It's full of religious tracts, all kinds. We gon' put 'em up careful for you."

"Thanks," said Kate dryly.

Somebody else in the office was laughing, and an old homicide friend of Benjy's came on the phone.

"Abundant life, peace and harmony," said Mitchell Moggins. "Tells you how to get it all."

"Well, I need it," said Kate. "It was an accident that just about got me, huh?"

"We don't know how or why it happened, Kate," he said more seriously. "But it wasn't a bomb, and I can't imagine that it was intended to swipe you off the escalator any more than the other folks who were on there."

"Hmm, they weren't in its path, it so happened. But I'm sure it was an accident. Thanks, Frank."

She hung up and went to greet Wayne.

"I've come to get you," the boy said, grinning and standing by his splendid equipage, a hand on the steering wheel as if he couldn't bear not to touch it. "Cheri and Grandma want you to see what they have been doing."

Oh-ho, thought Kate, *so it's "Grandma" already.*

She smiled and crawled in the car, which smelled grandly of enamel and shellac and wax.

Wayne skirted the Shining Waters Subdivision, taking a rough wagon road that was all but impassable and enclosed by trees with branches meeting overhead. It used to lead to the river and was one of hers and Benjy's favorite walking trails. But the subdivision had lopped off half its length and the rest was forgotten and left to grow up in sumac and Jersey tea bushes. Miss Willie remembered it and had instructed Wayne to go that way, probably because she didn't want her Shining Waters neighbors to know she was in residence yet.

And she was in residence, Kate saw when they walked into the yard.

There was a kerosene lamp burning in the front room, and Miss Willie and Cheri sat in cowhide-bottom chairs on the front porch.

"Come in and set!" Miss Willie called out happily. "We even got a settin' cheer for you."

They did, in fact, have three "settin'" chairs, enough because Wayne busied about his car, wiping streaks of dust and a sprinkling of leaves off its precious body before he took a seat on the steps.

"Miss Willie, you're furnished!" exclaimed Kate, standing and peering into the house. "A bed all made up and a lamp and . . . my goodness, a rug on the floor!"

"Jes' a old rag rug I crocheted a hundred year ago. I had it wrapped around my crockery in Lu Gilstrap's corncrib. But it does look homey, don't it?"

She fussed a little over the bed, tucking in a quilt at the foot.

"The electric ain't on yet, but I decided after what happened—" her voice wavered, "after what happened I'd better wait and let somebody knows more than I do be sure it's all right."

"Come see my room," said Cheri.

Kate followed her into the other room, where an iron bed, too plain to have interested the antique dealers who flocked to the old house when Miss Willie moved, was also neatly made up with sheets and a quilt. There was a nail keg for a night table and another kerosene lamp, not yet lit, sat in the middle of it. Kate was touched to see a bunch of joe-pye weed in a crock before the fireplace. Her own trick, she realized, and Cheri had copied it in an effort to substitute the dark empty maw beyond the hearth with beauty from the autumn woods. She hugged the girl.

There was warmth from the kitchen and Kate saw live coals graying in the front of the firebox of the old cookstove.

"You've already started cooking again!" she said, turning to Miss Willie.

The old lady nodded. "First thing I done when I got the place scoured out was to put on a pot of greens. They was good, too," she added, looking at the young people for confirmation.

"Wonderful," said Cheri.

"Yes, ma'am, mighty good," said Wayne.

"And the stove still works?"

"Lord, yes," said Miss Willie. "It ain't faltered or

failed in fifty year, and I know it ain't gon' give out on me and Cheri now.''

"When the electricity is working for sure I think I know where I can get them a pretty good refrigerator,'' Wayne said. "My aunt wanted one of them harvest gold-colored ones and she put a perfectly good white one out in the garage. I'm gon' ask her for it. There's some other stuff, too, they might want to use.''

Miss Willie and Cheri both looked at him lovingly, and Kate patted him on the shoulder.

"This is gon' be wonderful,'' she said. "We're gon' to have a great time getting you all fixed up again. You know I've got several of your quilts, Miss Willie, and it's going to be colder tonight. I'll send them back by Wayne. Unless . . . well, don't you want to come back and stay with me until everything's checked out and you're sure you're going to be comfortable?''

"Aw, no,'' said Miss Willie, "we gon' be fine, ain't we, Cheri?''

The girl put an arm around Miss Willie's ample old waist, which a black-checked apron still encompassed, and leaned her head against the old woman's shoulder.

"Yes, ma'am, this already feels like home.''

"Don't it?'' said Miss Willie happily. "It's such a thing, young'uns. . . .'' Her eyes took in them all, and she wiped back tears. "It's God-given to have a stay-place of your own.''

Kate had misgivings, but she didn't let them bother her as she made a pile of bedding for Wayne to take back. She added to Miss Willie's quilts a couple of good woolen blankets of her own and a pair of pillowcases with crocheted lace on them. Miss Willie had made them herself and she deserved to have some of her frills come home again, since so many of her possessions were scattered irretrievably.

"Wayne, you feel like they're all right over there by themselves?" she asked as she walked out to the car with the boy.

"I got a sleeping bag in the back," he said. "I'm gon' stay with them tonight to be sure. But you're here by yourself," he said, his eyes taking in the old gray log walls. "You feel safe?"

"Off and on, now and then," said Kate, laughing. And then more seriously, "I *am* safe. Pepper's a good watchdog, and I have my husband's pistol."

She didn't want to sound unduly squeamish and set up unpleasant thoughts for the campers, but she couldn't forget a murder had been done in that old house and there had been blood and vomit on the cellar steps.

"You know, after what happened over there . . ." she began hesitantly.

The boy nodded. "But it's all right. I helped Grandma scrub down the cellar steps and scatter sand from the creek over the floor. She said every old house in the country has likely had murder or something bad done in them, and you just make up your mind to overcome. If it hadn't been her son, I don't believe it would bother her at all."

Kate felt comforted. Miss Willie came from good sturdy no-nonsense stock. Not for her, sissy vibrations or girlish palpitations.

* * *

Kate was in bed when Mellie Alvarez called.

"I heard about you and the missionary," she said cheerfully. "That's one way of converting a sinner— send her tumbling down the biggest escalator in the country."

"Big sins, powerful action," Kate said smugly.

"You didn't burn the Haskinses' new chicken house, did you?"

"What?" cried Kate. "Not more trouble for them!"

"I'm afraid so," said Sergeant Alvarez.

"When? How?"

"Tonight. One of the country boys told us. He said the fire department got there too late to save the out-buildings, but the house's okay. They had to pull Mr. Haskins out. Poor fellow, I guess he was trying to save the thing and stumbled and fell. They treated him for smoke and some burns, and he's back home now."

So stunned was she by the Haskinses' latest catastrophe, Kate almost forgot to ask what the homicide crew had accomplished when they left the funeral.

"I don't think anything much," Sergeant Alvarez admitted. "We talked to some people. We have some ideas. I'll be back in touch."

"The fire," Kate said. "Could that have been arson?"

"The department is checking," Sergeant Alvarez said.

Kate went off to sleep thinking alternately of Miss Willie's soap-and-water-smelling house and the prospect of having her for a neighbor again, and poor Sam Haskins's tormented face.

Miss Marlowa came back from Twitty City and Dollywood earlier than she had planned. She didn't like the songs she heard there. "Ordinary," she said. Dancing was gauche and vulgar, not a polonaise or a polka in the lot. She had not even had her ball gown out of its linen slipcover.

"Couldn't dance, wouldn't stay," Ida sniffed to Kate when Kate swung by on her way to town to see them. "Pouted like a child."

"No such thing," scolded Miss Marlowa. "I was really worried about Willie Wilcox. Did you turn her over to the authorities?"

"Not exactly. Steve Sizemore talked to her and seemed satisfied that she was not guilty of murder."

"Ah, a Sizemore!" jeered Miss Marlowa. "What do they know? Willie deserves credit for getting rid of that villain. I think I'll call the chief myself."

Kate shuddered. More Tom Sawyer tactics.

"Please, Miss Marlowa, let's let well enough alone. Miss Willie has moved back to her own house, taking her granddaughter Cheri to live with her, and they seem so happy. The house is bare but clean, and it seems to have given Miss Willie a new lease on life."

Miss Marlowa was instantly diverted.

"The house is nothing," she said emphatically, "but it's home to Willie, and those old country places have a certain charm and should be preserved. What does she need? I'll share."

Kate looked around at the Empire secretary, the Hepplewhite sideboard, the Queen Anne chairs, and the crystal chandelier. She couldn't conceive of such ancient elegance being hauled out through the Corinthian columns and installed in Miss Willie's weathered old house with its scrubbed floors.

Miss Marlowa caught the look.

"Don't be obtuse, girl!" she commanded. "I wouldn't give up Grandmother and Grandfather's things. But the barn and the attic are full of our mistakes. Perfectly good stuff. Willie is welcome to it. Let's give her a housewarming!"

Kate had thought of taking her old neighbor a gift, maybe a rocking chair or a load of wood for her fireplace. But Miss Marlowa had taken over the project and was running with it.

"Saturday," she said. "We'll do it then. Ida, get your nephew who has that truck and does hauling, and we'll pick out some tables and chairs. And china, she will need something pretty to serve tea."

Kate smiled at the picture of Miss Willie in her faded checked apron with her scarred and callused old hands presiding prettily over a tea table.

Miss Marlowa had grabbed up a pencil and paper and was making a list. "Food, Ida, what should we take? Chicken salad or fried chicken, which shall it be? What about both with beaten biscuits and one of your banana puddings . . ."

Ida rolled her eyes at Kate.

"No rest for the weary or the wicked," she muttered.

Miss Marlowa's laugh tinkled like a small bell in

the big drafty hall. She put an arm around Ida and hugged her.

"Listen to the girl. Just back from a holiday in the mountains and she talks about rest! Ida, you know you want a party for poor Willie Wilcox after the trouble she's seen."

"Yes'm," said Ida, resignedly moving toward the kitchen.

"She'll do a feast," Miss Marlowa whispered to Kate. "Ida likes nothing better than a party."

Kate doubted that, but she felt with Ida that whatever Miss Marlowa wanted was irreversible and uncommutable.

She decided to take the car to town in case she had time to do a little shopping for the housewarming. It would be fun to pick out something for Miss Willie, but with Miss Marlowa on the job she would be hard-pressed to avoid duplication. Maybe bedspreads and curtains. She wouldn't have curtains herself. There seemed no point in living in the country if you were to shut out the view of sky and trees. She loved windows, wide open if possible. But Cheri might feel that curtains provided privacy and dressed up her little room, and whatever Cheri liked would please Miss Willie.

Kate parked at Rich's so it would be easy to shop after work. She walked along Forsyth Street toward the office, feeling almost lighthearted for the first time in days. She had to stop for the traffic light at Marietta Street, but she never minded that unless there was a push toward deadline, and then she jaywalked.

It was pleasant to look at the familiar landmarks—

the time-and-weather-greened statue of Henry Grady, the editor-orator, with his hand on his heart. Dead since 1889, he was now surrounded by buildings that always seemed to have reached the sky overnight. She remembered when so many of them weren't there, and sometimes she indulged in a rash of nostalgia for those that were gone, particularly the old Victorian pile on the corner where Woodrow Wilson had his first law office. The new, many-windowed federal savings structure there now had a near replica of Mr. Wilson's little office for tourists and history buffs to see. Kate had been invited to cover its formal opening. She thought often how like Atlanta, the pushy upstart town of Margaret Mitchell's big book, to tear down the old and replace it with a nice counterfeit.

As she stood musing, she felt a hand on her elbow and turned to see Baxter Winters looking early-morning crisp and fresh in a white shirt and a tweed suit she suspected came straight out of the hills of Scotland and cost him a month's salary.

"May I help you across the street, lady?" he asked.

"If you think I *need* help, no!" Kate said. "If you just want to be nice, yes!"

"Pleases and honors me to have a hand on the lady's arm," Baxter said. "And I certainly don't think you need it. By the way, Clay is excited over coming to the country. I told him about the donkey."

Kate stopped and stared at him.

"I forgot!" she said. "So much is going on. Miss Willie, the lady I told you about, has moved back to her old house and Miss Marlowa, the other lady I told you about . . . ?"

He nodded. "Back of the white columns, into Jeanette MacDonald and Nelson Eddy."

"The very one, and she wants to throw a house-warming for Miss Willie. We all have to help. Would you and Clay mind that? There's a creek in her yard where the kids build dams and waterfalls, and there'll be lots of food, and we'll get Sheena and Kim Sue and the donkey."

"Sounds good to me," Baxter said, "And I bet Clay will love it. What can we bring?"

"Oh, nothing . . . anything," said Kate, relieved.

"Wine?" he asked.

"Perfect," said Kate. *A lot better than white lightning laced with foxglove*, she thought as they walked into the building.

Work went fast, and by three o'clock Kate was ready to leave her office and duck over to Rich's to find housewarming gifts. She would go by the market on the way home and get pâté and wafers and fresh fruit and cheese and special gooey cookies for the children. She also picked from the store's buckets of cut flowers a mixed bouquet for Miss Willie's table-to-be, if Miss Marlowa came through, and some baby chrysanthemums for her own house. She wanted it to look loved and looked-after to Baxter, although he might not find a log cabin, no matter how waxed and polished and flower-garnished, to his sophisticated taste. She settled on the tawny, topaz-colored mums and mentally polished a copper pot that had been Benjy's to hold them.

She prepared to wheel her purchases toward her car when a woman she knew from church spoke to her.

"I read your story about the little Haskins boy," she said. "Very sad. But did you know they think his father set fire to his own chicken house? It was on television."

"No," said Kate. "I can't imagine that."

Remembering his face looking out beyond her at the old hound dog and her puppies, Kate could imagine it, and her afternoon was suddenly somber again. She stopped at a pay phone on the road and called Sergeant Alvarez.

"I think it was arson," Mellie Alvarez said. "That's what the fire marshal's office said. Gasoline in wood shavings and straw. Could have been Haskins himself. He's been acting funny, but I don't know. They hesitate to pin it on him because of all the grief he's going through."

"Oh, I hope they'll let him alone," Kate said. "Any word on anything else?"

"Some word," Sergeant Alvarez said in a low voice. "I'll call you later."

CHAPTER 11

October, Kate had long ago decided, was the prettiest month the world had at its disposal. And Saturday morning in the Cove was blue and gold. The leaves had reached the peak of autumnal splendor. Around every bend in the road there would be a maple or a sweetgum or a sumac of glowing, heart-stopping perfection. The frost had not yet gotten the asters or the goldenrod or the joe-pye weed in the low places. ("Queen of the Meader," Miss Willie called it, collecting it for winter ills.)

The muscadines had ripened and where there were no thrifty hands to gather them they had fallen to the ground, filling the air with the fragrance of new wine. The vines, climbing trees and hanging in swags, might have been wrought from finest gold.

Kate filled her picnic basket and committed her

spreads and curtains to tissue paper and ribbons. The Gandy sisters arrived wearing dresses.

Kate remembered the donkey.

"Mommer said no need to put on dresses," Kim Sue explained, "but if it's a party we thought we should."

"Oh, you look splendid," cried Kate. "Ribbons in your hair, even. Tell you what, wear the dresses long enough to make an entrance and let everybody see you, and then put on some shorts. It's warm enough to wade in the creek and Vic Ross is bringing his donkey."

"Ohka-ay!" yelped Kim Sue.

"Roger!" cried Sheena, and they departed to collect their everydays.

Watching them go, Kate wondered if the sight of the girls in Merthiolate-colored ruffles and bows would spook even the placid donkey.

Baxter and his little boy, Clay, arrived in the early afternoon. The father, at least, was properly impressed by the log cabin. The little boy, thin-faced and pale, Kate thought, stared silently at the logs, the dark pine rafters, the big stones in the chimney, and said nothing.

"Dry laid," Kate said, pointing to the big rocks stacked with clay in-between to make the chimney. "Family came over the mountains in wagons, cut the trees for the walls, and gathered the rocks on the ground to build the chimney. See that big rock way up there, Clay? Can you imagine one man lifting it into place?"

The little boy shook his head shyly.

"One man did that?" Baxter asked.

"I'm not sure," Kate said. "Maybe neighbors gathered for the house-raising. Or maybe he and his father rigged some kind of lift and did it together. The father was old, I understand, a veteran of the Revolutionary War."

Baxter let out a low whistle. "Hear that, son? The war that won our independence and made us a country."

The little boy looked at him, wide brown eyes like his father's, and said, "Wow."

Kate ended the tour in the house, where Baxter paused to scan her bookshelves and Clay picked up the cat Sugar and hugged her. The Gandy sisters returned and after a period of bashful appraisal of the little boy said, "Come on, let's play!"

Baxter and Kate elected to walk to Miss Willie's, skirting the subdivision castles, chalets, and manor houses, by taking the gouted wagon road, which was longer but retained the country look and feeling Kate was pleased to share.

"Little enough country left," she explained to Baxter. "I come this way if I have time."

He carried her picnic basket and she carried two bottles of wine, noticing that he had brought champagne. Vic Ross was already ahead of them, leading Job, his donkey.

"Job?" inquired Baxter, looking at the little animal swishing his tail and flapping his long ears at flies. "Suffered, huh?"

"You better believe," Ross, a retired airline pilot, said with a grin. "I raised three children on his back.

I'm going to leave him with you and the Gandys, Kate. I have to take Jessie shopping."

Miss Marlowa, true to her word, had sent a truck-load of odd tables and chairs ahead, and Miss Willie, helped by Cheri and Wayne, had arranged them in the big front room, moving the old Victorian bedstead to a smaller back room, which connected with Cheri's.

"The young'uns wanted me to have a parler," she explained. "Never had sich, but ain't it nice?" Then, "Nice for them," she added in a whisper. "Folks now-adays got something agin having a bedstead up in the front room."

"That's right," Kate said. "Now you have what the British call a reception room, where your friends and Cheri's can come and sit and visit. And your bed-room is private."

They looked at it with satisfaction—Miss Mar-lowa's round oak table, a turn-of-the-century fancy at Walton Hall which had lost favor, a fat-bellied glass and oak china closet of the same vintage, which Miss Marlowa had filled with dishes, and an assortment of chairs. Beneath it all was a shiny new lineoleum floor covering.

"How you like it?" asked Miss Willie, stepping carefully around the edge to avoid making tracks on the slick mélange of flowers and stars. "I always have wanted one, and them blessed young'uns, Cheri and Wayne, went in together and bought it for me."

"Oh, it's bright and cheerful and so cleanable," said Kate.

"It's an atrocity," pronounced Miss Marlowa,

who had arrived with Ida and Canary and baskets of food.

Not knowing what an atrocity was, Miss Willie smiled gratefully and took her seat in a split-oak-bottomed rocker, which she had given the Gandys when she was wrested from her house and which they had now returned.

Ida was wearing the snowy wig Miss Marlowa had thought to use to disguise Miss Willie on their trip out of town, and the old lady was delighted with it, and the day, and the other visitors, and the food. The pall of evil and death seemed to have lifted.

Kate and Cheri arranged the flowers in the center of the big table and Wayne took Baxter out to admire his car. The little girls, having made an appearance, divested themselves of their finery and badgered Clay to take off his shoes, astonished when he felt it necessary to get his father's permission first. The three of them were knee-deep in the creek, building a dam to trap enough water for some future swimming hole.

"Dad, can I come back and swim here?" he asked.

"Sure," said Baxter, "if you and these girls can get the creek deep enough for that."

"Hell, we've done it plenty of times!" lied Kim Sue before she caught Kate's admonitory eye on her and bent to catch a spring lizard that was trying to escape under a rock.

Baxter's champagne cooled in the creek, inspiring Miss Willie to find a small bottle of cherry cordial and set it in the creek next to the wine.

They spread dinner in the late afternoon, with the grownups filling paper plates Canary had thoughtfully provided and pulling their chairs out on the porch to catch the sinking sun as it deepened the blue of the mountains in the distance. The children ate fast and returned to some game which involved donkey rides up to the edge of the subdivision and back for the winner.

Kate was gratified to see that the Gandy sisters let Clay win the most. They accompanied him to the edge of the woods, calling out encouragement to rider and steed.

Baxter watched the slight figure of his son bouncing along on the donkey's back, and he smiled at Kate.

"He's really had a wonderful time today. And I have, too."

He looked out across the field, where the shadows were lengthening, and reached for the last bottle of champagne to refill the jelly glasses Miss Willie had rounded up from the smokehouse.

He lifted his glass: "A toast to the blue hour."

"Ah, *l'heure bleu!*" said Miss Marlowa. "I recollect, when Papa and Mama took me to France when I was a girl, we always sat on the balcony of our hotel overlooking the Champs-Élysées at this time of day. Papa would have a brandy, but of course I was not allowed to drink in those days."

She batted her eyes at Baxter, and Kate realized she had somehow found time to renew her makeup. The old girl was flirting! *Go to it*, she thought. *It's the skill of your age group, one lost to my generation, most certainly to me.*

Kate glanced at Miss Willie's glass, but the old lady shook her head. "A little of the cordial," she said, "and

I'm gon' show Ida and Canary where to catch bream. There's a hole in the river nobody else knows about."

Ida's dark face, looking uncannily chic under the silken white curls, glowed with interest. Canary took off her shoes and stockings to follow them barefoot. Cheri and Wayne made an excuse to take a run in the blue car. And Miss Marlowa invited Baxter ("because you are a journalist") to have a seat in her Lincoln and hear the news on the radio.

I bet she plays him the "Sweetheart Waltz," Kate thought as she collected the glasses and took them to the kitchen. It suddenly occurred to her that Sheena and Kim Sue, following the donkey and Clay riding it, had been gone longer than usual.

She put the glasses down and walked out the kitchen door along the path to Shining Waters. She had only been walking a little way when Pepper, ahead of her, suddenly stopped, sniffed the air, and shot out through the woods.

It was then she heard the screams.

The children, she thought, running down the rocky path as fast as she could go.

She rounded the last clump of trees and saw two figures in black standing over the children, who were piled up like players on a football field, with a pit bull slavering and tugging at one of them.

"No!" she screamed. "Get him, pull him off!"

The black figures weren't going to move, but at that moment there was an explosion from a shotgun. The dog fell dead, and the two figures, bleeding from scattered shot, stumbled toward the open door of a van.

Kate was on her knees beside the children in a second. Sheena was bloody but grinning. Kim Sue, the second on the heap, was less bloody and crying. And Clay, on the bottom of the heap, sat up, big-eyed, apparently unhurt.

"Oh, babies!" cried Kate, trying to take them all in her arms. "What happened? Did he bite you?"

Sheena held out an arm with an ugly tear in her young flesh. Kim Sue wiped her face on her shirttail.

"He slobbered on me," she said.

"He couldn't get me," Clay said. "Sheena and Kim Sue fell on me. I think—" he looked up and saw his father coming and tears belatedly filled his eyes, "I think they saved me."

"Natch," said Sheena with gallant flippancy. "Job threw you, and you're littler than we are."

"God bless you," cried Kate, tearing a swatch out of her cotton shirt. "Here. Let me bandage you."

They squatted there with Baxter cradling his son in his arms and choking up as he looked at the Gandy sisters. Officer Sizemore, accompanied by a whole retinue of other officers, came out of the Gardiners' house with the two sinister-looking figures in black in handcuffs.

Kate was too shaken to laugh. She just gaped and swallowed hard. Valerie Gardiner, slim as a pencil, was wearing a black leather jumpsuit and a ski mask. Voncile Wilcox wore an identical black leather jumpsuit—at least a size forty-eight. Both outfits were flecked with blood where shotgun pellets had sprayed and penetrated them.

Mellie Alvarez came from the other direction, carrying a shotgun and pushing Sam Haskins along ahead of her. He had come in search of the killer of his son and had arrived in time to save three other children from attack by another killer dog. But he wasn't satisfied.

"Man in there done it," he said, pointing toward the Gardiners' castle. "He killed my boy. And I helped him. I knowed he was in the dope business, and I give Troy my permission to be a runner or whatever they call it. He promised my boy he wouldn't see or touch the stuff—just deliver messages. I knowed it was wrong, but they paid him a hundred dollars a week and, God help me, I wanted it to build that chicken house. I thought—" He ducked his head and gave way to tears.

Kate wanted to put her arms around him, but they seemed full of the Gandy sisters.

"He burned his chicken house and tried to burn up himself," Sergeant Alvarez said.

He nodded numbly. "Couldn't stand the sight of it. Didn't want to live."

"Well, you saved our children," Kate said comfortingly. "We thank you for that."

He shook his head. "I was looking for that man."

"What man?" Kate asked, looking at Sergeant Alvarez.

"Your neighbor, Ron Gardiner, supplied the dogs and used the castle here and occasionally Miss Willie's buggy house to store the biggest cache of crack this county has seen yet. We already got him and his boss in jail. The kingpin had him or his pretty little helpmeet here to kill Garney for skimming off the profits from what he sold in the housing projects and condos around town.''

The pretty little helpmeet, Valerie, was in a very ugly mood. Her beautiful face was contorted, her usually expressionless eyes blazing. She and Voncile, Garney's partner in the business, had planned to kidnap Sheena and Kim Sue, who had committed the ultimate crime of knowing too much about their operation and trespassing in the house with Girl Scout cookies. They had meant to put them in the van and haul them to some spot where they could turn loose the pit bull dog and leave them. If Kate was in the way they'd take her, too, a prospect that no doubt excited and pleased the corpulent Voncile.

But the donkey and the presence of a third child had thrown their plans out of whack. The sight of the donkey had caused the dog to fling himself with such force against the cage in the van that the latch broke, and he was on his killing rampage in seconds. The little donkey, fleeter of foot than anybody suspected, had made a getaway.

''And the man in charge of all this?'' Kate directed the question to Mellie Alvarez.

''Oh, he was that slick-looking fellow who dropped the suitcase at the MARTA station and followed the Gandy girls. You saw him at Troy Haskins's funeral.''

Kate stood up with the idea of walking over and slapping the leather-suited idiots in their evil faces, but an ambulance arrived at that moment and she helped to herd the children into it. The medics bound Sheena's wound, discarding Kate's shirttail, and gave the little girl a shot, which necessitated her lying on a stretcher and being covered with a blanket.

The others were less solicitously treated, but they were also wrapped in blankets against possible shock. Another ambulance came for Valerie and Voncile, who were by now mixing sweat with buckshot blood.

Baxter climbed in the ambulance with the children.

"I'll go get the girls' mother and meet you at the hospital," Kate said.

She leaned over and kissed Sheena on her forehead, which was clammy and very pale.

"You're a good girl," she said chokily.

"*Pro bono publico*," whispered Sheena proudly.

"Oh, she learned it all. For the public good," Kate said aloud, and burst into tears.

CELESTINE SIBLEY has written for the *Atlanta Constitution* for more than forty years. Her first book, *The Malignant Heart*, a mystery, was published in 1958. She has since written fifteen books, including her recent memoirs, *Turned Funny*. *Ah, Sweet Mystery* is her second mystery novel.

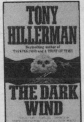